MARVEL

A NOVEL OF THE MARVEL UNIVERSE

MORBIUS
THE LIVING VAMPIRE

BLOOD TIES

D0833171

NOVELS OF THE MARVEL UNIVERSE BY TITAN BOOKS

ALSO FROM TITAN AND TITAN BOOKS

A NOVEL OF THE MARVEL UNIVERSE

MORBIUS
THE LIVING VAMPIRE

BLOOD TIES

An original novel by

BRENDAN DENEEN

TITAN BOOKS

MARVEL

MORBIUS: THE LIVING VAMPIRE – BLOOD TIES
Mass market edition ISBN: 9781789095654
E-book edition ISBN: 9781789095661

Published by Titan Books
A division of Titan Publishing Group Ltd
144 Southwark Street, London SE1 0UP
www.titanbooks.com

First mass market edition: January 2022
10 9 8 7 6 5 4 3 2 1

FOR MARVEL PUBLISHING
Jeff Youngquist, VP Production and Special Projects
Caitlin O'Connell, Assistant Editor
Sven Larsen, VP, Licensed Publishing
Jeremy West, Manager, Licensed Publishing
David Gabriel, SVP of Sales & Marketing, Publishing
C.B. Cebulski, Editor in Chief

This is a work of fiction. Names, characters, places, and incidents either
are the product of the author's imagination or are used fictitiously, and any
resemblance to actual persons, living or dead, business establishments,
events, or locales is entirely coincidental. The publisher does not have any
control over and does not assume any responsibility for author or third-party
websites or their content.

A CIP catalogue record for this title is available from the British Library.
Printed and bound in the United States.

This book is dedicated to Roy Thomas and Gil Kane,
the creators of Morbius; and to Don McGregor,
Rich Buckler, and Pablo Marcos, the creators
of Amanda Saint.

I'm guessing the latter three gentlemen never imagined
that a random supporting character they created in
1973 would return, co-starring in a novel,
forty-seven years later.

PROLOGUE

M

JOHNNY SWEAT was nervous.

He'd followed instructions. He *always* followed instructions, at least when there was a payday promised at the end of the job.

When there wasn't anything in it for him? Not so much. That attitude had gotten him in trouble his whole life, but he got by. At least that's what he had always told himself.

He'd been troubled since he was a kid… emotionally and sometimes even physically abused by a single dad who couldn't hold down a job and kept searching for happiness at the bottom of any given bottle. Johnny had fled their tiny Midwest town when he was fifteen and had never looked back. New York City looked great on TV and in the movies. All those people and opportunities. He knew he could make something of himself in a place like that.

Or thought so, at least.

His entitled attitude didn't serve him well, though. He followed orders when he was slinging French fries at a burger joint, but he sometimes did it with a sneer. And one night when his manager told him he had a bad attitude, Johnny rewarded the guy with a right cross to the nose. He was promptly fired and arrested, in that order.

Once he had a criminal record, Johnny could no longer find legitimate work. Which, when he thought about it, was just fine with him. When he took on his first *illegitimate* job, working as a bagman during a convenience store robbery, he knew he had finally found his calling.

As time passed, he did his best to keep his deep-seated anger in check. It was a little easier when surrounded by other low-level criminals like him. They were *all* angry.

Johnny started making some money. Not insane amounts, but enough to enjoy life a little bit. Buy a nice steak dinner now and then. Buy a bottle from the top shelf every month or so. Go on a date with a pretty girl. There was almost never a second date.

That's fine, he would tell himself. *I didn't really like that one anyway*.

He did what he had to in order to survive in an increasingly crazy world. Had worked for some of the biggest names in New York City crime. Owlsley. Lincoln. Russo. Even Fisk. Sure, he'd only been a grunt, following instructions—but he did his work to the letter, doing his best not to talk back when his bosses talked down to him. As a result, the work was steady.

Until it wasn't.

With all the super freaks swinging and flying around the city, the jobs had started to thin out. Steak dinners were replaced with greasy fast food. He could only stare longingly at the top shelf before buying a handful of those airplane-size bottles of booze. And there were no more dates.

He'd let himself go. Hair was longer. Stomach was bigger. Couldn't remember the last time he'd taken a real shower. His hot water had been shut off weeks ago. So, when Johnny Sweat heard from a friend of a friend about an easy score, his ears perked up. Things had been hard for a while. At this point, Johnny deserved a little "easy."

The instructions were simple. Weirdly simple, but still…

Go to the Second Avenue subway stop at 72nd Street, at 3 a.m. Head to the front of the platform—the north end. Wait until everyone gets on a train. When there's no one in sight, walk down the stairs and into the tunnel. Keep going for a quarter mile.

"There aren't a ton of trains at that time of night but walk fast anyway," the guy said. *"You never know. When you come to the third door on your right—make sure it's the* third *one—open it and walk down another long set of stairs. Then wait. Someone will meet you."*

It seemed pretty bizarre, but in the last five years, Johnny had done stranger. Had seen things his father

wouldn't have believed. Gods flying through the air—
at least they *called* them gods. Robots walking through
walls. A guy made out of orange rocks—and that was
when Johnny *wasn't* drinking.

He entered the station, went through the turnstile.

He'd heard stories about the subway tracks. About
homeless people who lived underground. Sometimes
nine-to-fivers caught glimpses of them on their way to
work or home or wherever the hell nine-to-fivers went.
He'd never seen any of those tunnel dwellers himself,
but he'd heard the rumors. Had heard that some of
them could get crazy, could get violent… That some of
them were even mutants.

So he brought his favorite knife with him when
he headed toward Second Avenue at 2:45 a.m. on a
Sunday night… or Monday morning, or whatever the
hell it was. He couldn't afford a gun, but he figured the
knife would do just fine. It always had. Johnny knew
how to handle a knife, especially this one. It was the
only thing he'd stolen from his father when he'd left
home all those years ago.

Even so, as Johnny hit the bottom of the stairs and
waited for the train to arrive and pick up the few people
scattered across the platform, he was nervous.

He'd forgotten his flask on the small table by the
door of his run-down, dingy apartment. There wasn't
much left in it, admittedly, but even just a swig right
now would have calmed his rattled nerves. He didn't
like this job already. He didn't even know who he was
working for, or what the job was, but he needed the

scratch. Bad. He was late on rent… *very* late… and he hadn't had a decent meal in a couple of days.

This gig could change everything.

Finally, the damn train came screeching into the station, the conductor a dark shadow behind smudged glass. The people got on board and, after the train sat there for what seemed like forever, the doors let out their telltale two-note ring and then closed.

The train didn't move.

"Come *on*," Johnny said out loud.

As if in response, the train lurched forward, then picked up speed and headed down the tunnel into the growing shadows until it was gone, its echo reverberating and then fading away entirely.

The subway station was silent.

Johnny looked around. During the entire five years he'd been in the city, he had never been totally alone like this on a train platform. Lights flickered on and off silently overhead. Rats emerged and scurried along the tracks, hunting for discarded food.

Taking a deep breath, Johnny stepped over the small chain that ostensibly kept people from entering the tracks, and walked down the several metal stairs that led into the subway tunnel itself. A cool breeze wafted toward him from the darkness, carrying a smell of garbage and urine that almost made him gag. Suppressing the urge, he trudged forward.

After a few minutes, Johnny stopped and looked back. The subway station wasn't that far away but its lights already looked dim, as if he was looking at them through gauze. He realized that his eyes were watering from a combination of the smell and fear, and he cursed himself. Then he turned back around and continued walking.

He passed one graffiti-covered door, and then a second a minute or so later. He glanced back again. He could barely see the subway station at all anymore. He fought the urge to bolt, go home and figure out another way to make some money.

And that's when he noticed it.

Headlights. Heading toward the 72nd Street stop behind him. Squinting, he quickly realized it wasn't a regular train. It was one of those "Out of Service" cars that blasted through subway stations. And it would be on top of him in no time at all. Even if he wanted to go back to the platform, he'd never make it in time.

Johnny whipped around and sprinted. He had no idea how close that third door would be, but figured he didn't have much time. He could hear the train rumbling closer behind him, louder than a normal engine. Never a religious man, not even close, he nonetheless prayed out loud for God to save him as his feet pounded the damp and uneven concrete strip that stretched next to the tracks.

The train hurtled closer, its horn blasting repeatedly, its brakes beginning to screech. Its light filled the tunnel, throwing sharp-edged shadows against the ground and walls. The conductor must have noticed a crazy person running along the tracks. Even with the brakes activated, though, there was no way the train could stop in time. Johnny felt the wind from the oncoming train swirl against his back just as he spotted the third door up on the right. He pushed himself harder, moving faster than he thought possible, and threw himself toward the door.

If it was locked, he was a dead man.

Johnny Sweat closed his eyes.

His shoulder hit the metal door.

It slammed open and Johnny fell forward, landing with enough force to knock one of the sneakers right off his foot. The train barreled past, brakes still screeching even though there was no longer a need. The door slammed shut again on its own.

He lay there on his back for several minutes, panting, eyes screwed shut, his chest on fire. Then he turned over and roared vomit all over the metal on which he was lying.

A few long moments passed, the sound of the train receding and then disappearing completely. Johnny caught his breath, swallowed, tried to ignore the terrible taste in his mouth. He suddenly realized how quiet it was. Opening his eyes, he got to his feet and took in his surroundings. Or attempted to.

It was dark in here… wherever he was.

Johnny blinked against the darkness and, after a few moments, his eyes adjusted to the relative gloom. He was standing on a small metal platform with a single bar at waist height, presumably to keep people from falling. If Johnny had moved a little farther forward while he was puking…

Peering over the metal bar, Johnny's stomach turned as he realized that all he could see from where he was standing was inky blackness. He wasn't a fan of heights... never had been. He'd worked plenty of rooftop jobs where he'd had to hide his terror, but it was always there, like some kind of childhood monster come to life.

Off to one side, a rusty metal staircase disappeared into the shadows. He glanced over his shoulder at the door through which he'd just come. There was still a chance to walk away from this. To head back to his tiny apartment and figure some other way out, maybe even try to get a legit job again. It had been something he'd been thinking about for a while... Maybe even go home and look up his dad? He'd been having dreams about him lately... realized maybe he even missed him.

Johnny shook his head, willing the emotions away. No. This was a good opportunity. The friend who'd told him about it said the pay was good and the work was easy. Johnny spit a wad of phlegm and leftover vomit into the darkness. Then he headed down the stairs.

They seemed to go on forever.

He felt like an idiot, tromping down the metal stairs wearing only one sneaker. His foot was cold, and wet. No telling what he had stepped in. He should've opened the door and looked for his other shoe, but the experience with the subway train had freaked him out too much. He didn't want to risk having his head lopped off while he crawled around looking for a sneaker that had holes in its sole anyway.

So he continued down. Fifteen steps, then a small landing, turn a hundred and eighty degrees, and then another fifteen steps. Over and over again. The railing was rough against his hand, occasionally shifting under his grip where it had almost rusted away. Every now and then he could hear a train rumbling past overhead, but even that noise began to fade into the background after a while.

Finally, twenty—forty?—minutes later, Johnny reached the bottom. He was out of breath, even though he'd kept an even pace. Yep, there was no question about it, he'd let himself go over the last year or so. Too many cigarettes, too much booze. Not enough exercise, except when he was beating someone down on a boss's orders, or running from the cops.

He stood at the bottom of the stairs for a moment, hands on his knees, bent over and sucking in big breaths of air. After a while he felt his heart stop hammering and resume a reasonable pace.

Johnny stood up, wiped the thin layer of moisture from his forehead, and smiled. "Sweat" wasn't actually his last name. He'd been born Jonathan Wasberski. But after he'd done a few jobs when he'd first moved to New York, following the incident at the hamburger joint, one of the other goons had mentioned how Johnny never seemed to sweat, no matter how many windows he broke or how many apartments he snuck into—and then out of, hauling bags of stolen goods. After that, all the guys started calling him "Johnny Sweat."

It was good to have a cool nickname when you were looking for work with some of the top criminal masterminds in the city. And he took pride in the fact that he never sweat. It meant he was always cool and collected… or at least appeared to be.

But now, standing at the bottom of an insanely long set of rusty metal stairs, way beneath the subway, Johnny had finally cracked a sweat. He laughed quietly. At least no one was around to notice and bust his chops about it.

A clanking sound pulled him out of his reverie, causing him to spin around as he searched for the source of the noise. There was light down here, enough to see a few details, but he couldn't tell where it was coming from. The ceiling was high—so high he couldn't see it above him—and the walls didn't seem to be concrete. It looked as if the tunnel had been carved through solid rock.

After a moment, he heard the sound again.

He stepped in its direction.

"Hello…?"

He took several more steps and then realized he was approaching another metal door. He raised a hand to knock, but stopped himself.

"This is stupid," he whispered.

"You must be Johnny," a voice intoned from behind him.

Letting out a little cry he whipped around, his stomach dropping, reaching into his pocket for the knife. Standing in front of him was a tall man in a dark red robe. He was bald and had a black-and-gray beard, which was thick but trimmed extremely short.

"Uh… yeah, that's me," Johnny replied, swallowing

nervously and keeping his hand in his pocket.

"I'm Brother Thaddeus," the man said, stepping closer. His voice was deep. "Thank you for coming." Where had this guy even come from? All Johnny had seen were impossibly tall stone walls and this one door. How did he get behind him?

"Sure, my pleasure," he said, trying to gather his confidence. "I heard you had a job, and I have a little time in my schedule."

A large, unpleasant smile appeared on the man's face. "I'm sure," he responded. A painful moment of silence stretched out. The unnerving smile remained in place while the man's dark eyes… shimmered?

"So… uh…" Johnny said, struggling to come up with words. "What's next? What's… where's the job?"

"It's right here," the man answered. He looked amused by Johnny's question.

"Huh?" Johnny blurted, looking around. They were surrounded by those high gray walls and the door, and nothing else. He couldn't even tell where that damn light was coming from. "I don't get it."

"Oh, you will."

Johnny felt a sharp pain in his neck and whirled around, whipping out his knife and slashing. He'd always had good instincts… it was part of what kept him alive while working for the best of the worst, and today was no exception. He slashed someone across the chest and watched as a second man in a red robe crumpled soundlessly, blood pooling out on the floor beneath his prone body.

"What the *hell*?" Johnny shouted, staring up at "Brother" Thaddeus, his dripping knife raised. Thaddeus stared down at his companion for a moment, and then back up at Johnny.

"Impressive…" he murmured, still with that infuriating grin.

Johnny's neck began to pulse and he looked down again at the second man. A needle was clutched in his hand. Johnny grabbed his neck, felt how hot it was. His vision began to blur.

"What'd… what did you do to me?"

"Good night, Jonathan."

Johnny took a step forward, tried to swipe at the man, at that damned grin, but he tripped on his own feet and went down, hard, next to the guy he'd stabbed. He tried to raise his free hand to stop his fall but failed, miserably, and hit the floor face first. He felt the blood flow from his nose, watched through heavy lids as it pooled out, mingling with the other man's.

Johnny's vision went dark.

And then absolutely black.

JOHNNY SWEAT woke with a gasp.

He was still face-down but the stone floor was gone, replaced by packed dirt. He took deep breaths, confused, and then broke into a coughing fit as dust filled his lungs. He dry-heaved for a moment, but there was nothing left in his stomach to expel. Finally,

Johnny found enough strength to sit up.

He was in a strange-looking room... wait, it wasn't even a room. It was oval-shaped and the walls went up about fifteen or twenty feet, topped with incredibly sharp razor wire. Light radiated down but once again, Johnny still couldn't see the source. Staggering to his feet, he turned in uncertain circles, confused, trying to figure out what the hell was going on.

Then he heard it. A sound.

Voices. A lot of them. Up in the shadows. Above the...

Arena. He was in some kind of arena.

"Hello?" he said, then he shouted. "Hello!"

The voices went silent.

"Help me!" he screamed.

The voices returned, but they were no longer speaking. It was laughter now. Johnny felt his face flush with anger. When he got out of here, he would find those laughing bastards and show them exactly how he—

A new sound echoed out, and Johnny turned again, trying to figure out where it was coming from. He noticed for the first time that there was an outline along one of the walls... no, two outlines, on opposite sides of each other. He squinted and tried to figure out what they were.

He realized that the outlines were actually slabs of metal, and they were lifting up as he looked back and forth at them, revealing darkness on the other side. They screeched as they moved, making the hairs stand up on the back of his neck. Doors. Some kind of makeshift doors.

Maybe a way out.

Johnny hesitated, and then hobbled toward one, shambling on one sneaker and one sock, pushing his aching body forward. The voices above him grew louder, but he did his best to shut them out. He'd make them all pay.

As he approached the opening, a sound made him stop. A low roar came from the darkness, rising in intensity… a sound so primal and rage-fueled that Johnny froze. The chattering voices above him grew even more excited.

Johnny backed up, and then turned for the other opening. If he could only make his way into the shadows, he was sure he could escape. And there were plenty of shadows in this second entrance. Shadows that seemed solid, seemed to be moving.

Johnny stopped again. The shadows were *literally* moving. How was that possible? He peered into them, trying to understand what he was seeing, when he realized that two huge red eyes were staring back.

He spun in place, looking first at the darkness from which the roar had emanated, and then at the living shadows, over and over again, trying to decide which horror scared him the least. Sweat ran down his face, down the back of his neck.

He didn't have time to make up his mind.

Two shapes burst forth from the doors simultaneously, one a blur of fangs and claws, the other a slithering mass of blackness, and they reached him at almost exactly the same time.

"Daddy…"

That was all Johnny Sweat had time to whisper. On one side, claws dug into his shoulder, sending bolts of pain down his arm and into his chest, then pierced his leg, while on the other side something wrapped around him and pulled flesh out in great chunks. He didn't even scream as he was ripped apart, and then discarded as the monsters crashed into each other.

Discarded as if he had never even existed at all.

ACT ONE
CITY OF SHADOWS

CHAPTER ONE

MICHAEL MORBIUS was hungry.

The lights of New York City fought hard against the dark clouds that had stalled overhead, but the incessant rain made it a losing proposition. Morbius was perched atop a four-story building at the corner of Fulton and Gold Streets, watching the occasional person pass by. It was three thirty in the morning, so most of them were drunk or well on their way, or heading home after a long shift at a restaurant or a bar.

Even from such a height, he could smell their blood.

It was intoxicating.

He swallowed his urges down, closed his eyes against temptation. It had been almost two full weeks since he'd drank blood from a living victim, the longest he'd gone since the experiment that had changed his life, since the beginning of his curse.

Then again, could he call it a curse if it had been self-inflicted?

Morbius raised his eyes to the steel-gray sky. *Let the water fall, let it sting.* His mind turned back on itself, returning to the beginning, like it always did, even when he attempted to will it otherwise.

He used to have such hope. A brilliant young mind at odds with an imperfect body, but full of idealism regardless. For as long as he could remember, he had suffered from a rare blood disease, had been told by doctor after doctor that there was no cure, but he'd refused to give up. And then came the opportunities: the chance to attend a prestigious college, to find a best friend, and even to fall in love.

Martine.

Her face flashed in his mind and he writhed in a response of physical agony. He missed her so much, longed to see her again, to hold her in his arms—but it was impossible. Even if he knew where she was, how could she love a monster like him?

He'd been so certain that his experiment would work. Electrifying samples of bat's blood, mutating it in a very precise way. It made sense, worked on paper, worked in the laboratory when he and Emil Nikos conducted their secret, controlled tests. But when they followed through with the experiment, out on the ocean, away from danger—or so they thought—everything changed.

Michael the human died that day.

Morbius the living vampire was born.

It hadn't been all that long ago but it felt like ages. So much had happened. He had murdered Emil. Had battled other beings with incredible powers. Lost Martine to an organization with otherworldly ties. Had succumbed to an undeniable thirst time and again, draining the blood of innocents, hating himself every time he did. Faced a cult that sought to sacrifice a young woman named Amanda Saint.

Morbius laughed and opened his eyes. The rain increased, washing down his pale skin in rivulets. He didn't laugh often, hadn't even before the experiment, and there was no humor in the bark that came from his thin lips now.

In an ironic twist, he had targeted Amanda himself, back in San Francisco. Had stalked her through the streets. The memory was still vivid. Her blood smelled so good, so pure. But he hadn't been the only hunter that night.

The Demon-Fire cult had set their sights on Amanda, too, and Morbius shocked himself by saving the young woman, and then protecting her from the cult over and over again. He hadn't understood why he did it, still didn't, when she represented a meal, with blood so enticing that it made him ache. Yet the two had formed a friendship, if a living vampire was capable of such a thing.

He felt for Amanda. Like him, she had lost so much. Her mother, who had abandoned their family to join the cult, and who was killed in front of Morbius. A death he still didn't have the courage to reveal to Amanda. Her father, searching for his wife, lost somewhere in the vastness of America and unaware that the woman he sought was already dead. And Amanda's sister, Catherine… another member of the cult, who died in battle with Morbius.

Amanda had no one. Morbius had no one.

So, they had each other.

Morbius shook the water from his long black hair. The rain was increasing, so the streets below had grown empty. He was alone.

Again.

AMANDA SAINT looked around, made sure no one was watching.

It was 6 a.m. and the hospital was relatively quiet. She'd only been working at St. Gabriel's for a few weeks, but she'd already figured out the ebb and flow of the place, knew when this particular hallway, the Pathology section, would likely be empty. There was a camera near the ceiling in the far corner, but she knew from talking to Jerry, the overnight security guard, that half of the cameras in the place hadn't worked in years. No one seemed to care. The hospital continuously struggled for funding, often losing patients to the larger and more modern Downtown Medical just a few blocks away. Only the most desperate of patients ended up at St. Gabe's.

Amanda was pretty desperate, too.

As she slipped into the Blood Issue room, her mind

cycled through the last month. It'd been a harrowing series of events, a blur of blood and betrayal. Bad enough when her mother ran off to join a cult, made worse when her father stupidly decided to save her.

So naïve, she thought. All he accomplished was to leave Amanda and Catherine alone to wonder and worry. She had no idea where the hell he was, or if he was even still alive.

Catherine had been her rock during that time, older and wiser, and she always seemed to know what to say. Always told Amanda that things were going to work out. That Catherine would take care of everything. It had made the abandonment a bit more bearable.

Amanda also had Justin. It'd been a random encounter—or so she had thought—shortly before her mother took off. Back when life was still normal.

They got to talking at a coffee shop, and minutes stretched into hours, their untouched drinks getting cold on a small table. Even when they left, they'd walked around the city, sharing stories about their lives and their dreams and their passions. Amanda had never been in love before, had never even been close, but this certainly seemed to have all the hallmarks of falling, hard and fast.

If she could have frozen time, Amanda would have done it then. Her parents, still at home and seemingly in love, if sometimes distant. An older sister who watched her back, and a thoughtful man who focused on *her*, who didn't rush her to do anything before she was ready. Everything was perfect.

Only, it wasn't.

Catherine and Justin had betrayed her, one after the other. They were both part of the same cult that had ensnared Amanda's mother. Hell, her own sister had been ready to sacrifice her to a demonic creature. Arachne.

Amanda shook her head to clear the memory of that giant spider as she closed the door behind her. It was too much to even think about sometimes. It didn't seem real. If it hadn't been for Morbius…

She smiled ruefully at the thought of Michael.

She had befriended a vampire. A living vampire, he was always quick to point out. Had almost been his victim, but when she'd been attacked by the cult, something had changed. And now they were…

Friends?

She didn't know what they were, but she cared about him. Which was evidenced by the fact that she was currently skulking around in a shadowy storage room in a run-down hospital, ready to steal a few more packets of cold, preserved blood.

She reached the refrigerator that held the containers and squatted down, looking at the sleeves of red liquid through the glass door. Michael told her repeatedly that he didn't care what kind of blood she brought home, but she knew he secretly preferred AB-negative.

Opening the glass door, she extracted a couple of packets, making sure there was enough left behind that no one would notice the theft. St. Gabriel's records programs were as bad as their security. She felt guilty about it—did every time she stole blood from the hospital—but she knew she was actually saving lives by doing so. Michael had managed to keep from murdering anyone for a couple of weeks now, and the blood Amanda stole had been the reason why.

She couldn't imagine the thirst that drove him.

Quickly placing one packet into each of the two pockets of her scrubs, she moved toward the door, then froze. There were voices in the hallway. She struggled to keep her breath even, to control her heart, which had already increased its beating. She didn't know what the authorities did to people who stole blood, but she didn't want to find out.

A pair of doctors walked past the door, visible through the little window, but didn't even glance in. Then they disappeared from view.

Amanda let out the breath she hadn't even realized she'd been holding. Laughed at herself. Everyone was so wrapped up in their own worlds. They had no idea that one of the new custodians was trying to keep a vampire... a living vampire... from killing again.

LIZ GREEN sipped at her coffee as the vampire slipped in through the window.

She had to stop herself from physically recoiling as he glanced from side to side. His huge bloodshot eyes landed on her, and went wide. He was ugly, there was no way around it, with his alabaster skin and long stringy black hair and sharp teeth. Yet she also had to admit to herself that there was something undeniably compelling about him, a magnetism that was hard to dismiss.

Still, Liz was terrified every time she was in his presence.

Slowly placing the coffee mug on the table, she felt sweat break out along the back of her neck, and forced a smile.

"Morning," she said.

He grunted a response, then strode past her and into her cramped extra room where he and Amanda had been sleeping. There were two mattresses on the floor, but Liz didn't ask any questions. It was none of her business what happened in there, even if Amanda had said repeatedly that she and her new bloodsucking companion were just friends.

When the door shut behind Morbius, Liz let out a small laugh at her own fear and took another sip of coffee. Sure, she lived in a city full of super heroes and monsters and mutants, but it was still pretty damn surreal to be sleeping one room over from a modern-day Dracula.

She stared out the window of her two-bedroom apartment and took another sip. As her mind drifted, she absent-mindedly played with a strand of her long, dark hair, most of which was pulled back into a tight ponytail. Liz and Amanda had been close when they were young, almost inseparable, really. They'd been two socially awkward teens in a small school, and had clung to each other the way outcasts at that age often do. During those years, they forged a quintessential bond—at least it felt that way—and vowed to always stay in touch. To always remain best friends.

But then graduation had happened, and the unraveling of that bond. Amanda and her family moved across the country. The two of them would sometimes see each other at holidays, and laugh that their lives had gotten so crazy, promised that they would be better, but then the time between communication would grow longer and longer, until it was like they had never known each other at all.

Liz had regretted the death of their friendship, found herself thinking about Amanda much of the time, but her life was such that she hadn't been able to dwell on it. She'd become busy bartending most nights and auditioning for off-off-off-Broadway plays and bad student films during the day.

She'd come close to being "discovered" once, had been approached one night after a play she'd directed and starred in. A guy in a nice suit carrying a business card emblazoned with an agency name she recognized, the kind of company that represented major stars. He'd told her to call him, which she did three days later… didn't want to seem too desperate.

But she never heard back. Maybe she had waited too long. She eventually convinced herself that she had *definitely* waited too long. Liz called a couple more times, but it didn't matter. He'd clearly forgotten about her, or had never been all that serious about connecting with her in the first place. Since then, the jobs had been sporadic at best, and she wondered what the hell she was even doing with her life.

Then there was her dad.

He'd helped her out so much over the years, lending her money when she needed it, but now he was sick. Really sick, and the medicine he needed was expensive. He was a proud man, *too* proud, but she knew he was in trouble. He'd lost so much weight in recent weeks, and his skin was so thin, like paper. She told him he should move in with her, that she was between roommates and had extra space, could help take care of him, but he refused and scoffed at her concern. He was fine, he insisted. Just going through a bad spell. The medicine would work, and then he could get back to hunting for a job.

Tears appeared in her eyes. Liz wiped them away and laughed at herself. She had an audition in a few hours, and didn't want to look puffy or depressed. It didn't take much for a casting director to move on to the actor behind you.

As Liz headed to the sink, the apartment door opened and Amanda trudged in, wearing her hospital scrubs. Liz smiled. Even though things were weird—to say the least—with Amanda and Morbius staying there, it was still a thrill every day for Liz to see her best friend.

Or whatever they were now.

"Hey," she said and a smile crossed Amanda's face, too, even though she looked exhausted.

"Hey there," Amanda replied, walking over to the table and slumping down into the seat Liz had just been occupying. "Is that coffee? It smells—"

Before Amanda could finish her sentence, Liz

placed a steaming cup in front of her friend. Amanda's entire body appeared to relax as she leaned over the aromatic steam.

"Oh my god," she said. "*Thank* you."

"Of course," Liz replied, mussing her estranged friend's hair, something she used to do back in high school. Amanda smiled and then took a long sip of the coffee, her eyes shut in apparent ecstasy. Liz sat down across from her and just watched her for a minute. She'd missed this.

"Is he...?" Amanda said, her eyes still closed, nodding toward the small room with the closed door.

"Yeah," Liz answered. "Came in a few minutes before you."

"Hm." Amanda opened her eyes and put the coffee down on the table. "I wonder if he..."

The two women stared at each other for a long moment.

"Attacked someone, murdered them, and drank their blood?" Liz finished for her in a monotone voice. Silence hung heavy for a minute and then the two women burst out laughing.

"It's not funny!" Amanda blurted.

"I know it isn't," Liz answered, and the two continued to laugh until it finally died down. Amanda chugged the rest of her coffee. It was still hot, and she waved her hand around her throat, as if that would help.

"Whoah," Liz said, her eyes wide.

"Ha, yeah, guess I needed the caffeine. It was a long night. Hell, it's been a long *month*."

"I know it has," Liz responded. "Anything new on finding your mom? Or your dad?" She still couldn't quite fathom everything that had happened to her friend.

Amanda released a long sigh, as if she'd been holding it in for hours, if not days.

"No. I mean, there was that note Morbius and I found back in Maine, telling us to go to Nevada, but I don't exactly trust it after everything we went through. I'm still reaching out to people who knew them… to people who may have been involved with Demon-Fire back in San Francisco, or Maine, or here in New York. But when I do, they either deny having any information or hang up on me as soon as I mention the cult. They sound so… *scared* when I even bring it up."

"Well, from what you told me, the people in that cult *are* pretty scary."

Liz's eyes wandered to a nearby window. From where she sat, she could just make out a sliver of sky above the top of the building next door. The dark gray rainclouds were moving on, making way for a radiant blue and a quickly rising November sun. The dichotomy, split almost evenly through the glass, was beautiful, but she found herself having trouble appreciating it.

"Yeah… that's an understatement," Amanda said finally, dreamily, also watching the blue overtake the full slab of sky that was visible. "I don't think I'll ever get the stench of that giant spider out of my nose… or the sight of its gaping mouth… those fangs… out of my head."

"I still can't believe that guy Justin was part of it all along," Liz said. "And your sister! I… I thought I *knew* Catherine. Can only imagine how painful it was. That cult, the way you've described it, is pure evil. I know I've already said it, but I'm sorry you had to go through that. I'm just surprised…"

Amanda pulled her eyes away from the window and looked at her friend. Liz's face was scrunched up as she searched for her next words.

"Surprised what?"

"I'm just…" Liz said haltingly, then blurted, "… surprised that you'd keep going… keep hunting for your mom and dad, after everything that's happened. If I were you, part of me would just want to run away and find a place to hide and never look back."

Amanda let out a laugh that contained no humor whatsoever.

"Trust me, I've thought about it," she said, "but I… I have to find my parents. Even if they're already dead, or a part of the cult. Even if it kills me, I can't just let them go. I love them too much to just abandon them. You know?"

"Yeah… I know," Liz responded, smiling sadly at her friend. "I'd do the same for my dad."

A long moment passed as they stared at each other, the sounds of an awakening New York City rising up to greet them. Cabbies laying on their horns, cops rushing to their destinations with sirens wailing, locals grumpily pushing their way past starry-eyed tourists.

"What a world," Amanda said finally.

"Seriously," Liz concurred, "but at least we get to see Thor fly by every once in a while."

Amanda rolled her eyes at her friend.

"I mean, have you seen his hammer?"

A spurt of laughter burst out of Amanda's mouth, followed by deep guffaws, and then she was laughing so hard that she could barely catch her breath. Liz couldn't remember the last time she'd seen her friend laugh so hard.

"You are the *worst*," Amanda said, wiping the tears from her eyes.

"Yep," Liz replied, sitting back in her chair. "And that's why you love me."

Amanda adjusted in her seat, as if something was poking her in the side. She reached into her jacket's inner pockets and pulled out the two packets of blood, dropping them down onto the table with an audible slap.

"Gross," Liz said, even though she'd been expecting it. She said the same thing every time Amanda came home and revealed her stolen goods.

As if in response, the door behind her opened.

Violently.

Liz stiffened immediately, all the mirth in the room dissipating in an instant. She could feel the vampire walking toward them, even though she didn't hear a thing. His ability to remain silent like that might have been the most frightening thing about him. She closed her eyes.

When she reopened them, Morbius was standing

next to the table, staring down at the packets with a look of dissatisfaction on his face.

"Only two?" he growled.

Amanda's expression went as dark as his, and Liz held her breath. Her two houseguests had a contentious relationship, to say the least, which would have been bad enough if they'd both been… you know… human.

"I'm doing the best I can, Michael," Amanda said sharply, staring daggers up into his pale face. In response, he grunted and grabbed one of the containers. Liz tried to will herself to look away, but she couldn't resist. It was like watching a car crash. She didn't want to see the monster feed, not really, but it was as fascinating as it was stomach-churning.

Morbius held the packet almost gingerly, staring at it with excitement despite his earlier words and attitude. He slowly raised it up and sunk his long fangs into it, through the plastic sheathe and into the plasma within. The gentle slurping sounds were almost as unnerving as watching the vampire's throat trembling as he chugged the dark red fluid.

When it was empty, he dropped the container back onto the table, drops of blood leaking out, and quickly grabbed the other, sucking it down just as quickly.

Liz made eye contact with Amanda and her friend opened her eyes a little wider, as if to say, *This is nothing compared to the things I've seen.* Liz nodded, wishing she had the courage to get up and walk away from the table. Before she could even process the thought, Morbius dropped the second packet as well. Empty. Both sat on the table, slightly crumpled, twin holes in the skin of each with the drops of blood still oozing out.

Swallowing down nausea, Liz looked up at Morbius.

The vampire's eyes were closed, head raised up to face the ceiling. From her angle, he looked almost peaceful, and Liz wondered if perhaps she was being too judgmental, too harsh about this haunted figure. Based on what Amanda had told her, despite everything that he'd done, the man had suffered through his own share of tragedy.

But then his huge eyes sprang open and found hers, and she recoiled. Any sympathy she felt instantly washed away as he wiped the blood from his mouth with the back of his hand and strode back toward the extra bedroom.

"Anything you'd like to say?" Amanda called out after him.

He stopped at the door, his clawed hand resting on the handle.

"I need more," he said, almost a whisper, and then he disappeared into the room. Amanda shook her head and looked over at her best friend, picking up the coffee cup in front of her.

"I was hoping for a 'thank you,'" Amanda said, staring at the bottom of the cup for a long moment, and then letting out an exhausted sigh. She looked up again, her eyes dark. "But what do you expect from a vampire?"

CHAPTER TWO

THE HOSPITAL was quiet. Very quiet.

Amanda walked down a hallway, pushing a mop and a bucket of water. Her job tonight was to clean up the floors in the southeast wing, a part of the hospital that had been under construction for months following some kind of super-powered battle, but was reopening shortly. She had never been down here and was unnerved by how silent it was. Even the car horns and sirens out on the street echoed softly in the distance.

The overhead fluorescent lights blinked on and off.

Apparently those needed fixing, too.

She stopped and pulled the mop out of the dirty water, cleaning the next section of floor. The peacefulness should have been nice, but too much had happened to Amanda recently for her to really enjoy it.

In the couple of weeks she'd been working here, she was almost always surrounded by people, something that had taken some getting used to after being on the road with just Morbius, but she had started to like it. She'd forgotten how much she enjoyed the company of others. An easy thing to forget after all the betrayal she'd suffered. Her mother. Her sister. Justin. It was almost too much to contemplate.

Amanda shook her head against these thoughts and focused instead on the burgeoning strength she had begun to find in herself, as a result. On the odd friendship she had with Michael. It was far from normal but, in many ways, it was the most stable thing in her life right now. She laughed at that thought and continued mopping.

The lights continued to flicker overhead and then went out altogether. The blackness was absolute.

The breath caught in Amanda's throat. She had always been afraid of the dark, going as far back as her childhood. Amanda would awake screaming from a nightmare, the darkness closing in around her, only to find a room just as dark. Her mom would come into her room, would push the hair back from her sweaty forehead and tell her that it was okay, that everything was going to be okay. She would sing quietly until Amanda slowly drifted back into unconsciousness.

What had happened to *that* woman? When had that person turned into someone who would run away and join a murderous cult? Yes, her parents' relationship had grown strained over the years, but her mom's abandonment of the family was still shocking.

Amanda's fingers tightened on the wooden mop

handle. She could feel the splinters pushing into her skin, but she ignored the pain, her eyes attempting desperately to see through the pitch blackness. There were no windows in this stretch of hallway and all the doors were closed due to the construction, the glass covered with yellowing newspaper.

A noise reached her from the end of the hallway. A skittering, and was that… *laughter?*

"Hello…?" she called out, her voice breaking slightly.

"Hello…" a voice replied… or was it her own echo? She wasn't sure, but she could feel the hairs on her arms standing on end. She took a step forward and then stopped. The laughter sounded again and the lights flickered for a second.

At the end of the hallway, a woman stood against the far wall, staring at Amanda. She had a sick smile on her face.

It was her sister. Catherine.

Her *dead* sister.

It can't be.

The lights went off again and a rushing noise filled the space, seemed to swell in the air around Amanda, and she held up her hands to stave it off. Terror rose up from her stomach and filled her lungs, the mop handle slapping down onto the ground loudly, and she almost screamed.

Then the lights came back on, nearly blinding her with their brightness.

The hallway was empty. She was alone.

"The hell…?" she whispered. "I'm losing my mind."

Amanda laughed at herself, secretly hoping the laughter would quell the fear. She leaned down to pick up the mop, then nearly cried out when she saw a pair of shiny black shoes.

Looking behind her, she saw a man wearing a security uniform.

"Jesus, Jerry, you scared the crap out of me," Amanda croaked, but she smiled and stood up straight. They'd become friendly since she started, and she made sure to always bring him a cup of coffee before her shift started. In return, he'd give her inside info about the hospital, like the details she needed about the Pathology section.

Her smile faded as she took in Jerry's demeanor. His arms were folded across his chest and his mouth was a straight line beneath his mustache. His eyes were dark and serious.

"Come on," he said without warmth. "Boss Man wants to see you."

"YOU'RE FIRED."

Amanda stared at the man sitting behind the desk. She tried to remain calm, even though she could feel the sweat breaking out all across her body. She had only been working at the hospital for a little while, but she had come to like the job, even if she'd originally taken it to help Morbius. She had made some friends, was learning about medicine, and had even thought about maybe going to nursing school someday.

"What…? Why?"

She knew exactly why.

"This meeting gives me no pleasure," he said through pursed lips. The nameplate on the desk said Matthew Costello, but he had instructed her to call him Matt when they'd met at her initial interview. The job was "only" a custodial position, but Matt had said that it could lead to bigger things, that she seemed bright and that this hospital—unlike Downtown Medical—often promoted from within. If Amanda could eke out six months or a year as a custodian, they might even help pay for classes.

That was all gone now.

"I like you, Amanda," he said. "I really do, and I had high hopes, but we do not tolerate theft at this hospital. Did you really think we wouldn't notice? I'm just chagrined that it took us this long. Our resources are stretched too thin, and this kind of thing does nothing to alleviate that situation."

"I… I can explain," she stuttered.

"What were you even doing with the plasma? Selling it?" he probed, confusion wrinkling his face. "I can't imagine it would fetch all that much. Why risk your job for so little reward? I'm genuinely baffled, Amanda."

"I was… I was saving lives," she said. She knew it made no sense but she thought it was important to say it. It was the truth.

Matt continued to stare at her with that confused look. Finally, he spoke.

"You're just lucky I'm not pressing charges," he responded. "Like I said, I'm fond of you. I'm so disappointed, but I don't think you're a bad person. Desperate maybe, but not bad. I just hope you'll make better choices in the future."

"Matt, can I—?"

"Jerry will see you out. You can collect your personal items from your locker, and you won't be welcome back to this hospital. If you ever require medical attention, I hope you'll avail yourself of Downtown Medical's services... though I hate to give them any business."

Amanda stood up, nodded. Were those tears in his eyes?

"I... I'm sorry, Matt."

"So am I, Amanda."

THE PHONE behind the bar rang, rattling Liz and causing her to drop the pen she'd been holding.

It was almost closing time... 1:45 a.m. and the bar was nearly empty. Liz was working on a crossword puzzle and about to pull her hair out. She hated these things, wasn't sure why she kept trying to do them, but her mom had always said they were good for you, that it was good to push your brain a little harder than it wanted to be pushed.

She missed her mom. She'd died years earlier. Cancer. It had happened so fast. Liz had never been the same, and neither had her dad, even though the two were divorced. She swallowed down sadness as the image of her dad's pale face rose unbidden in her mind. It was almost too much to handle sometimes. She just wished she could do more.

Liz turned around and grabbed the phone a little more aggressively than she'd intended.

"Dive Inn, whaddaya want?"

"Liz? It's Amanda."

"'Manda? What's up? Are you okay?"

"Yeah, yeah… um… I'm fine," the voice on the other end of the line breathed. "But I need help. Do you know anyone who works at any hospitals? I can't get any more plasma for Michael, and I'm afraid of what might happen when he finds out."

THE NIGHT settled on Alphabet City, that part of the Lower East Side where the avenues were named with letters, rather than numbers.

Liz had taken a spot at a table inside the bar, sipping from a glass of bourbon on the rocks, staring out onto the streets of Manhattan. She didn't usually drink at work, but it was past closing time, she was the only one there, and she figured she had earned it. It had been a busy night earlier, so much so that she'd barely been able to catch her breath until about 1 a.m., but her boss was too cheap to hire an extra bartender on crazy nights like this.

It had mostly been regulars, but there was one creepy-looking guy who'd sat alone at a table and never touched the drink he'd bought. Liz had caught him staring at her more than once, but it was New York City, so what was she gonna do? She'd seen and experienced worse.

Then on top of everything, the panicked phone call from Amanda. She had managed to talk her friend down and deal with a pissed off, drunk customer rolling into the bar at the same time. Multitasking was one of the many talents her boss ignored. Well, a glass of his best bourbon after-hours was the least he could do for his best—and often only—employee.

Sighing, she stared at the ice cubes as they melted into the brown liquid. It tasted *so* good but she wasn't getting much pleasure out of it right now. Today's audition had been a mess. Between her dad and her waning acting career, and the bloodsucker sleeping in the room next to hers, life hadn't been going exactly as she'd planned it.

The front door rattled. Liz looked up to see Fabian standing there, backlit by a passing car, his features disturbingly blacked out. But she knew his posture, the way he hunched his shoulders, that same green army jacket he always wore. Good ol' Fabian. The best worst person to know in a city like this.

Liz lifted herself out of her seat, at the same time finishing her drink in a single gulp. The ice cubes clinked against her teeth and she smiled as the bourbon burned her throat. Walking over to the door, she unlocked it and ushered Fabian inside.

"Hey," he said, walking in like he owned the place.

"Hey yourself," she responded, smiling, closing the door behind him and locking it. They had dated on-and-off for years, the kind of mind-bending, whirlwind romance she had only read about as a kid. Of course, it was messier than the books and movies she'd experienced when she was younger, never as neat or clean as the happy ending of a fictional story. Too many tears shed on too many drunken nights. But Fabian was generally a good guy, even if he did run with some tough characters now and then. He didn't mess around on her when they were together, and was always up front when he needed a break, never got angry when she asked for one. Always showed up when she needed help.

Like tonight.

Fabian walked behind the bar and poured himself a shot of cheap tequila, downed it without batting an eye. She sat back down at a table by the window, watched him while he poured another. He looked different tonight. There were worry lines etched into his forehead and he seemed tense, which wasn't a word she would normally use to describe Fabian Jones.

"You okay?" she asked.

"Huh?" he said, the second shot at his lips. His eyebrows rose and fell, as if attempting to answer her question, then he drank the alcohol and walked back around the bar, sitting down across from her. "Yeah, I'm fine."

"Okay. You just look—"

"I said I'm *fine*," he said, slamming his open palm on the table. Liz recoiled as if she'd been hit. Fabian was never violent, at least not around her, despite what she heard about the things he did out on the streets. She looked at him more closely as the sound faded. His eyes were bloodshot and puffy.

"Sorry," he mumbled. "It's… it's been a long night."

"It's okay. Really," Liz answered. "I'm sorry that I even bothered you. I know your nights can get crazy, and I know my request was really weird. I just figured you might—"

Fabian interrupted her by reaching into his leather jacket and tossing a plastic vial of blood onto the table.

At least it *looked* like blood.

The color was off. Almost black. Liz had never seen blood like this before.

"What… how?"

"You wanted blood, right?" he answered. "Well, there you go." He sat back, his usual cocky grin finally slithering back onto his face.

"But I just told you I needed it, like, a couple hours ago. I just figured you might know someone who works in a hospital, that maybe you could connect me with someone or get some in a few days or something. I didn't expect… wow."

"You happened to catch me at the right time," Fabian said, looking out the window as a loud group of teens ran by. "A friend of mine works at Midtown General and was just getting off when I called him. He was able to grab this one. That's it, though. He said it was too dangerous for him to get any more."

"No, this is great," she said. "I honestly wasn't expecting… but why does it look so weird?"

Fabian glanced at the packet of dark red fluid that lay between them.

"No idea." His expression said he didn't care. "You want it or not?"

"Sure, thanks. Beggars can't be choosers." She picked it up, suppressing a sudden wave of nausea. It even *felt* strange. "Which friend?"

"Huh?"

"Which friend works at Midtown General? You never mentioned him before."

"Oh. Uh… Francis."

"Francis?"

"Yeah, Francis. Why you givin' me a cross-examination? Did I come through for you or what?"

"Yeah," she said, scrutinizing him. She had never seen Fabian act so twitchy before, but maybe he'd just had a bad night, like he said. She heard the rumors about some of the stuff he did, some of the people he ran with, and she always made a point of not asking too many questions. She liked him, and didn't want to hunt down any reason to feel otherwise. "Yeah, you came through for me, Fabian. What do I owe you?"

"Well, it cost me an arm and a leg… but how about you and me go out this weekend on a date. Like, a real one. Dinner and a movie. Something like that."

He stared at her for a long time and she watched as he visibly relaxed. This was the Fabian she knew, the one she had originally fallen for. A confident guy but gentle underneath. Never really worried, even when life threw curveballs in his direction. She hadn't recognized the Fabian that had appeared a few minutes earlier. She was glad that guy was gone.

A grin broke open on Liz's face.

"Deal," she replied.

CHAPTER THREE

M

MORBIUS HELD the packet of dark blood in his hands.

He could feel Amanda's and Liz's eyes on him but he ignored them, instead tried to discern what he was looking at. He was, after all, a Nobel Prize-winning scientist. He knew better than anyone the intricacies of blood and its components. He'd studied this vital liquid more than any of his super-powered contemporaries, and certainly drank more than them, too.

The thought almost made him laugh… a mirthless humor that sometimes threatened to consume him.

Michael Morbius had never seen blood like this.

"Here, why don't we do this a little differently," Liz said, walking over to the kitchen and rummaging around in a couple of drawers and cabinets. Morbius looked over at Amanda, his only friend in the world. She smiled and shrugged. She had told him that she'd lost her job at the hospital, and he knew she was upset about it. Some distant emotional corner hidden within him felt bad about that fact.

Liz returned after a moment with a gold-colored chalice and a pair of scissors.

"Where did you get *that*?" Amanda asked, laughing. With the darkness of night lurking outside the apartment's dirty window, the laugh reverberated with a gallows humor.

"The goblet? Medieval Fun. My dad dragged me there a few years ago. Before, you know. It's tacky as hell, but I couldn't bring myself to throw it away. Seems appropriate now."

Liz gently placed her fingers on the plastic vial, and Morbius' head snapped up. His eyes locked on hers, and then ventured down to her bare neck. She had never let him come this close to her before. At least not willingly. She couldn't stop her fingers from trembling.

"Here," she barely got out. "Let me help you."

After a moment, the muscles in Morbius' face relaxed, then his hands, and he let go. Liz nodded nervously and brought up the scissors, slicing open the top of the packet. Like the experienced bartender she was, she poured the dark liquid into the goblet without spilling a drop. Its smell was nearly overwhelming. He had never experienced anything like it before—not unpleasant, but not exactly pleasant either.

Liz's expression, however, made it pretty clear she didn't like it.

"Bottoms up," she whispered, holding the goblet out to Morbius. He nodded his head slightly, and took hold of it. His claws gently raked her skin and she shivered visibly, though she held her ground.

Morbius held the goblet up and inhaled deeply through his flattened, deformed nose. Every molecule in his body seemed to come alive at the mere scent of this blood. He held it away from himself for a moment, tried to see exactly what he was about to drink, but it was thick and opaque.

"This smells different than ordinary human blood," Morbius mused. "Where did you say you got it?"

"My friend, Fabian. He... knows people. I didn't ask too many questions."

Morbius considered this answer. His scientific brain told him to get more information, but the vampire in him told the scientist to shut up. He looked up at Amanda, who smiled and raised her chin.

Go ahead, she said with her eyes.

Morbius nodded and slowly tipped the goblet toward his lips. This was packaged blood, just like he'd been suffering through for weeks, but it was also different on a molecular level, he suspected. He hadn't felt this excited since his teeth had last sunk into the neck of an unwilling victim. He cursed himself for how much he loved that memory. How much he loved the memory of every single one of them. He'd never thought it was possible to love and hate something with such equal fervor.

The goblet touched his lips. Despite looking like metal, it was cheap plastic, but he ignored that and tipped the receptacle farther, the liquid slowly oozing down toward his tongue.

He took in a single breath.

The first drop of the blood touched his tongue.

And everything changed.

Morbius' senses exploded. The entire apartment tunneled. The ceiling seemed to explode and then reconstruct itself into a crystalline form. He could hear the two women breathing, could smell the sweat on their skin, but when he looked at them, all he could see were their veins, spreading out like mazes across the outlines of their bodies. The room went blindingly bright and then dark, then strobed different colors.

Gathering himself as best he could, Morbius gulped the rest of the blood, unable to feel the rest of his body as he did so. His skin was crawling, a strange warmth buzzing up and down from his stomach, his entire being seeming to fill up the room. A bizarre smile creased itself onto his face and a strange sound fell out of his mouth.

Laughter. Coarse and guttural.

Michael Morbius took two halting steps as the goblet fell from his clawed fingers, and then he burst through the window without opening it and out into the growing shadows of the night.

"WHAT THE hell was *that*?" Liz said, looking over at her friend. "Has he ever acted that way before?"

Amanda walked toward the window, careful to avoid the few pieces of shattered glass that had ended up on the floor. She peered out, straining to see over the nearby rooftops, but Morbius was long gone.

"No, never," she murmured. Silently, she hoped he wouldn't hurt anyone.

Including himself.

MORBIUS TURNED his face up to the moon and smiled.

Waves of pleasure rippled across his body, unlike anything he had ever experienced. He was back in his familiar perch at Fulton and Gold, a spot he liked because the darkness here seemed to wrap naturally around his body, shrouding him in almost perpetual shadows.

He closed his eyes, but the moonlight only grew more intense for him, pushing past and through his skin, traveling down his throat and into his stomach and extending through his limbs, exploding out of his fingertips and toes. He laughed and reopened his eyes. The moon was a tiny dot in the starry distance, then blazed a path back to its rightful place, pulsing to the same rhythm as Michael's own heartbeat.

He slowed his breathing, tried to get ahold of himself. He had seen and done so many unbelievable things in his life, especially since the botched experiment, but he couldn't remember ever feeling quite like this. Except perhaps when he was with Martine…

The thought of her sent his mind spinning.

He closed his eyes again as memories flooded into his reeling mind. For a moment, he was a boy again in Greece, holding his mother's hand as she walked him to school. He'd been a bright child… too bright, bullied for what was considered his strange appearance and preternatural gifts at math and science. But his mother had always supported him, no matter what.

Michael's father—a writer, artist, and filmmaker—was almost never home, so Michael and his mother relied upon each other. She told him to ignore those other children, that they were jealous. He was destined for great things, she said.

And then came the sickness.

Michael had been called to the front of the class despite trying to hide himself in the back row, behind the rest of the students. His teacher knew he was bright, suspected he needed as much support as possible, so she asked him to come to the front and finish the math equation that had been stumping everyone else. Michael had already solved it in his head, but he didn't want to stand in front of the others.

The teacher insisted.

The chalk trembling in his hand, not feeling all that well, Michael had begun to solve the equation when he coughed violently, and a splatter of thick, dark blood shot out of his mouth, spraying the chalkboard. The children yelled and some laughed, and the teacher recoiled. She had always been so nice to him—but now? Now she looked disgusted. Michael tried to apologize to her but instead he coughed again and this time the spray of blood covered her.

The teacher's innocent scream was the first of many he'd hear in his life.

Despite their relative poverty, Michael's parents somehow managed to have him seen by multiple doctors, but the diagnosis came back the same from each. He suffered from a rare blood disorder, and would most likely live a short, pain-filled life.

His mother never cried in front of him, but at night Michael could hear her weeping through the thin walls that separated their bedrooms.

BACK ON the rooftop, Michael opened his eyes and stared again at the moon, hoping its brightness would sear the painful memories from his mind. Yet even with his eyes open, the strange blood that Liz had given him coursed through his system, warping his senses, and more memories rose, unbidden.

HE WORKED hard in school, consistently coming at the top of his class despite his illness, and started a career as a scientist in Greece, happy to be free of the childishness and immaturity of his classmates. To his surprise and dismay, however, his unattractive appearance and brusque personality made him an outcast in the scientific community as well, even after he'd won a Nobel Prize. He had learned that academics acted like schoolyard bullies when presented with someone who didn't look or act the "right" way.

Undaunted, he moved to Athens, which beckoned to him like a tantalizing stranger, and the city had been everything he'd hoped.

At least at first.

On those streets, no one seemed to give Michael's strange appearance a second glance. The Nobel money was enough for him to rent a studio apartment and buy some used furniture. It wasn't much, but he was happy—when his blood didn't betray him and send waves of breathtaking pain coursing throughout his body.

He often found himself sleeping through the day and walking the still-busy streets at night. That was when he felt more at home, more alive in his own skin. The daylight revealed too much.

Eventually the money began to run out, so he started looking for work. It took a few weeks, but one of his former classmates—one of the only kind ones—named Emil Nikos reached out and told Michael about a job opportunity.

It was in a cutting-edge laboratory, hidden high in the hills outside the city, where they were studying the blood of animals, figuring out ways to better the human condition. It was perfect. Michael joined a team of dedicated scientists and no one seemed to mind his gaunt appearance or his quirky personality. In fact, they seemed to like both.

Emil, now his co-worker at the lab, continued to accept Michael as no one else ever had, and their friendship was a bond that would never be broken.

And then, one night, he met Martine. She worked in

a different section of the lab. She wasn't a scientist but she was brilliant. And beautiful. And funny. And when she looked at Michael, he couldn't detect any disgust at all. She seemed only interested in his intellect—his scientific curiosity and the kindness that was often hidden behind his biting words. He kept his sickness hidden from her, even though he longed to tell her the truth.

Michael refused to seem weak in front of her.

Martine liked Emil, as well, and the three of them bonded—in the facility and the world outside. They would often leave work and find places where they could continue their conversations and intellectual arguments, in particular at a bar in a small town near where their laboratory was located.

It was on one of those nights, after Emil had left early to see another friend across town, that Michael and Martine had kissed for the first time. He would never forget it. His first kiss. With the woman who would become the love of his life. It was perfect.

And then… it wasn't.

Michael's blood condition worsened. His doctor told him that there wasn't much time remaining. Weeks. Maybe months. He confided in Emil, and his friend promised they would fight it. Emil would do everything in his power to save his best friend's life.

BACK ON the roof, Michael looked away from the moon. The memories were so strong. It was as if they were playing out in front of him. He didn't want to see this next part, but the images followed his gaze even as goosebumps washed across his skin.

Despite the painful thoughts, the strange liquid he'd ingested still flooded his body with pleasure. He stared at a nearby building, and the memories seemed to play out across its walls like a flickering movie on a screen.

EMIL'S PASSION to save him led Michael to an idea. Something that he had been researching at the laboratory. A procedure involving bats.

Vampire bats.

What he and Emil did would be illegal, but they didn't let that stop them. Indeed, Morbius had no choice. He had a life now. Had a woman who loved him and whom he loved desperately. He wanted to *live*.

Theoretical science gave way to practical testing, and they reached the point where it was do-or-die. They decided to perform the procedure on a boat, out at sea, where no one could stop them, and Morbius spent every last penny he possessed outfitting a chartered yacht far from Greece, at an English seaport.

He and Emil returned to the lab for the final equipment they would need, and as they prepared to leave, Martine insisted on accompanying them. Morbius found himself unable to say no.

They booked a ride on a tanker that took them through the sun-drenched Mediterranean and eventually dropped them off at the seaport, where they made their way to the yacht. Despite Martine's curiosity at what her lover and his friend had planned, they kept the details a secret from her. Morbius sometimes wondered if everything would have turned out differently had he told her the truth. About everything. Perhaps she would have talked him out of it.

Perhaps all the lives he had destroyed could have been spared.

Emil fought with him. He wanted to tell Martine what they had planned, but Morbius forbade it.

The night of the experiment, Michael and Martine had dinner on the deck, talked quietly, and watched as the sun set over the water. It was one of the most beautiful things Morbius had ever seen, perhaps the happiest he had ever been. Which made saying an early good night to her that much harder. He had to work, he told her. Her final words to him, before his transformation, were heartbreaking.

"Of course," she said. "I understand, my love, but do not work *too* long. You seem… so pale."

They kissed, and then Michael made his way below decks, where Emil greeted him. The machinery was ready.

First, Morbius donned an insulated suit he would be cursed to wear in perpetuity. After that, Emil helped him climb into gear that made it look as if he was about to walk on the moon. Once the helmet was locked in place, Emil stared through the glass and looked his best friend in the eyes.

"Are you sure...?" Emil asked. "This is highly risky, Michael."

One last opportunity to avoid his fate.

"Unless this shock treatment succeeds... against all hope, all odds," Morbius had answered, his voice muffled, his eyes wild with desperation, "I'll measure out my life in days. Perhaps hours."

"I... know," Emil had responded, turning to the computer and beginning to input the commands necessary to begin the experiment. "But electrical creation of blood cells is something that's never before been attempted," he continued, "let alone achieved. If only we had time to gauge all possible results, all potential side effects..."

Morbius closed his eyes. He knew the moment had come, and heard Emil's final words before they reached the point of no return.

"As you say," Emil agreed, "we have no choice. What side effect could possibly be worse than death?"

IF ONLY Morbius had known. If only he had listened. He had learned since that night that there were many things worse than death.

The images continued to play out in front of him as he crouched on the Manhattan rooftop. It was surreal, as if he were both watching and experiencing the events simultaneously. Emil hit the button that began the procedure, and in the present he could almost *feel* the pain of the electrical shocks that had coursed through his body, that sent the altered vampire bat's blood coursing through his veins.

The pain had lasted a moment.

Had lasted a lifetime.

The next thing Morbius knew, Emil was helping him get the helmet off, helping him out of the chair. Michael felt so weak at first, so cold, and the overhead lights burned into his eyes. His brain. That was the first indication that something had changed, that something was very wrong.

Poor Emil.

He helped Michael to another room. To rest, to recover.

The world went red, and without knowing how it had happened, Michael found his hands wrapped around his best friend's throat. Squeezing. Ignoring the gurgling cries of the man who had tried to save his life.

Until Emil was dead at Morbius' feet.

Michael had wept in the moments after he realized what he had just done. He had *killed* a man—something he never could have imagined. He stared at Emil's corpse for several long minutes, then climbed back up to the deck, desperately needing to get some air, to think.

And then the thirst overwhelmed him for the first time.

The absolute need to drink human blood. He could smell Martine's, even from the other side of the boat. It smelled so *enticing*.

Realizing what was about to happen, he came to his senses and threw himself off the side of the ship.

From that day onward, his life had become a perpetual hellscape. He had transformed into a monster—there was no other way to describe himself. Had murdered his best friend. Watched the love of his life placed in thrall to a powerful man named Reverend Daemond. Killed the innocent, over and over again.

SCREAMING, MORBIUS launched himself into the sky, almost hoping he would somehow be engulfed by the light of the moon and burned to a cinder.

As he rode the wind currents, another wave of ecstasy wracked his body, pushing the memories out of his mind; he *smiled*, taking in the metallic beauty of the city. The lights shimmered and humans milled about, oblivious to the bizarre creature hovering above them.

"No!"

The voice echoed from below.

At first, Morbius wasn't sure if it was real or a product of the bizarre fluid he had imbibed. He looked around, didn't see anything. It had been a figment of his imagination, after all.

"Please!"

The voice again. Desperate. Pleading.

Morbius' mind cleared somewhat and his eyes found the source of the cries. Gold Street ended in little more than an alleyway, where the trash had piled up and shadows congregated. There, a woman was being pulled deeper into the darkness by a man whose face Morbius couldn't make out. But it wasn't just any woman.

It was Martine.

Without thinking, Morbius dove. The wind pushed against his face but he could barely feel it, was barely aware of anything except the shock of blond hair that belonged to the love of his life. He had been looking for her for so very long, ever since she had been abducted by Daemond. But her trail had gone cold, and Morbius had found himself diverted by Amanda's plight, focusing on that rather than his own.

And now, here she was. Martine. How was it possible?

It didn't make sense.

It also didn't matter. They would be reunited.

Finally.

Morbius landed and dropped into a crouch just behind the female figure, then rose up to his full height. From this new angle, the moon's light revealed the face of her attacker, and Morbius felt the breath sucked from his lungs. Reverend Daemond stared back at him, a cruel sneer on his face.

Morbius hesitated but Daemond didn't. He pushed Martine aside and lunged, shoving a knife deep into Morbius' stomach. Dark blood spilled out, but Morbius barely felt it. Normally, he was strong— incredibly so, ever since the transformation—but being stabbed should have yielded much more pain. Perhaps it was another side effect of the strange blood, he mused in a distant corner of his mind.

Daemond stared down at the blade protruding from Morbius' stomach, a look of surprise and consternation crossing his face. As the black blood slowly leaked onto his hand, Daemond let go of the knife and attempted to pull back his arm, but he was too slow. Morbius' claw-like fingers clamped onto the man's arm and wrenched it to the left, easily breaking the bone and sending it exploding out of its flesh casing, followed by a spurt of blood.

Daemond screamed and collapsed to his knees.

Morbius smiled. He had dreamed of this day.

The moonlight hit Daemond's face and neck, and Morbius realized at that moment, with absolute shock, that he felt no hunger whatsoever. He had no interest in draining the life from his opponent, at least not using his fangs.

Morbius blinked, his senses still scrambled, and watched as Daemond's blood poured from his ruptured arm and flowed onto the dirty ground below. But then the man's hair began to grow, and became… lighter? Was this some sort of trick? Certainly the man had access to dark magic, but no, this didn't seem to be his doing. His face was transforming as well, scruff appearing, and multiple rings in each ear.

It wasn't Daemond at all.

Thinking his brain was playing tricks on him, Morbius turned quickly. Martine was there. She had pressed herself against the nearby wall, eyes going back and forth between the two combatants, terrified of both.

"Martine… it's me," Morbius said as softly as he could, while the man continued to groan behind him. "It's Michael."

"Stay away from me!" she yelled and her features began to change, too. Hair growing shorter, darker. Nose elongating, eyes changing color. This wasn't Martine—it was a woman he didn't recognize. Morbius had inadvertently stopped a mugging, had done the right thing for all the wrong reasons.

A growl escaped his lips as he leapt away, back to the top of the nearby building and the safe shadows therein. From there he watched, his skin still prickling, as the woman ran back to Fulton and flagged down a police officer. Within minutes, several emergency vehicles arrived. The criminal was treated, and placed into the back of the ambulance, where he was handcuffed to a stretcher.

The first officer put away his notebook and spoke to the woman. She shook her head and began to walk away as the incident faded away from the city's consciousness. At the end of the street, however, the woman stopped and looked up into the darkness. Morbius wondered if she could see him. The smallest smile appeared on her face… or did he imagine that?

And then she was gone.

New York pulsed around him and Morbius sat back, moving out of the shadows, letting the moonlight wash over him. Despite the fact that his mind was playing tricks on him, his body was alive with intense sensory palpitations. He couldn't remember the last time he had felt this at peace with himself and his surroundings.

Michael Morbius closed his eyes again, and smiled.

CHAPTER FOUR

AMANDA AWOKE from a nightmare where she was covered with thousands of tiny spiders.

It was the same dream she'd been having ever since she had nearly been eaten by a giant, demonic arachnid. Since she had been tagged as a human sacrifice by her boyfriend and her sister. *Her own sister.* It still didn't seem real. The memory of the betrayal was a hundred times worse than the horrifying image of the spider.

How could Catherine do that to her?

Drawing in a deep breath, Amanda counted to three, and then released it. She had read in a book that this simple exercise could greatly reduce stress and anxiety. It usually worked. But right now?

Not so much.

A noise came from outside her small bedroom, the one she shared with Michael, and she realized it was the same noise that had woken her. She blinked rapidly, willing the sleep out of her mind, then stood up. Opening the door slowly, she peeked out and saw Michael standing at the kitchen table, washing his hands. The hot water handle glistened red.

Off to one side, a makeshift patch of cardboard and tape hung from the window.

"Michael…" she said quietly.

The living vampire whipped around, his fangs bared, but then instantly checked himself, his entire body relaxing at the sight of his friend.

"Amanda, I'm sorry. Did I wake you?"

She had never heard his voice sound quite like that. It was softer somehow, maybe even… happier? That didn't seem possible. Michael was often short with her, sometimes downright rude, though she knew the bad attitude came from a place of pain. This seemed like a very different Michael Morbius than the one she had come to know over the last several weeks and states.

"No, I was awake," she lied. "But what about you? Are you okay? You drank that weird blood and then blasted out of the window. Where have you been?"

Morbius walked over to the table and sat down, pink water dripping from his fingers and onto the floor. Liz and Amanda had spent half an hour cleaning up the shattered glass and taping cardboard over the gaping hole. Michael had pushed back through it during his re-entry. He wasn't exactly the dream roommate.

She smiled at the ridiculousness of the thought, of the idea that she was debating the merits of bunking with a vampire, and took a seat across from her pale-skinned companion.

Morbius closed his eyes and sat silently. For a moment, Amanda thought he might have fallen asleep. And then he spoke without opening his eyes.

"I can still feel it," he said. "That strange blood. Working its way through my body. The effects are diminished... I suspect they'll be gone entirely within an hour, but it's still there. I... I've never experienced anything like it before."

Amanda took that in. He had told her some of the things that had happened to him since he'd turned himself into a vampire. Stories of other worlds and superhuman beings. So this was quite an admission.

"Is that good or bad?" she asked.

Morbius opened his eyes and stared into hers. It usually unnerved her when he did this, because she could sense the hunger he was fighting, even when he was doing his utmost to hide his desire to bite into her neck and drink her dry. But not now. She saw no such desire in his expression.

"Good," he said, sounding surprised by his own answer. "It's good. My hunger was gone. I felt at peace with myself. I saw the world laid bare, as I think it was meant to be seen." Each word was tentative, as if he didn't trust them to be true.

"That's... that's amazing," Amanda said. "I'm really happy for you. It must have felt so great to be out there and..." She paused, and looked at his hands. "And not have an urge to attack anyone."

"Well…"

"Well, what?"

Michael looked down.

"I may have attacked someone."

"Michael, you just said—"

"It was a criminal, Amanda," Morbius said, looking back up. Despite what they were discussing, she fought another smile. He looked almost like the child he had once described to her. That bullied little boy in Greece. It was moments like this where her heart bled for this poor, cursed man. Vampire. Whatever. He wasn't evil. At least, she didn't think he was. Not when she got right down to the deepest part of his soul.

"He was mugging a woman," Morbius continued, "and I… well, I broke his arm in half. But I saved her."

"Huh," Amanda responded, inwardly cringing at the image. "Well, I guess that's… positive, then?"

Morbius stared at her for a long time, looking as if he was wrestling with his next sentence. She waited, gave him the time he needed, and then he finally said it, quietly. Almost a whisper.

"I thought the woman was Martine."

"Oh," Amanda said, her stomach turning. She knew how much Michael missed the love of his life, how worried he was for her. It was a devastation that Amanda knew all too well. "But it wasn't her."

"No," Michael answered after a moment. "That blood Liz gave me, it… it *did* something, to my brain. It took time for me to get control of it, of myself, but by the end of the night I figured out how to sort through

what I was seeing, to use the side effects to my benefit."
He leaned forward. "That blood might just be the
answer to all my problems. I may never need to feed on
a living person ever again."

"That's… that would be amazing," Amanda said,
and she meant it. She knew that Michael agonized every
time his thirst led him to murdering an innocent victim.
Deep down, she was afraid of him, too. Always had been.
She often wondered if she would wake up in the middle
of the night and find him hunched over her, his long
teeth sinking into the soft flesh of her neck. "I'll ask Liz
if she can get more."

"Thank you, Amanda. I…"

She looked up at him and saw that he was struggling
to speak. She had never seen him like this, and fought
back a laugh, didn't want him to think she was making
fun of him. This was a new side of the living vampire,
and she liked it.

"You what, Michael?"

"I'm sorry that you lost your job because of me. I
know you liked it."

"Oh," she said, unable to hide her surprise. "It's okay.
I mean, yeah, I did kinda like it, but I only took that job to
help you in the first place. Besides, this will give me more
time to research Demon-Fire. I'm starting to feel like the
trail has gone cold. Maybe New York City was the wrong
place after all. We can always move on. There was that
note someone left us back in Maine about Las Vegas. And
I'm sure Liz will be happy to get us out of her hair."

"She's kind," he said quietly. "Like you."

"Yeah, she's a good one. We go way back. Hit it off immediately, the second we met. We were freaks. Guess we still are."

"I like freaks," Michael said.

"Yeah, me too," Amanda replied, sitting back in the chair and closing her eyes. She was tired, but surprisingly content. In a couple of hours, when the sun rose, she would resume her search for mother and her father. But for right now? Amanda Saint was happy.

LIZ GREEN wasn't happy.

It had been a long night. There had been some kind of corporate function at a hotel near her bar, and a gaggle of black-suited jerks had descended on the Dive Inn, taking over the place with their loud drunken voices and flailing arms and expensive haircuts and big stupid faces, driving her regulars out. They were too drunk to tip well and overstayed their welcome, until she'd been forced to turn off the music and turn on most of the lights to get them to finally leave.

One straggler had tried to convince her to go home with him, but she laughed in his face and literally shoved him out onto the sidewalk. He stood there for a minute, pouting, looking like she'd ripped apart his favorite stuffed animal, until he finally got the hint and grabbed a passing cab.

It took her a long time to clean up the mess they left behind. Fabian was supposed to stop by around

2:30 a.m. with another package of blood, but that time came and went, and still no Fabian. She called him, but it just kept ringing and ringing. He had never been the most reliable guy, but she was annoyed anyway. Amanda had told her about the effect it'd had on Michael—how they both saw it as a potential cure for his... well, murderous personality.

Sure, the broken window had been annoying, but if they really had cured a vampire, then Liz figured having to clean up some broken glass was a small price to pay.

At 3 a.m., the bar was finally in reasonable shape. She tried Fabian one last time, but he still didn't pick up. She growled inwardly. What else could she do? Maybe he'd call later, and Amanda could pay for a car to bring him to the apartment, deliver the blood directly to the vampire. Besides, Michael had been sleeping all day, apparently the soundest sleep Amanda had ever seen him get. Maybe he'd sleep all night, too.

The trip back to her apartment wasn't much better. Her train broke down between stations, and they were stranded there for twenty minutes, the lights flickering, the air system off, and a weird odor getting worse and worse every second that went by. She tried to move to another car, but neither door on either end would open.

"This is a fricking coffin," she whispered.

Finally, the fans came back on, then the engine, and with a lurch the train finally lumbered forward. After a few more starts and stops, it deposited her at the station closest to her apartment building. She ignored the random guy cat-calling her a block away from her place, and then dragged herself up the four flights of stairs. She was ready for a huge glass of water, a couple of aspirin, and about four hundred hours of sleep.

"WHERE IS *it?*" Morbius demanded the instant she entered the apartment.

He looked terrible. His already pale skin was whiter than usual, and there were huge bags under his giant eyes. His long black hair was greasy and messy. She'd never thought of him as particularly monstrous looking—she'd dated a few guys with a similar esthetic, after all—but he sure looked like a monster right now.

Amanda stood nearby, her eyes wide with fear.

Liz had seen terror in her best friend's eyes when they were teens. Hell, the two of them had been afraid of almost everything. But since Amanda had showed up again, Liz had been amazed at her friend's newfound confidence. She might even credit it to Morbius. Hanging out with a vampire—one who left you alive out of pure friendship—had to have a profound effect on your sense of self-worth.

But that was gone now. Amanda looked like the scared teenager Liz had known so well.

"What's… going on?" Liz said quietly, leaving the door unlocked in case things went south.

"Where is it?" Morbius repeated, taking a couple of unsure steps in her direction. "I need that blood!"

Liz fought to keep herself from turning around and running, calling the cops or the Avengers or whatever. She had convinced herself that Morbius would never hurt her, or maybe Amanda had convinced her of that, but right now she wasn't so sure. But no, she couldn't leave her best friend alone with this bloodthirsty lunatic.

For a moment, she wondered what her dad would do if she was found dead, two bloody holes torn in her neck. Who would take care of him? She forced the image away and instead held up her chin, staring directly into the vampire's bloodshot eyes.

"I'm waiting to hear back from Fabian," she answered, managing to keep her voice steady. "He told me he could get it, and I believe him. He probably just got busy or something. I let him know it was important."

She held her breath, waiting.

Morbius moved away from her, a low rumble sounding in his throat. Liz released the breath. He reached the window and tore away the cardboard, a cool wind immediately pushing in and causing his hair to undulate behind him. Liz almost yelled at him, but she checked herself.

Pick your battles, Lizzie, she told herself.

Amanda looked over and her eyes said "*I'm sorry.*" Liz shook her head. "*Don't worry about it.*" The two of them had these kinds of silent conversations all the time when they were kids. They smiled at each other. Despite the insanity of this situation, it was nice to have each other again.

"Michael," Amanda said, stepping toward the vampire, "I know you're in pain but you're doing great. I'm sure Fabian will—"

"Shut up!" Morbius yelled, turning and facing her. Amanda recoiled, surprise etched onto her face. "I am *so* sick of your constant sniveling. You've dragged me halfway across the country, searching for your father, and what do we have to show for it? *Nothing!* I should have minded my own business when I saw you on the street."

He stopped. Amanda's eyes went wide with shock, then narrowed in rage. Silence filled the room, seeming to press against each of the three people within, and no one spoke for a long moment, didn't even seem to breathe.

"You really are a monster," Amanda whispered, then she turned and walked into the apartment's extra room, slamming the door with enough force that the walls shook.

Liz looked at Morbius, and saw a range of emotions playing across his features, from rage to confusion to… sadness?

Enough of this, she thought, anger growing within her. She went to the table, grabbed a pad of paper, and started to write. When Morbius turned to look at her, she tore the sheet off the pad. Stepping closer to him, she glared and held it out, refusing to show any fear.

"Take it," she said.

"What is it?" he growled, though clearly intrigued.

"It's Fabian's address," she said, her eyes wide and angry. "He's the kind of guy who doesn't mind a pop in, and he owes me one from last New Year's Eve. Even if he doesn't have the blood, he can let you know where he got it. Tell him I sent you and that we're even. He'll know what you mean."

"I—" Morbius said.

"One more thing," Liz said sharply.

"What?" he snapped back.

She stepped even closer, surprising both of them. He looked hungry.

She was pissed.

"Don't ever come back here."

His lips curled back, revealing his sharp fangs. They stared at each other for a long time, and then without another word, he turned around and dove out the open window.

The tension went out of Liz in an instant. She wobbled over to the kitchen and poured herself a huge glass of whiskey. After drinking it down in one slow, smooth gulp, she headed across the room and tapped lightly on Amanda's door.

CHAPTER FIVE

MORBIUS GLIDED above the city, trying to ignore the growing ache that gnawed at his stomach.

He was hungry, there was no denying it, but some of the pain came from an overwhelming sense of guilt at treating Amanda so poorly. She was his only friend. He needed her.

"No!" he bellowed into the wind, shaking his head, angry with himself. He was Michael Morbius. He had gone toe-to-toe with super-powered humans and mutants and monsters, and he had never allowed anything to stand in the way of his goal. He wouldn't start now.

Pushing the image of Amanda's crestfallen face out of his mind, he continued toward his destination. He was close to the apartment building where he would find the man called Fabian. He would acquire more of that strange blood—as much as possible, slake his thirst for as long as he could—and then deal with the matters he'd left behind.

After a few more minutes, he descended and landed on top of a five-story brick building like so many in Hell's Kitchen, that part of Midtown Manhattan infamous for drugs, prostitution, gangs, and violence. But Hell's Kitchen had its own defender, and he had to be careful here. Even monsters like him were wary of the devil.

Morbius walked across the rooftop, gravel crunching underfoot. It was still dark out and there were a few hours before dawn. Plenty of time to take care of business. Reaching the door that led down into the building, he noticed that it was padlocked; an impressive lock that must have cost the building's landlord a pretty penny. Morbius tore it off with barely a thought, dropping it to the ground where it clanked noisily.

Then he ripped the door open, nearly pulling it off its hinges. He was in no mood to proceed gently or with caution. Fabian was somewhere below. Fabian would make things right again. Or there would be hell to pay.

The old wooden stairs led into darkness, and Morbius slipped into the shadows. Creeping down, he could smell the helpless humans sleeping behind the closed doors, heard their soft murmuring as they stirred, could almost *feel* the blood pulsing through their veins. He experienced a momentary vision of going apartment to apartment, draining the blood from all who lived there. Every neck would be different, each person's blood having a slightly different tang. The thought thrilled him, sending goosebumps all along his flesh.

Amanda's face appeared in his mind, and he quelled his hunger.

Yet he couldn't erase the look on her face. The fear, and betrayal. Even though he possessed great strength, and often reveled in it, deep in his heart, in a part of himself that he barely recognized anymore, he hated what he'd become. His hunger showed him no mercy, yet every time he fed, he would sink into a period of self-loathing. Often, he contemplated ways to end his suffering, and thus everyone else's.

Until the hunger rose again.

It was a vicious cycle. One that had seemed endless… until now. If he could get his hands on more of this wondrous fluid, discover more about it, perhaps even learn to synthesize it, he might cure himself of his hunger, yet retain his incredible powers. Perhaps the name "Morbius" could come to represent… a hero.

He nearly laughed out loud as he continued down to the third floor of the dilapidated apartment building. Michael Morbius was no hero. He had killed too many people, had fought against *real* heroes, had nearly killed them, too. The best he could hope for was to stop being a monster.

One thing at a time, Michael, he told himself.

He reached the third floor.

The one working bulb was flickering, casting elongated shadows along the dirty walls. Morbius crept down the hallway, his other senses making up for the lack of light. He could smell cigarette smoke and sweat and fried food. The nighttime noises were louder down here, snoring and coughing and quiet conversations among other nocturnally minded people like himself. Morbius, however, was silent.

He reached the end of the hallway and stood in front of apartment 3D. He couldn't remember the last time he'd simply knocked on a door, and just as he was about to do so, he noticed that it was slightly ajar. He glanced back down the hallway.

It was still empty.

Morbius put his clawed hand against the door and pushed. It creaked open. An unpleasant mix of smells grew stronger, as did the sound of a television, and the scent of blood. His body tensed, and he entered the gloom of the apartment.

Inside, it looked as if a bomb had gone off. He couldn't tell if Fabian was naturally messy or if someone had ransacked the place. Cautiously, he made his way through the kitchen, past a sink filled with dirty dishes and counters covered in fast food take-out wrappers and bags, and then into what could only generously be described as a living room. All the lights in the apartment were off. Across from him, a TV blinked imagery across the room, the only source of luminescence. The noise was distracting.

The back of a reclining chair faced him. At this close proximity, Morbius could smell body odor and bad cologne and still the slight scent of blood.

"Fabian," he said over the sound of the television. "Liz sent me."

The TV continued to flash its images, but otherwise there was no movement. The shadows appeared and faded, a surreal tableau as Morbius made his way around the chair. First he noticed an arm, covered in black hair, and then a hand wrapped around a television remote.

Morbius continued around and then finally faced the chair's occupant, who stared glassily at the TV in front of him, eyes wide open. He was unmoving.

And quite dead.

There were no marks on him, but Morbius heard no heartbeat, and the man's face was unnaturally pale. Morbius fought his urges, his hunger.

Fought, and lost.

He surged forward, sinking his fangs into the dead man's neck. The skin was still warm, and so therefore was the liquid that lay within. The flesh gave way easily and the blood filled Morbius' mouth, running down his chin as he drank greedily. With the heart stopped, he had to work harder to extract the fluid from the veins.

The taste of the blood told him that this man had poisoned himself for much of his life, with alcohol and drugs and nicotine. As a result, it was highly unpleasant.

Morbius didn't care.

His hunger was so great that any distaste was overwhelmed by the pleasant sensations that spread out from his stomach and toward the rest of his body. He drank his fill, and then kept going—but as his hunger disappeared, the taste became more evident. The blood, while satisfying, was incredibly bitter, and while Fabian's questionable lifestyle could account for much of it, there was another flavor present, subtle but undeniable.

Without warning a wave of agony ripped through Morbius' stomach. He belched bloody vomit all over the corpse. Then he blinked at the gory body, slowly realizing what had just happened.

"Idiot!" he growled at himself. He'd been poisoned. In his desperation for sustenance, he'd ignored all the warning signs and let himself be tricked into consuming his own defeat.

At that moment, something was shoved into his back. There was a crackle, and he was wracked with pain as electricity blasted through his body. Morbius attempted to remain on his feet, but another burst of agony shot through him, this one emanating again from his gut. As he collapsed, the person behind him began raining blows onto the side of his face and the back of his head.

As he threw an elbow at his attacker, connecting viciously and hearing a cheekbone crack, his lips actually curled back in a rueful smile. Whoever had planned this, Morbius was impressed. But the smile disappeared as he gasped from another spasm of pain.

A second assailant came rushing from the shadows and kicked him in the face, sending him flying against the wall. Morbius left a trail of his own blood across the floor. He recognized the irony, but clenched his jaw as a third attacker landed another blow.

His head was spinning, black spots forming in his vision, but he fought to remain conscious. If he could just get his fangs into one of these men... get their untainted blood into his system, there was still time to save himself.

As another foot came toward his face, Morbius used all his remaining energy to grab it and twist. A loud cracking sound filled the air and the man screamed, pulling himself away and curling into a defensive ball on the floor. Morbius pushed himself against the wall, barely getting to his feet, trying to get his bearings, to figure a way out of this trap.

One of the men—or a new one—appeared in the flashing shadows created by the television. Morbius was unsure how many people were attacking him, but there were at least three. He landed a powerful haymaker across Morbius' face and blood exploded from the vampire's already deformed nose.

The same attacker, a huge slab of muscle with a buzz cut and a nasty look in his eyes, threw another devastating punch, but Michael was able to slap it away, the blow slamming into the wall, leaving a hole where before there was only paint and plaster. The man struggled to remove his fist, his body nearly pressed up against Morbius as a result of the deflected blow.

Morbius could smell the man's sweat and the iron of his blood, which was completely unlike Fabian's. This man was healthy, clearly took good care of himself. Michael blinked as his enemy grunted and tried to free himself. His jugular vein pulsed in his neck, as if in invitation.

His body flooding with endorphins at the prospect of regaining some of his lost strength, Morbius leaned forward. Just as his teeth touched the man's neck, however, another burst of pain erupted in his stomach—the worst one yet. Morbius gasped, pulling away slightly just as his assailant pulled his fist free and once again planted it on Michael's face.

The other attackers surged forward as Morbius stumbled along the wall. He reached the corner and attempted to keep moving, but there was nowhere else to go. Fists rained down on him, and then someone held out an object, jabbing him in the gut. Electricity coursed through his body again, but this time the device wasn't pulled back. It was held against his body and waves of intense pain radiated out, making the poison in his system seem like a minor bruise in comparison.

Morbius screamed.

Another electrical device was placed against him, and then another. He had never experienced pain like this, not in his entire life, and yet still he stood. He swiped blindly at his attackers but landed no blows. He couldn't even *see* them anymore, could only see the flashing light from the damn television. On it, a young couple stared at each other, apparently in love. Slowly their lips came closer, and met.

Martine… Morbius thought. *I'm sorry.*

The darkness fought for control, and finally won.

Morbius fell to the floor, unconscious.

CHAPTER SIX

"HE'S GONE."

"What do you mean?" Amanda asked. "Where?"

"I gave him Fabian's address and told him never to come back," Liz answered, her forehead wrinkling in confusion. The situation seemed pretty obvious to her. Morbius wasn't just an abusive jerk, he was also… you know… a *vampire*. Amanda should have been thanking her.

After the creep had hurled himself out of the window, Liz had checked on her friend and found her passed out from exhaustion. *Poor thing*. She'd repaired the damn window, *again*, then caught a few hours of shut-eye herself. When she woke up, she made herself a huge omelet and a full pot of coffee. She had a day full of errands, a couple of auditions, and then another night at the bar.

When Amanda had finally come out of her bedroom, she was surprised that Michael wasn't sleeping the day away on the mattress across the room from her, like he usually did.

"Crap," Amanda said to Liz's news. She headed over to the door and put on her shoes.

"What's that supposed to mean?" Liz said, annoyed.

"Nothing, I'm sorry." Amanda stopped to look at her. "It's not you. It's just…"

"*What*, Amanda?"

"Morbius isn't normal…"

"You think?"

"He isn't *normal*," Amanda repeated, as if that made her point. "But he isn't evil. He says the worst things to me sometimes and trust me, I've thought about just walking away from him a million times, but he *cares*… he cares about me. He's not capable of showing it—not really—but every now and then there's this different side of him that comes out. It's usually when he's talking about Martine, and you can feel the pain radiating off him, and it's just heartbreaking.

"But it's also little things, little gestures that he does," she continued. "And he's saved my life more than once. I know it doesn't make any sense, Liz, but nothing in my life makes much sense anymore. My mom, my dad, Justin, my sister. I mean… honestly? Michael is probably the least messed up thing I have going on right now."

Liz stared at her friend, and then burst into laughter. It had an edge, though.

"Do you know how crazy that sounds?" she said. "A 'living vampire' is the most normal thing in your life."

"I know!" Amanda said, and she started laughing, too, heading back over to the table. "Trust me, I'm not exactly happy about it."

Her words caused Liz to soften.

"So… what are you gonna do?"

"I should go over to Fabian's place, and see if Michael's there," Amanda replied. "See if I can help. It's what he would do for me." Tying the second shoe, she added, "Can you give me the address?"

"No," Liz said, and Amanda stared. "Fabian lives in a pretty bad neighborhood. The area's improving, but not his part of it. Even during the day it's dangerous. Michael's a big boy, to say the least. He can handle himself." Amanda started to protest, but Liz cut her off with a raised hand.

"Trust me on this. I'm right, and I've got a ton of stuff to do. So you chill out here for the day, do some digging on that cult of yours, and then meet up with me back here later. I'm only working the evening shift today. We'll drink a bunch of Long Island Ice Teas, like we did at Tommy DeGarro's party after Junior Prom."

"Oh my god, I forgot all about that," Amanda said, her face immediately going red. "Was that the night we stole his little sisters' tiny bikes and rode them down that *huge* hill across the street from his house?"

"That was *exactly* that night," Liz said. "I think I still have grass stains on my knees from wiping out over and over again at the bottom. But you wouldn't stop! You kept making me drag that My Pretty Pony bike up the hill over and over and over again!"

Amanda laughed and sat down. "Give me a break. You loved it."

Liz looked at her best friend and smiled.

"You're right. I did."

MORBIUS' EYES fluttered open, then they closed. Then opened again.

There was something covering his entire body, some kind of thick cloth, and his arms and legs were bound at the wrists and ankles by what felt like some kind of metal. Tentatively he flexed against his restraints, careful not to draw attention to the fact that he was awake, but he could tell that the metal was formidable. He could lift his arms, but not pull them apart. In his weakened condition, he doubted that he had the strength to break free, much less get the jump on his captors.

He struggled to clear his head.

The events in Fabian's apartment started to reemerge in his mind, like the pieces of a puzzle slowly slipping back together. He could still feel the poison pumping through his veins, but its intensity was finally starting to fade. Between that and his overwhelming hunger, Morbius felt hollowed out, a shell of a human—or whatever he was now—yet he was determined to escape.

When he swiveled his head slightly, the cloth covering it moved as well, revealing a small hole through which he could narrowly see.

He was being carried by two people, one of whom

he could make out, at least partially. They were hauling him head-first, so he could see the man at his feet. The other he could hear, steady breathing coming from just above his head. Wherever they were, it was dark except for an occasional muddy light that passed overhead as they walked.

Strong odors assailed his senses, such that he couldn't sort them out. The air was cool and damp. There were distant sounds that he thought he recognized. With concentration, he put the sounds and smells together. They were underground. A subway tunnel. He wasn't sure what time it was, but it felt like it was still the middle of the night.

"How much farther?" the man at his feet panted.

"Almost there," the other answered, less out of breath. "The door's up here on the right. Hurry up before we get flattened."

"Did you see the look on that guy's face, back at the platform?" the first remarked. "Fricking *priceless*."

"Shut up and keep moving," the man above Morbius growled.

After another minute, they stopped and a metal door creaked open with a rusty screech. They started moving again. As they made their way through, the man at his feet stumbled slightly and lost his grip, causing Morbius' body to lean toward his captor. He used the momentum to lunge forward, headbutting the man directly in the nose and causing the cloth to pull away. Blood burst from the man's face. He fell back onto the subway tracks, and didn't move.

"What the hell?" the man behind Morbius said, letting go.

His hands and feet still bound, Michael attempted to stay upright and twist around. He barely dodged a fist thrown at his face, and found himself staring at the large man with the buzz cut from Fabian's apartment. A disquieting smile spread across his assailant's face.

"I was hoping I'd get another shot at you."

In response, Michael smashed the man across the face with his bound fists, a spray of blood arcing out into the air and falling down into darkness. As the man shook off the blow, Morbius attempted to retain his balance and took in his surroundings. They stood at the top of a steep set of metal stairs which descended into blackness. With his preternatural vision, he could see a great distance, and the height was dizzying, even for someone who was accustomed to gliding above cities.

Behind them, he could hear the rumbling of a train.

The big man landed a nasty blow to Michael's stomach, knocking the wind from his lungs. He'd let himself be distracted, and exhaustion wasn't helping. The man brought up a knee and it connected with Morbius' face, pushing him back to the brink of unconsciousness. He fell on top of his other captor, who was still knocked out.

A glaring light appeared in the corner of his eye, the light of a subway train barreling toward them.

The large man loomed overhead, that cruel smile still etched onto his face.

"They told me to bring you in alive, but they didn't

say what shape you had to be in," he said with sadistic glee. Morbius took this in, and made a decision. If this was the moment he died, then it would be on his terms.

He launched himself forward, hearing behind him the sickening crunch of the unconscious man as the train struck him. Morbius hammered into the large man, his momentum sending them through the metal railing. Their bodies careened into the yawning darkness, seeming to hang there for a second.

The two men fell.

Time seemed to stand still. As the light from above drifted away and they plunged into darkness, the metal staircase whipped past. Morbius marveled at the surreal beauty of the situation. The stairs reflected the diminishing light, while the sound of the train rattled and then faded away entirely. Echoing the silence, the shadows swallowed them.

His reverie was interrupted by yet another blow to the face. The man continued to fight despite their impending doom, which was vaguely impressive. Morbius was too weak, and the man was too heavy to attempt any kind of gliding.

The pitch darkness only lasted a few moments, and then light appeared from below. The ground had to be approaching. Fast. Yet the man didn't seem to notice, just kept pounding on Morbius' face, pushing him closer and closer to unconsciousness. Still he took the abuse, used the man's clinging, violent embrace as an opportunity to adjust their bodies as they rushed toward the ground below.

"Was it worth it?" Morbius whispered.

"Freak," the brute replied, pulling his fist back.

The last thing he ever did.

Morbius and the man landed with a horrific impact, his captor's body careening up and then violently back down. The sound of breaking bones reverberated out into the dark space, blood spurted from his ears and nose and mouth. Morbius took a fair share of the impact, as well, grunting in pain and rolling away until he slammed into a wall, coming to a stop in a crumpled heap of agony and exhaustion.

After a long moment, he got shakily to his feet and looked around. The impact had knocked loose his bindings. He was in a small hallway, high stone walls reaching up into the darkness, where he could faintly hear another subway car rumbling by. There was light, not a lot but enough, though he couldn't see where it came from.

Morbius was hurt. Badly. He couldn't remember the last time he'd endured such damage, but he was also free. He'd defeated his would-be abductors, and now all he had to do was climb the metal stairs.

As he limped toward them, his mind went back to the events in the apartment. It had been a trap. They'd been expecting him, which meant they knew of Liz's involvement. Amanda might be in danger, too. He had to get back, to protect her. He remembered the last words he had spoken to her.

"I should have minded my own business when I saw you on the street."

The look on her face…

"You idiot," he said to himself, placing his hand on the metal railing, ready to ascend.

"You took the words right out of my mouth, Michael."

The voice came from the darkness down the hallway. Morbius turned, every muscle screaming. He attempted to see through the shadows, and failed.

Letting go of the railing, he hobbled toward the speaker, realizing that any attempt to escape made no sense at this point, not in his current state. Better to face any adversary head-on. After a few steps, he realized that a man was standing near the far wall. No, not a wall. A large metal door. The man sported a thick beard and a bald head, and most distinctively, he wore a familiar red robe.

Demon-Fire.

Morbius' stomach dropped. All this time he and Amanda had been looking for the cult, and the cult had been watching them. Just how far-reaching was this group's grasp, he wondered, standing up straight, attempting to convey strength where there was none.

"Hello, Mr. Morbius," the man hissed.

Morbius bared his teeth in response, too tired to engage in banter. He had to dispose of this priest—or whatever he was—and get to the surface, warn Amanda.

"I have to admit," the man continued, "I'm surprised you fell for our bait. I said the plan was too simplistic, but the others assured me that your history and personality made you an easy mark. And here you are. You will be a highly prized addition to the games."

The games?

What the hell was he talking about? Morbius blinked, tried to clear his head, and decided it didn't matter. He tensed, ready to lunge, to drink every drop of this man's blood, when he felt something sharp enter his neck. He yelped, more from surprise than pain, and whirled. Two more robed figures stood in the shadows, their hoods pulled up, hiding their faces in darkness. One of them held a syringe.

Where had they come from? How had he *missed* them?

He clasped his hand over the spot on his neck, and the skin there was already burning. He attempted to step toward them, but instead fell to his knees. He heard the first man—the one with the beard—approach from behind, but was unable to turn, was barely able to keep upright at all. His head was swimming.

"Shhhh… it's okay, Michael," the man said. "You did your best. You had a good run. You killed so many people. People who *mattered*. But now you… you and Amanda… are ours. Again. And this time, nothing will save either of you."

The man laughed quietly as Morbius fell to his side. He fought to keep his eyelids open, to crawl toward his enemy, but his body refused to obey his mind's commands. Feet surrounded him, possibly more people than just the three he had seen.

It was impossible to tell.

He grunted, tried to tell them all that he would kill them, but instead his eyes finally closed and Michael Morbius slipped into unconsciousness.

CHAPTER SEVEN

LIZ GREEN walked down Avenue C. She was smiling. Despite the way it had started, it had been one hell of a day. Things had really picked up.

Finally.

It was cold out, but the sun was shining and the sky was a bright blue, the kind that instantly made her happy when she saw it. After running a few errands, Liz had gone on the first of two auditions she'd scheduled, and *crushed* it.

The casting director offered her the part right there in the room, something she had never experienced before—had only heard about from other actors. "Friends" who only came into her bar when they wanted to brag about their successes.

It was a starring role in a short film, which normally wasn't a huge deal, but its director had been a director of photography on a number of big Hollywood releases. She was making her first foray into directing her own material. The casting director told Liz that the Sundance Film Festival had already expressed interest in the script. The director's agents had insisted that she cast a star, but she wanted to find an unknown, thought the part would get lost beneath someone famous.

Liz would be playing the role.

She had decided to skip her other audition—for an off-off-off Broadway musical that honestly sounded really dumb, something about a war between the rats and cockroaches of New York City. Instead, she decided to treat herself to a nice lunch, something she never did. Liz could barely afford a deli sandwich, let alone a nice meal.

There was a restaurant she passed almost every day. She would stare at the people inside and dream of someday sitting by the window, watching New York pass by.

Today was that day.

There were tables available, but she waited for a seat with a view. She ordered a steak and mashed potatoes and carrots—her favorite meal growing up—and a glass of Pinot Noir that was almost as expensive as the meal itself. She sipped it slowly while she ate, savoring its taste as juxtaposed with the perfectly cooked meat.

The waiter was handsome and flirted subtly with her, even filling up her glass halfway for free and walking away with a wink. For a moment she thought about Fabian, and felt slightly guilty, but she hadn't heard from him. He hadn't returned any of her calls. So, she left her phone number on the receipt, and wondered if the guy would call.

Even if he didn't, that was fine. Either way, she was going to star in a short film for someone with credits. Real credits. This could change everything.

She couldn't wait to tell Amanda. She thought about calling her but then decided to wait until they met up back at her apartment that night. She wanted to see her best friend's face when she heard the news. Liz had whispered this kind of dream during many sleepovers when they were kids, how she hoped someday to be famous.

Liz had just taken a huge step in that direction.

After lunch, she visited her dad in his apartment. He wasn't feeling well, but a huge smile crossed his face when she told him the news. He patted her hand and she noticed how thin his skin looked, almost like tissue paper. He needed better care, which meant she needed more money. And this short film might be the start... for both of them.

He was tired, said he might take a nap, so she kissed the top of his head and told him she'd stop back in tomorrow, to hang out with him all day. It was her day off and she didn't have any auditions. It would be a straight-up daddy-daughter day. He smiled at that as he drifted off.

The sun was still shining as Liz made her way down the avenue, deeper into Alphabet City. There was the same amount of trash on the sidewalks and streets, the same number of people asking for spare change, but the city seemed more beautiful than ever. She had come here with one purpose, and had nearly given up several times.

Nearly. But not quite.

Liz laughed as she reached the Dive Inn. She was only working the evening shift today, which was fine with her. She would head home afterward and hang out with Amanda, help her friend figure out her next steps.

But she was excited to see her regulars, to tell them the news. They were her family, too. More so than her blood relatives, if she was being honest with herself. Her mom's family didn't understand, told her she should give up acting and come home. She pushed them out of her mind. They never asked about her dad, either—hadn't since the divorce, and then her mom's death.

The joke would be on them, when she was starring in a movie that was shown at Sundance.

Unlocking the door, she turned the sign from CLOSED to OPEN. Not that she expected anyone to show up just yet. They didn't serve food, so it wasn't like anyone was going to be looking for a burger and a beer. Anyway, she welcomed the quiet. The casting director had slipped her a copy of the script, and she was excited to read it from beginning to end. Very carefully, taking in every single word she'd be saying on camera in just a couple of months.

She situated herself behind the bar and opened the script to the first page, then quickly reached into her purse and withdrew a yellow highlighter. She laughed again. She'd been highlighting her lines since the first play she'd done in middle school, and now here she was. Highlighting lines for her first—

The door opened.

Liz looked up, but the sunlight was reflecting off the window of a car parked on the street. The person standing in the doorway was just a silhouette, but she could tell it was a woman. Liz squinted, tried to see who it was. She was bummed that she couldn't dive right into the script, but this might be one of her regulars. Maybe she would be the first person to hear Liz's good news.

"Can I help you?" Liz said.

The woman walked forward, and Liz's mouth fell open.

She wasn't a regular, but Liz *did* know her.

MORBIUS AWOKE with a start, breathing in deeply, and dust filled his lungs.

He coughed and spit, a dirty mix of blood and saliva, and blinked rapidly, slowly coming to realize that he was lying face-down on packed dirt. He could hear voices murmuring above him… a lot of them. They echoed indistinctly, as if he were in a large chamber.

Slowly turning himself over, he squinted at the incredibly bright lights that greeted him, raising a clawed hand in an attempt to shield his eyes. After a moment his vision adjusted and he sat up, grunting in pain at the effort. There was something tight wrapped around his neck, and he reached up to touch it. A thick metal band had been affixed there. He tugged at it, but it was pointless—the metal was strong, and resisted his attempts to remove it.

I'll deal with that later, he thought absently as he looked around. He was sitting in what could only be described as an arena, an oval-shaped expanse of packed dirt surrounded by high walls that were topped off by nasty-looking razor wire.

As he lurched to his feet, the unseen voices grew louder, morphing into excited shouts and even laughter. He tried to see through the shadows and could barely make out what looked like faces up there, dozens... maybe hundreds. He turned in a circle, trying to see past the lights, to see who these people were, but they were almost completely obscured by the brightness. Likely on purpose.

He could smell their blood. So close, yet...

Across the arena there was a banging sound, and he saw a metal door. That was what had made the sound, or something behind it. Morbius slowly came to understand what was happening.

The games, the man had said.

When the metal door began to rise, the voices became an uproar as the hidden crowd whipped itself into an ecstatic fury. The screams and cheers and laughter increased, and Morbius placed his hands over his ears. His enhanced auditory abilities intensified the headache that was pounding through his skull. Added to the many bruises and cuts on his body, the pain was almost unbearable.

He attempted to blink back his dizziness.

The metal made a screeching sound as it lifted, revealing darkness on the other side. Morbius couldn't see what lay within, but he could *smell* it. It was a strange mix… almost like tar and burnt leaves and sulfur. And there was another smell beneath those, something familiar.

A low rumbling emitted from the darkness. Quiet, almost mournful, and Michael felt himself relax. Perhaps whatever opponent he was being forced to face was as reluctant and confused as he was. Perhaps there was a reasonable way out of this. He was already in so much pain…

A huge creature suddenly burst from the darkness, scuttling on six huge, hairy legs, bloody slobber falling from its jaws. Huge fangs glinted in the glaring light, multiple rows of them in a gaping mouth. The creature's eyes were set deep in its misshapen head, but they were locked on Morbius. There was no question what the monster had in mind.

Its hunger was not mournful at all.

In addition to the razor-sharp teeth in its cavernous mouth, the thing also sported long claws on its bear-like paws, already caked in dried blood.

"Wonderful," Morbius muttered as the creature barreled toward him.

The crowd roared.

It struck him head-on before he could even contemplate dodging. Morbius thought he felt several ribs crack as he was slammed into the concrete wall.

He brought his hands up, pressing against the creature's face, its rancid breath curling out and nearly suffocating him. The multitude of teeth were just inches away from his head. The creature pushed harder, and Morbius grunted, pressing back with all the strength he had left.

Which wasn't much.

Suddenly Morbius let go, surprising his assailant, and slipped down beneath the leathery skin of its stomach, shimmying along the dirt floor. Thrown off-balance, the creature smashed hard into the concrete wall, resulting in an unnerving crunching sound.

Morbius rolled along the ground and got to his feet as quickly as possible. The crowd screamed louder, crying out for blood. And sure enough, the creature turned, revealing the ruined shell of an eye socket, mucous and dark red fluid pouring out of the open wound. It let loose with an insane roar, a clear mix of pain, anger, and hunger. Morbius tried to steady himself while glancing around the arena, desperate for an escape or anything that might give him an advantage.

By the time he looked back, the creature was almost on him. It was incredibly fast despite its size. Morbius leapt, even got a foot or so off the ground, but the creature caught him mid-ascent, its claws sinking into his leg, pulling him down to the ground in an excruciating burst of pain. Michael screamed and rolled away again, his own blood flowing out and mixing with the creature's on the ground.

The crowd's excitement only escalated.

The monster ran toward him, but Morbius surprised both of them by launching himself up again and catching the creature under what could only generously be described as its chin. He struck with both of his fists, sending the creature flying backward as it tumbled in a mass of muscle and short, bristly fur.

Morbius landed and tried to catch his breath, glancing down quickly at his leg. The wound was deep and was certain to become infected. Despite the momentary respite, this fight was not going his way.

The creature raised itself back up onto its six legs and made its way toward Morbius, slowly now, circling around the perimeter, eyeing its opponent cautiously. Morbius walked in the opposite direction, taking in his opponent as well. Staring into its one good eye, he suspected there was intelligence there, and briefly felt bad for the behemoth. It was most likely in the same situation as him, forced to fight for survival.

Quickly he shook the thought away. That kind of compassion would only get him killed.

The crowd grew quieter, and then someone began to boo. Others joined in, until it was a roar. Apparently they didn't like these kinds of lulls in the action. The creature seemed to shudder at the sound—perhaps it had been trained to avoid displeasing its masters, whoever these sick bastards were.

Then it launched itself at Morbius, striking him squarely and knocking him down onto the ground, pinning him beneath its weight. Again the knife-like teeth were inches away from his face, and he pressed his forearm against them, his arms wobbling, almost all strength gone.

His arm slipped, and the creature's teeth ripped a long gash across his skin. Blood flowed and fell against the monster's tongue, which seemed to increase its fury. Or desperation.

Perhaps both.

Morbius shifted and placed one hand above the creature's mouth, the other just below. He gripped as hard as he could, his fingers digging deep into the thick, leathery skin until it nearly broke open. A sound of pure rage bubbled up from the creature's throat. Morbius did his best to ignore it, as well as the blood that was gushing from both his arm and his leg. There wasn't much time left.

Unconsciousness was closing in yet again.

An image of Martine appeared in his mind, and it was all he needed. He summoned whatever reserves he had left, gripped the creature's flesh even tighter, and pushed his arms apart, screaming with the effort.

Almost immediately, the jaws cracked violently open. There was a sudden spasm, and the creature went limp, collapsing at Morbius' feet. Its huge body shuddered, and then finally went still. Blood poured from its dead, gaping maw. Morbius stared down at it. If things had gone only slightly differently, it would be him bleeding out on the dirt floor.

The crowd roared its approval.

Fighting to catch his breath, Morbius stared at the creature's blood as it pooled at his feet. Its scent rose up and filled his nose, and then everything clicked. That strange blood that Liz had given him, the package Fabian had provided. It smelled almost exactly the same.

Without hesitating, Morbius fell on top of the monstrous corpse and sank his teeth into the thick flesh of its neck. It wasn't easy to get through the fur and scaly skin, so Morbius redoubled his efforts, desperate for the creature's blood. At last, he pierced the epidermis, and the dark liquid entered his mouth, flooding his mind and body with pleasure.

Just as he managed to gulp down a single mouthful, the metal device on his neck made a clicking noise and a blast of electricity shot through his body, many times stronger than he'd suffered in Fabian's apartment. Crying out, he fell back, away from the monster's corpse, and writhed in the sand.

The crowd cheered, jeered, and laughed.

A pair of cult members approached, one holding a device that clearly controlled the electronic collar. The other held one of the electrical devices that had incapacitated Michael previously.

Smiling, the first man shut off the neck device. The pain receded, gradually, and Morbius slowly came to his feet, a feeling of rage rippling through him. A tiny voice in the back of his head told him to stand down, to save his energy for when he would really need it.

He didn't listen.

Morbius lunged at the man who held the remote control. He knew it was a stupid move, but he didn't care. At this point, as far as he was concerned, it was all or nothing.

The man looked surprised at the vampire's burst of speed, glanced back down at the device in his hands, and attempted to hit the button before his attacker could reach him. But the few drops of monster blood Morbius had managed to ingest energized him, and he leaned into the feeling, grabbing the man's head and twisting.

The snapping noise was deeply satisfying, but it was followed quickly by a painful burst of electricity as the other man shoved his weapon into Morbius' ribs. He screamed, fell to his knees, and collapsed into the dirt.

As unconsciousness claimed him yet again, he stared up into the lights. The roar of the crowd grew louder and then quieter, until it finally faded altogether.

CHAPTER EIGHT

AMANDA SAINT wanted answers.

After Liz had left, Amanda had taken her friend's advice and spent a good part of the day doing more research on the Demon-Fire cult. There wasn't much out there, but Amanda dug deeper than she ever had before.

Leaving the apartment, she headed to a small bookstore in the West Village that specialized in horror novels and non-fiction books about the occult. The small building looked as if it was falling apart. Even so, it was a treasure trove. In addition to all kinds of obscure, hard-to-find books, it had an impressive back-catalog of old newspapers from across the country, some that couldn't be found anywhere else in the world, or so they claimed.

The old woman working there smiled as if she'd been expecting Amanda her entire life. She wore huge glasses that reflected what little light there was, making it impossible to see her eyes. Spooked, Amanda tried to smile at her but had difficulty making it happen.

The woman led Amanda down a short set of wooden stairs and showed her how to use the microfiche reader, a technology she had never used before. The machine seemed like a creature from another planet, but she found its quiet whirring sound to be almost peaceful, a Zen-like trip through some very dark history.

The woman explained in quiet tones that her deceased husband had been an avid traveler—"I barely ever saw him," she murmured quietly—but he had sent home hundreds of newspapers from every trip, and brought dozens more back in stuffed suitcases. When he'd died in a private plane crash in Europe, he'd left her enough money to keep her small bookstore going, even if wasn't generating enough revenue. Or any. That inheritance also enabled her to put the mountain of clippings on film, which she maintained for curious persons like Amanda who sought to delve into the unknown.

The woman eventually stopped talking and just stared. Amanda still hadn't seen the old lady's eyes.

"Um... thank you?" Amanda said kindly.

The woman simply nodded and then headed back upstairs to her empty shell of a bookstore. Amanda turned and opened her laptop next to the humming machine. She had enough details from previous research to know general topics and time periods to search. It took hours but slowly, page by page, she discovered more information about the cult that had ripped her and her family apart.

What Amanda found disturbed her deeply.

The Demon-Fire cult had its hands in crimes and sacrifices around the world. Clues in one story led to yet another, making Amanda realize that the cult was much larger than she had ever realized.

Her mind went back to the night she'd been kidnapped by the cultists, by its high priestess Poison-Lark, who turned out to be her own sister, Catherine. Poison-Lark had said words that Amanda had barely registered at the time, but now they filled her with dread.

"*Demon-Fire is everywhere.*"

There were news stories of stomach-churning murders, entire families tortured and mutilated, arcane writing found on victims' walls. Claims of demonic creatures being summoned, something Amanda herself could verify after her run-in with the giant spider that the cult had called Arachne.

There were even reports of Demon-Fire having multiple cells in major metropolitan areas, including here New York. According to the accounts, some of which sounded more like fiction than fact, they had built an infrastructure that led throughout the underbelly of the city. Sewer systems, aqueducts, and subway tunnels. They made blood sacrifices in dingy basements and high-priced penthouses. Authorities called the claims "ludicrous" and "the work of overactive imaginations."

But there was no denying it.

The cult's reach was staggering.

Even so, actual eyewitness accounts were few and far between, relying on reports from the very few people who had managed to get out alive. They all said the same thing, however, mirroring the words Catherine had spoken on that horrific night, all those weeks ago. The Demon-Fire cult was looking to bring about the terrestrial victory of Satan.

A sudden noise grabbed Amanda's attention. She blinked at the shadows that surrounded her, juxtaposed with the bright screen at which she'd been staring for…

She had no idea how long she'd been down in the basement. It was entirely silent upstairs. There were no windows down here and the overhead light had gone out, or been turned off at some point. The only light came from the machine in front of her.

"Hello…?" she called out.

Another noise reached her… a kind of shuffling sound.

She stood and looked around for a weapon, finally wrapping her fingers around an old stapler. It might not be much, but its weight felt good in her hand. Cautiously, Amanda walked around the basement, stepping into the shadows. There were stacks and stacks of books and magazines and newspapers down here, with narrow pathways between.

The silence was oppressive.

She fought an urge to run upstairs. *No.* She'd been running scared for too long. She was at the point where she'd resolved to face her fears, whether literal or figurative.

The noise sounded again. Close. She tightened her grip on the stapler, ready to bash whoever—or whatever—was down here. Holding her breath, she turned a corner and raised her arm up, ready to fight.

She let out a laugh that sounded more like a cough.

The light from the microfiche machine barely reached this far back into the basement, but there was enough to see the small cat that stood in the corner, looking just as scared as Amanda.

"Hi there," she said, bending over and scooping the skinny creature into her arms. It purred noisily and licked her finger.

A bony hand wrapped around Amanda's shoulder, causing her to jump. The cat's claws dug deeply into her arm, immediately drawing blood. The animal jumped down onto the dirty ground and disappeared into the shadowy stacks of books and newspapers.

"I'm sorry, I didn't mean to scare you," the old woman said, smiling a toothless smile up at Amanda. She must have taken her dentures out and forgotten to put them back in, or simply chose not to. Regardless, the result was unsettling to say the least.

"It's… it's okay," Amanda replied. "Quite a maze you have down here."

"Yes… I keep meaning to get it organized, but there's never enough hours in the day. Speaking of which, I'm sorry to say it's closing time. You've been down here for hours, sweetie."

"Oh. Sorry about that," Amanda said, following the woman back toward the staircase. "I got lost in my research."

"That's quite all right. I like knowing there's

someone else in the store with me," the old woman said, pulling herself up the steps. "Life is so short and often so heartbreaking. Other people are what make it bearable, wouldn't you say?"

You don't know the half of it, Amanda thought, her mind turning to Morbius, how he had saved her from the Demon-Fire cult on more than one occasion. She hoped he was okay.

"Yes," Amanda said, following her back up out of the shadows. "I would absolutely say that."

MORBIUS' ENTIRE body ached.

He blinked awake, realizing that even his eyelids hurt. He laughed at the thought, and then doubled over in a fresh wave of pain. Several of his ribs had to be broken. He looked down at his leg, ready to see it still bleeding, but was pleasantly surprised to find it professionally wrapped in gauze, with just a small spot of blood having leaked through. Ditto his arm, which pulsated with pain to the rhythm of his heartbeat.

Slowly, he sat up and tried to ignore his pounding headache. He was exhausted. And starving. And in so very much pain. But he was alive.

Looking around, he half expected to still be in the arena, but discovered instead that he was in a small room with walls made up of large rocks, and a nearby door composed of metal bars. There was a bare bulb hanging from the ceiling, providing the only light.

He was a prisoner.

Morbius shook his head, infuriated with himself for being so stupid. He'd played right into Demon-Fire's hands, and now he was at their mercy. Destined to be dumped into that damn arena for God knows how long. He'd barely survived that last encounter. His luck wouldn't hold forever.

And then there was Amanda.

He'd been so cruel to her, and now she was completely vulnerable. Perhaps she was down here, too. She might even be dead, or sacrificed to some demonic creature like Arachne. Michael audibly cursed himself yet again.

"Take it easy over there, pal."

The voice came from nearby.

Still on the ground, Michael looked around, attempting to ready himself for an attack, knowing full well that he would be easy prey for anyone who wanted to kill him. But the cell was empty except for him. He peered intently, trying to pierce the shadows. Other than a small metal slab in the corner that must have been intended for sleep, and a hole in the floor that was intended for obvious purposes, the room was bare.

"Over here," the voice continued. Morbius realized it was coming from near the "bed."

He dragged himself up onto his feet and made his way over to the slab, collapsing onto it. Despite the pain in his body and the hardness of the platform, it felt incredibly good to lay down on it. He took several deep breaths and listened as his heartbeat returned to its normal tempo for what seemed like the first time in days.

"First bout?" the voice asked.

"Go to Hell," Morbius answered.

The voice laughed, then sighed. "I suppose we're already there, friend."

Despite himself, Morbius smiled at the remark. He turned himself over slightly and realized he could see through a wide crack in the stones, opening into the other cell. A man sat on the floor against the far wall, dressed in nothing but a ripped pair of jeans. Fresh wounds and cuts ran across almost every visible part of his flesh. His hair was brown, long and unkempt. He sported several days' worth of a beard, and a deeply sad look in his eyes.

"I suppose we are," Morbius said, through the hole. He leaned against the wall.

The man looked up, and an expression of mild surprise appeared on his face.

"I know, my appearance…" Morbius said.

"Oh, ha," the man said, laughing. "It's not that. My last neighbor was a gelatinous blob, so I haven't spoken to anyone in weeks. It's nice to meet you. My name is Jacob, but everyone calls me Jake."

Morbius stared at the man. He looked so skinny, so weak. How had he survived for so long down here?

"I'm Michael."

"Hey Michael," Jake said, waving his hand and smiling sadly. "Welcome to monster fight club."

CHAPTER NINE

NIGHT HAD fallen hard on Manhattan.

Amanda was surprised how dark it was when she left the bookstore. It had been bright when she'd entered, with shocking sunlight streaming down through a cloudless sky. Now it was covered by steel-gray clouds, and tiny pieces of the moon could be glimpsed every few minutes. There was a smell of the inevitable rain in the wind.

She had trouble getting a car, so she decided to take the subway, which left her feeling unsettled after reading about Demon-Fire's alleged use of the underground system for who knew what kinds of evil purposes.

As she sat by the grimy window inside the subway car, she stared out into the darkness, intermittent subterranean lights flashing by and then vanishing as if they had never existed at all.

The train suddenly lurched to a stop and the lights

went out, then back on, then off again. She tried to keep her breathing calm. The things she had just read about in the basement of that dark little bookstore, they lingered in her mind like a nightmare she couldn't shake. Some of the pictures she'd uncovered, blurry crime scene photos that only hinted at the real horror and gore, were burned into her memory.

The lights snapped back on but the train remained motionless between stops. She hated this feeling. Trapped in a tin can under the earth. A coffin. She was basically sitting in a coffin. Amanda wondered if other people thought of it this way.

Noise from the other end of her car caught her attention. A man was standing over a couple of teen girls, whispering something Amanda couldn't hear. Based on the terrified looks on their faces, she knew the gist of what he was saying.

Without hesitation, Amanda stood up and strode down the unmoving subway car, directly toward the man. The girls noticed her first, their frenzied eyes locking on hers, silently begging for help. Amanda nodded. The man glanced over and at first looked nervous, but then a nasty smile split his face open when he realized who his potential adversary was. He licked his lips and stepped toward her.

"You got something you wanna say, baby?" he asked, his foul breath washing over her. "Or even better, something you wanna *do*?" His face was pock-marked with acne scars and his thinning red hair clung to his head with a fervor that was almost impressive. Dried saliva caked his mouth and his pupils were huge, full of the excitement of intended violence.

In response, Amanda kneed the man directly in his nuts, and his face immediately drained of all color.

"Oh," he said quietly.

As he instinctively leaned forward in pain, Amanda brought her leg down and then raised the same knee again, as fast as possible, striking him once again, but this time in the nose, breaking it on impact. The sound was like an egg dropped on the concrete from a third-floor window. Blood exploded out from his nostrils as he collapsed onto his back, sputtering.

Morbius had been teaching her some moves over the last few weeks while they traveled. She had wondered how effective they'd actually be in a real-life situation.

She didn't wonder anymore.

The girls gaped up at her and she winked at them, then walked back to her seat and made herself comfortable. They hurriedly got up and avoided the pooling blood as they followed her to her end of the car, continuing through the door and into the next. As she stared out the window, the darkness didn't seem so bad anymore.

She had enjoyed that. Way more than she expected she would, perhaps more than she should have...? Her eyes refocused and she found herself staring at her own reflection in the window. She didn't realize until this moment that she was smiling. Sweat from the encounter dotted her forehead, her cheeks flush with blood. There was a crazy look in her eyes. Amanda didn't recognize herself in this moment.

It energized her.

It terrified her.

Her mother had joined a cult, had probably done unspeakable things. Her sister had tried to sacrifice Amanda to a demon. Evil ran in Amanda's blood—or so she feared. What if she was like them? What if their father had been turned, as well? Why else hadn't he been in touch?

Amanda turned away from the window. Her momentary burst of confidence had been shattered, and she felt herself falling back down into the pit of fear and uncertainty that had defined her for most of her life. She allowed people to walk all over her, which explained how both her sister and her first real boyfriend had betrayed her so easily.

She wanted to change, to be stronger, but not if it meant selling her soul to the dark forces that had claimed her family.

At last, the subway car shuddered, and started moving again.

The man with the shattered nose still lay on his back, muttering incoherently and occasionally spitting blood out onto the floor. The rest of the passengers had fled to the adjacent car. Only Amanda remained. She should have been afraid of him, of the possibility that he would get up and want to exact some kind of violent revenge on her.

She should have been afraid, but she wasn't.

MORBIUS DRIFTED off again, then slowly awoke, still in an upright seated position with his face pressed against the wall. He groaned as he pulled his sweaty cheek away from the cool stone.

"Good nap?" Jake asked from the other cell.

Morbius' stomach rumbled. He felt a little better after finally catching some sleep, the kind that wasn't forced on him from blows to the face or attacks from an electrical prod, but he was still incredibly hungry. All the sleep in the world wouldn't matter if he starved to death.

"Fine," he growled.

Jake seemed nice enough, but Morbius didn't trust him. Didn't trust anyone, for that matter. Except Amanda. He grimaced at the thought of her, then put her out of his mind. Guilt wouldn't help save her if she was in danger. He had to keep his wits about him, figure out a way to escape. First things first.

"You must be hungry," Jake said, as if reading his mind. Morbius thought about ignoring him, but then decided that it would at least pass the time. He would simply be careful with how much he revealed.

"Yes... I am," he said simply, peering through the hole in the wall. Jake sat in the exact same spot, staring off into the distance, that strange bemused smile still on his face. He was an odd character, this Jacob who most people called Jake. Morbius didn't want to like him, but on some level he already did. They seemed to be kindred spirits. At least on some level.

"Well, these guys are pretty good about feeding their prisoners, but everyone gets their own special meal."

"Oh?"

"Yeah, for instance, the blob that was in that cell before you? They would shove these huge rats through the door... and I mean huge, and it would just, I guess, suck them up into its body. You could see them being digested in there, through his... what, skin, I guess you'd call it? Pretty awful. I kept telling myself not to look but there I was, staring through that hole at a bunch of rats being digested by a big pile of goo." Jake laughed at the thought.

Morbius shook his head and smiled.

What the hell kind of place is this?

"And you?" he asked.

"Me?" Jake answered, finally looking over at Morbius, his smile still there but sadness in his eyes. "Well, they feed me when I... when I don't look like this. Last time it was some stray dog they must have found on the street. I didn't want to eat it. I fricking *love* dogs, you know? But I wasn't exactly in control of myself. It—it's hard to explain."

"I... understand," Morbius said, locking his eyes onto Jake's. The two men stared at each other for a long moment, and then Jake nodded.

"Yeah, I'll bet you do."

"You said, 'when I don't look like this'?"

"Believe it or not, Michael, I didn't always live in a stone prison beneath New York City." Jake laughed but it was a humorless sound. "I was jogging in Central

Park one night. I guess it wasn't *that* long ago, but it feels like a million years. Anyway, I was running. It was probably too late at night to be in there… I should have known better. But I got jumped. I offered them my credit cards but they weren't interested.

"They actually didn't say anything at all. They just beat me up a little bit and shoved a needle in my arm. When I woke up, I was in a lab. And they… did something to me. Changed me. So every now and then—I'm not really in control of it—I change, Michael. Into something really, really horrible, and when I'm like that, I don't have full control of myself. I wish I did. I'm working on it. I hate it. At least, that's what I tell myself. But it's part of me now. Part of my blood."

It was Morbius' turn to nod.

"And they only feed you when you're… transformed?"

"A few scraps here and there, to keep me alive," Jake answered, looking away. His smile had faded. "But they want to keep me hungry for when my next fight comes along. Which must be pretty soon. I don't know. I've been down here a *long* time. Sometimes they even put a regular human in the arena with us. To get us all frenzied, I guess. It's evil… but it's also damn effective."

Michael looked around his cell, wondered how long they would leave him down here before he would be forced to fight again.

"I'm sorry," he said without looking back at Jake.

"Me too, buddy," his new friend said, his voice sounding more distant. "Me too."

CHAPTER TEN

M

A COOL, light rain began to fall as Amanda emerged from underground.

When the subway had reached the next station she'd decided to get off, even though it wasn't her stop. She passed a couple of police officers who were hurrying to the subway car, to find out what had happened, and she thought about telling them, then decided against it. For all she knew, she'd be the one to get interrogated and arrested, and she had learned from Morbius that it was sometimes prudent to walk away from a situation before it became a situation.

She saw the two girls as she exited the platform through the turnstile, and one of them mouthed "thank you" to her. Amanda smiled and kept on walking.

She had to walk almost a mile to reach Liz's apartment, but the crisp air and cold rain were bracing in the best way possible. She knew it was ridiculous, but after she had wiped the proverbial floor with that thug in the subway, her senses felt more attuned to the world. The sounds of tires on the wet pavement, the smell of the rain hitting the sidewalk, the taste and feel of the water on her tongue—it was all so crisp and clear, like she was the only one in the city who was aware of everything that was happening in those moments.

She wondered if this was how Michael experienced the world.

Michael.

At the thought of him, she hurried her pace to the apartment, hoping Liz had connected with Fabian and had answers.

The walk up the four flights of stairs was less exhausting than usual, which she chalked up to the adrenaline still running through her body. It almost made her laugh. Her skin felt like it was on fire. She wasn't sure if she had ever felt so alive.

She arrived in front of the apartment door and went to unlock it, but discovered that it was already open. *Must be home*, Amanda thought. *Maybe she got out early.* She couldn't wait to tell her friend about the encounter on the subway.

The apartment was dark except for Liz's room, which was lit by a small lamp. *That's weird*, Amanda noted. Liz usually turned on every light in the place. She was about to call out to her friend and turn on the lights when Liz's silhouette suddenly appeared in her room's doorway.

"Hey!" Amanda called out and she walked across the

room, turning on the light over the small kitchen table. She plopped down into one of the chairs, smiling up at her friend. "You won't *believe* what just happened to me."

Liz walked into the kitchen and stood there, forcing a smile but not saying a word. Amanda's forehead wrinkled in confusion. Her friend looked pale—or even paler than usual—and it looked as if her mascara had run a bit. Added to the fact that the lights in the apartment were still off, Amanda was concerned. Maybe something was wrong, despite the smile. Maybe something to do with her auditions or…

God, her dad.

Despite everything, Amanda wished Michael was there. The day had just been so… weird. Liz was her oldest friend, but something about being with Michael just made her feel better, despite his sometimes bad attitude. She stared at Liz, waiting, didn't want to push. She knew Liz. She'd talk when she was ready.

The rain came down harder outside the window.

Amanda shucked off her wet jacket and let it fall back, inside out, on the back of her chair. The overhead light was old, and didn't throw out much luminescence. Liz moved again, grabbing two glasses from the cabinet and a bottle of bourbon. The good stuff that she saved for special occasions. She sat down across from Amanda and poured them each a drink, then pushed one of the glasses forward.

The dim light reflected against a mirror above the kitchen sink. The reflection gave the glow a distilled effect, hazy, like a memory that has only just resurfaced.

"Bottoms up," Liz murmured.

"You okay?" Amanda asked, picking up the glass but not looking at it.

Liz smiled again, sadly, and placed the bottle down gently on the table, as if it was the most important thing she had ever done. Then she quickly downed the liquor in her glass.

"Yes? No. I don't know."

Liz looked at her friend.

Amanda had been right. Liz's mascara was a mess. She'd been crying.

"What happened?" Amanda asked, reaching out and putting her hand on her friend's.

"It's… it's my dad," Liz said, her eyes wide and filling with tears.

"Geez, is he… did he…?"

"He's okay, Amanda," Liz said looking away and pouring herself another drink.

"Oh thank God," Amanda breathed, taking a sip of the bourbon. She wasn't the biggest fan of alcohol, but after the day she'd been having she decided a sip to calm the nerves was in order. "So, what's going on with him? You can tell me anything."

"He always liked you," Liz answered, looking over and staring dreamily at the mirror on the wall. "He thought you were a good influence on me, and he was right. After my parents split, I acted out. Probably just trying to get attention. I remember being in so much pain, and causing other people anguish made me feel better. At least for a little while."

"I remember," Amanda said, smiling sadly.

"But you loved me anyway. Never judged me. Always had my back. I'm not sure I ever told you how much I appreciated that."

"Liz. You never had to."

"I—" Liz started, a single tear rolling down her face. "I had to say it now."

She inhaled the shot in front of her and then stood up, wobbly. She's drunk, Amanda realized. Liz could hold her alcohol, had always been able to. Whatever was happening, it was serious. Amanda stood, too.

"Whatever's going on," Amanda said, walking around the table and putting her hand on her friend's shoulder. "I can help."

"That's just it, Amanda." Liz looked at her sadly. "You're helping just by being here."

"What? What do you mean, Liz?"

A noise from behind her caught Amanda's attention. She turned, trying to remember if she had left the door open. One of Liz's neighbors was incredibly nosy and pushy.

"Sorry," she started to say, "now's not a good time but…" The sight of a silhouette by the open door made the words dry up in her mouth. The shadow, definitely belonging to a woman, was impossibly familiar.

The woman's hand was on the door and she closed it, the faint clicking sound reaching Amanda's ears, filling her with dread despite the relative innocence of the action. She could feel the hairs on her arms standing on end. Suddenly, her final night at the hospital, when she thought she was seeing things, started to make sense.

"Hello, Amanda. I've missed you."

The voice was like a knife to the gut.

"Ca… Catherine…?" Amanda managed to get out, unable to catch her breath, feeling like she might vomit out the one sip of alcohol and whatever else was in her system.

The silhouette strode forward and Amanda's "dead" sister Catherine appeared in the eerie light emanating from above the kitchen table. A cruel smile was etched onto her face. Her hair was down, a style she'd sported for most of her life—though the last time Amanda had seen her, when her sister called herself Poison-Lark and tried to feed her to a demonic spider, it had been pulled up into a severe-looking bun.

Amanda still couldn't catch her breath. She looked over at Liz, who was staring at the floor, her face flushed.

"Liz…?" Amanda asked quietly.

"I'm so sorry," her friend whispered. "I am so, so sorry. I had to. For my dad…"

The truth of the situation washed over Amanda and her stomach knotted immediately. She had been betrayed.

Again.

She locked eyes with her sister. The smile was still there. Resembling a smile she used to love, to emulate. Now it just filled her with terror.

Without even thinking about it, Amanda threw a punch and it landed on her sister's cheek, hard. Catherine staggered back but then righted herself, fixed her hair, and stood motionless, still with that infuriating grin on her face.

"I'll kill you," Amanda whispered.

"Oh, sweetie, I know," Catherine replied and then she looked past Amanda, into the shadows of the apartment, and nodded.

Men in red robes emerged from the darkness, swarming around Amanda and binding her. She screamed but it was a small sound as the rain increased and pelted the windows like bullets. One of the men placed a strange-smelling gag into her mouth. She fought them, but within moments darkness encroached on her brain and she passed out.

"YOU SAID there's a fire exit, correct?" Catherine asked.

Liz nodded, still looking at the floor. "Yes, out in the hallway, to the left."

Catherine's eyes flashed at the men and they carried Amanda past her and out into the hallway. Liz heard the door slam shut, and she suddenly burst into tears. Catherine appeared next to her and gently ran her hand down Liz's hair.

"Shhh," she said quietly. "It's okay. You did a good job. You were always my favorite of Amanda's friends growing up. You had such a spark, even as a little girl."

"You… you won't hurt my father, right?" Liz choked out between sobs.

"Of course not," Catherine answered, still smiling. "We were never going to hurt him in the first place."

Liz looked up into Catherine's face, confusion wrinkling her features.

"You weren't? But you... you said if I didn't... didn't help you get Amanda, you would kill him."

Catherine continued to run her hand along Liz's hair, slow, even strokes with a rhythm that was in time with the beating of the rain against the window. The shadows in the apartment seemed to grow, now that it was just the two of them.

"You're right, Elizabeth, I did say that, but I knew the threat would be enough to get you to do whatever I asked. I never once suspected that you would do anything stupid, and that I would be forced to slit your father's pathetic throat. I remember how much you idolized him when you were young... how you looked at him with so much love in your stupid little eyes. Sad, really."

Liz looked at Catherine's face, the tears having dried up but her chin still trembling.

"Thank you, and I promise... I won't say anything. To anyone. Ever. It'll be like this never happened."

"Why, you took the words right out of my mouth," Catherine said, raising up her other hand from the darkness.

Liz gasped.

Blinking against a sudden burst of pain in her stomach, she glanced down. Catherine had slipped a long knife into her gut. Small rivulets of blood began to leak out in several places around the blade.

Liz looked back up at Catherine, utterly astonished. Her mouth opened and closed several times, like a dying fish.

"But…" she managed to get out.

"Shhh. It's okay." Catherine continued to rub her hair. "It'll be over soon."

She withdrew the blade and then reinserted it, just above the previous wound. Liz gasped again but didn't scream. Catherine was impressed. Blood poured onto the kitchen floor, rolling out and across the old, cracked linoleum.

"As you slip into that beautiful darkness, Elizabeth, know that your death is in service to a much greater good. You won't be here to witness my transformation into Amaymon, the truest and most powerful servant of Satan, but this moment has been an important step in bringing about my coming change. So, from all of us…"

Catherine withdrew the knife a second time and then plunged it directly into Liz's chest.

This time, she screamed.

"Thank you," Catherine finished.

She took a step to her left and dislodged the knife for a final time. Liz collapsed onto the floor and shuddered for several seconds. Catherine walked across the kitchen and cleaned the blood-covered blade on a dish towel.

Taking a deep breath, she caught her reflection in the small mirror above the sink. For the first time in a while, she noticed the imperfection on her face from where she had fallen asleep on the *Lemegeton* all those years ago. The book of spells had left its mark. She would have to work harder to keep it covered. At least until her own transformation was complete. Then it wouldn't matter anymore.

For the briefest of moments, Catherine questioned what she was doing. She had just murdered her sister's best friend. Yet another death on her hands. She glanced down, clenched her teeth, and then looked back up. Her eyes looked different.

Powerful.

Determined.

This was the way it had to be. Throughout history, great people had to make very difficult decisions in order to accomplish important and essential things. In this case, some people had to die, unfortunately. But Catherine Saint was going to save the world.

Even if it meant burning it to the ground.

CHAPTER ELEVEN

MORBIUS HAD inherited Amanda's nightmare. She had been talking about it since the night after he had saved her, when she awoke screaming. Over time, he had gotten used to her late-night agonies.

But her trauma had made its way into his subconscious.

He stood in a dark hallway in some unknown building. The fluorescent lights overhead blinked, creating a strange, unsettling strobe effect. The walls seemed as if they were breathing.

He was alone there.

Until he wasn't.

Martine stood at the other end of the long hallway. She saw him and a sad smile crept onto her face.

"Michael," she whispered.

"Martine!" he cried out in response. Morbius sprinted forward. A part of him knew this was only a dream, but he didn't care. As he ran, the hallway grew longer and longer, and he screamed in rage. Martine continued to stare at him, her eyes filled with confusion. Why did he refuse to help her?

Morbius felt a crawling on his face, and he slapped at whatever it was, feeling something moist explode onto his palm. He pulled his hand away and saw a dead spider, its blood and guts splayed out on his pale skin like an expressionist painting.

More crawling sensations, more spiders on his face. He swatted at them and saw that they were climbing all over him. The floor was covered with them and they were dropping from the ceiling. Thousands and thousands of spiders of all shapes and sizes. Biting him, entering his mouth, his nostrils. Covering his entire body.

The weight of them caused him to collapse onto a knee. Martine was closer, but he couldn't stand. He raised a spider-covered arm, reaching toward her.

"Martine…" he whispered, spiders running along his tongue and teeth.

"Why won't you help me?" she responded.

She disappeared into darkness.

MORBIUS WOKE up screaming.

Slowly, he caught his breath and looked around. He was still in the cell. His body hurt less but he was hungrier than ever. He couldn't remember the last time he had gone this long without a meal.

"You okay there, buddy?"

For a second, the voice confused Morbius, caused him to tense and ready himself for an assault, but then the memories returned to him.

Jake. His fellow prisoner.

"I'm fine," Morbius said, more harshly than he'd intended.

"Glad to hear it," Jake replied, appearing to ignore Morbius' bad attitude. "Trust me, you'll hear a *lot* of screaming down here. Plenty of nightmares to go around."

Morbius grunted and stood, stretching his arms over his head. He walked around the cell a couple of times, getting the blood flowing in his legs and examining the walls, looking for weak spots.

There were none.

After a few minutes, he sat back down on the stone slab and stared at the floor. He wasn't sure what was going to kill him first: the hunger or the boredom.

"Pretty awful, right?" Jake said, as if reading his mind.

"What do you do to pass the time?" Michael asked.

"Well, I used to talk to the blob—you know, before you got here. But he... she?... never said anything, probably didn't have vocal cords, now that I think about it. But it was good even to just talk *at* a living creature, you know?" Jake laughed, then sighed. Something he did often, apparently.

"Other than that? Talk to myself, I guess. Do pushups. Sleep. Scream. The usual prisoner stuff."

Morbius grunted again. Jake laughed.

"What?" Michael asked.

"You're a man of few words. I respect that."

"It's… it's been a long day. A long year, really," he said, adding, "I just don't know how to talk to people anymore. I'm so angry all the time. I have trouble controlling myself, can barely stand to look at myself in the mirror. When I do, all I see is a monster. And then I start to think, maybe the monster was there all along…"

Jake started to respond when a noise silenced both of them.

The man with the beard stood motionless at the door to the cell, on the other side of the bars, still wearing the same blood-red robe. His eyes were fixed on Morbius, hatred burning out from them, but a saccharine smile adorned his face.

"Good morning, Michael."

With lightning-like speed, Morbius sprang from the slab and rushed toward the metal bars and the man just behind them.

"Michael, don't!" Jake yelled but it was too late.

Morbius got one hand through the bars and his claws found purchase on the man's face, three jagged lines ripping open almost immediately. But as soon as Morbius' shoulder touched the metal, a burst of electricity lanced through his entire body, throwing him back onto the ground, his skin bubbling and smoking from the contact.

He lay there for a few seconds, blinking, then rolled over and stood up, nearly falling over in the effort.

The man's smile was gone. Morbius was in incredible pain but he took a small pleasure in having rattled the cultist. The three cuts in his face were deep, extending down his cheek and into his beard. Blood poured out, dripping down and darkening the already red robes he wore.

"I hope that was worth it," the man growled.

"It was," Morbius responded, a rare smile appearing on his pale face. He was enjoying the moment and licked at what little of the man's blood and skin had ended up on his claws. While it tasted good, *so* good, it only made him hungrier.

"Then I'm going to enjoy this next part even more," the man replied. "Do you know who I am?"

Morbius stared at him, looking more closely at his face, and searched his memory. As far as he knew, he had never seen this man before in his life. Then again, since he had become a living vampire, many incredible things had happened—things beyond the imagination—so it was possible that he had forgotten, or had encountered the man and simply never registered his existence.

"No," Morbius responded. "Should I?"

"Perhaps not," the man said, "but I know you. My name is Thaddeus. And I've been waiting for this. To do to you what you've done to me."

"And what exactly have I done to you?"

"You took the most important thing in my life away from me. You killed my son."

Morbius swallowed. He had killed many sons since the accident that had turned him into a bloodthirsty monster. After he fed, after the lust for sustenance faded, he would often berate himself. That person was someone's child. And here, at last, was that very renunciation in the flesh. He could hardly blame this man for his anger.

"It's certainly possible," Morbius answered, doing his best to keep his voice level. He had no interest in showing weakness to his captor, despite any guilt he might feel.

"Oh, you didn't kill him yourself, Michael," Thaddeus said, anger flashing in his eyes. "You didn't drink his blood, like all those others who you've murdered, but your actions were responsible for his death. And for that, you must pay."

"Who was your son?" Morbius asked, his curiosity getting the better of him.

"His name was Justin. He seduced Amanda Saint and was on track to join me as a high priest of Demon-Fire, but your actions destroyed *everything*. All for a pathetic woman you had *just met*!" the man screamed, his face turning red.

"Ah yes," Morbius answered. "I remember your son now. The last time I saw him, he was running away. Like a coward. Like his father."

At that, the anger built in Thaddeus, and Morbius was counting on it. Then the man's demeanor relaxed, and he smiled.

"You are going to die slowly, Michael. I'm going to make sure of that—but not today." He spoke calmly, and looked to his right. In response, two more men in red robes appeared, and quickly opened the cell door. The action so surprised him that Morbius didn't have time to react as they shoved something inside, then closed the door again.

Not something. Someone.

It was a woman, unconscious but alive. Her long hair was strewn across her face, so Morbius couldn't see what she looked like. But he *could* see one thing.

Her neck.

The carotid artery pulsed as she breathed slowly, and it was like a beacon calling to him, insisting that he come closer. His stomach rumbled. His hands trembled.

He had been so good. He hadn't killed.

He had made Amanda proud.

But Michael Morbius hungered.

Laughter filled the cell. Morbius pulled his eyes away from the meal—from *the woman*—in front of him, and looked up. Thaddeus was laughing, his hand pressed against the gashes in his face. Blood leaked between his hairy fingers.

"What's the matter, Michael? Isn't this what you wanted?"

Morbius ignored him. Tried also to ignore the body on the ground, and failed. He looked at the woman again. She murmured softly in her sleep, or her unconsciousness, or whatever it was, and Morbius nearly screamed in agony. For what he wanted to do. For what he knew he shouldn't.

"Enjoy," Thaddeus said, and he turned to walk away. The other men had already vanished. "We'll be back later to clean up your leftovers. If you leave anything behind, that is."

Morbius crawled closer to the woman. Her blood smelled so good. So fresh.

"You okay, man?" Jake asked.

"Don't look at me!" Morbius screamed, peering at the hole in the wall near his bed. Jake didn't respond. The quiet that descended was almost unbearable. He could hear the woman's breathing, a delicate sound, precious. Fragile.

As his mouth drew closer and closer to her neck, Morbius' mind cast back to the first time he had drained the blood from a living human. It had been an older man, shortly after the experiment, after he had murdered Emil. Morbius had fled the boat upon which Martine still slept, had even attempted to kill himself in the ocean, but was unable to do so. He'd swam for a long time and had finally come across a boat.

Sneaking aboard, he attacked the first person he saw. Acting purely on instinct. The man had looked at him with an expression of such shock and betrayal as Morbius sank his teeth into his flesh. Had yelled a single word as Morbius fed.

"*Please!*"

But Michael's mind had gone bright red with hunger, with desperation. He wasn't able to fully comprehend what he was doing—what he had done—until the man was a lifeless husk on the deck in front of him. When he came to his senses, Morbius fell to his knees, shaking the man gently, imploring him to wake up. But he knew. Knew the old man was dead.

Knew what he had done.

What he had become.

A monster.

All these months later, here he was again. *You don't have to do this*, a part of his brain cried out. *You can control yourself.*

No, you can't, another said. Louder.

Morbius' teeth met flesh, hesitated for the briefest of seconds, and then pierced it, the sweet warm blood immediately filling his mouth. He thought it was the most delicious thing he had ever tasted. Hated himself because of that fact, but the self-loathing didn't stop him from digging in deeper, from sucking down the hot liquid even faster. The woman moaned slightly but didn't wake up. Morbius silently thanked the universe for that.

He drank and drank as the woman's breathing slowed. He wanted to stop. He tried, but he was so hungry. Had been so hungry for so long.

"I'm sorry, Michael," Jake said, his voice far enough away that Morbius knew the man in the other cell wasn't watching. The apology was agonizing regardless.

Damn them! he thought fiercely. *I will make them* pay. Despite his determination, tears streamed down Morbius' face as he fed. He choked back sobs, fresh blood dripping from the corners of his mouth, but slowly felt the strength returning to his body.

A strength he needed, and loved, and despised.

ACT TWO
ARENA OF BLOOD

CHAPTER TWELVE

CATHERINE SAINT had been a happy child.

She was born to Myrna and James Saint, both teachers at the same high school, both in the same social studies department. They had met because of a shared love of history, brought together by a mutual friend during college who thought they might get along.

An understatement.

They hit it off immediately, retreating to a corner at the party where they'd been introduced and falling into a conversation that spanned centuries. He was obsessed with forgotten or misinterpreted dynasties and leaders who came in second in national elections, while she found the "bad boys of history" as she said—like Genghis Khan and Hitler—at the same time interesting and somewhat baffling. Their often unlikely rise to power, their ability to sway otherwise good people to do horrible things, their undeniable charisma.

When Myrna and James kissed at the end of the night, James had thought to himself how unlikely their pairing was. He was about as far removed from a "bad boy" as one could get. He was a meek academic, someone who lost himself in books, never in action. He was a classic example of a passive-aggressive person. James literally feared confrontation, and would complain about something minor when he really wanted to dive into something much deeper.

Regardless, they fell madly in love, helped each other pass their classes, and found teaching jobs at the same school immediately after graduation.

Catherine arrived a year later.

She was the apple of their collective eyes. They spoiled her, took endless pictures, bought expensive and ridiculous outfits upon which strangers would stop and remark, much to their pride. At night, the three of them would lie together in the queen-size bed in their tiny apartment, Catherine nuzzled between them, snoring softly, her parents staring at her until they, too, drifted off.

As the years passed, James was quickly promoted to department head after the existing head quit unexpectedly. There were rumors of an illicit affair with a student, but these whispers were quickly silenced by a heavy-handed administration. Myrna was a little surprised that they had chosen James over her, especially given how much he had started to drink after the arrival of Catherine. But then again, she wasn't *really* surprised by his promotion at all.

He was a man.

She wasn't.

The first seed of bitterness toward her husband was planted deep in Myrna's mind.

On Catherine's second birthday, her parents told her that they had a surprise for her. In her young mind, she thought it would be a pony, or something equally amazing. But it wasn't. Not even close. It was something she had never wanted.

A sister.

She had cried. On her own birthday. Screamed at her parents. Had an absolute meltdown. Told them she didn't want a sibling. Everything was perfect the way it was. They'd had to tell her friends' parents that the carefully planned party was canceled. It was embarrassing, but less so than having the guests all arrive to a screaming, sobbing birthday girl.

Catherine's behavior eventually recovered, but the level of happiness she'd felt—up to the moment of her parents' revelation—never did. Not really.

She learned that she should act happy about her incoming sister, but she didn't actually feel that way. And when they moved into a new house so that they would have enough room for their growing family, she resented the baby even more. That little apartment had been her entire life, and it became just a memory.

When Amanda arrived six months after the move, Catherine was shocked to discover that something changed inside of her as she stared into those tiny little eyes. She had wanted to hate this new human, and still did on some level, but she also realized something else, something that dismayed her.

She loved Amanda, too.

The convergence of absolute hatred and deep love confused Catherine profoundly, and she would often cry herself to sleep at night because of it. She would feel the rage building in her when she watched her parents doting on the helpless infant, but then laugh out loud when Amanda's chubby fist wrapped around one of her fingers.

One night, about a year and a half later, when her father had passed out early after consecutive sleepless nights, Catherine found herself in the nursery, standing over Amanda's crib. The baby was asleep, a cute pink smile curled up into her cheeks, her small eyelids fluttering with some delightful dream, Catherine assumed. The smile enraged her. Even asleep, the baby's life was better than hers.

Without realizing what she was doing, Catherine reached out and slowly wrapped her fingers around Amanda's neck. Gently at first... and then less so. The baby was so fragile in her grasp. Catherine tightened her fingers around the soft flesh.

Amanda's eyes suddenly burst open, her forehead wrinkling with concern and confusion.

Catherine squeezed more. It felt so good.

Amanda managed to suck in half a breath and tried to cry out, but couldn't. Catherine realized that all her problems could go away if she just held on for a few seconds more. But then their eyes locked again, and she thought back to the hospital, to the first time she'd seen her sister. Those beautiful blue eyes and the hidden depths behind them.

She loved her sister.

Catherine let go and stumbled back. There was a moment of absolute silence in the house, and then Amanda screeched louder than Catherine had ever heard a human scream before.

She scrambled out of the nursery and sprinted down the hallway, hurtling into her room and collapsing into bed. Pretending she was asleep but keeping her eyes open just enough to see what was going on. Seconds later, her father hustled past her door, calling out to his daughter. Catherine could hear him in there, soothing her. It took a long time for the crying to subside. She watched as her dad passed by her room once again, holding Amanda tightly against his chest.

Catherine wondered vaguely where her mother was.

Amanda looked at her as they passed.

The baby was probably too young to fully understand what had happened, but Catherine could have sworn she saw a question in her sister's expression. *Why?*

After that, Catherine made a silent resolution to herself—to be a better person, a better sister. She spent as much time with Amanda as possible, playing make-believe and hide-and-seek and super heroes with her, much to the delight of Myrna and James.

TIME PASSED.

Even though they were nearly three years apart, they became as close as twins. When Amanda was bullied in school, Catherine would get involved, putting the fear of God into those mean little girls, having her friends say hi to Amanda in the halls, elevating her sister's social status. A third grader who was acknowledged by sixth graders? Immediate badge of honor.

However, their friendship grew more strained as Catherine's entrance into middle and then high school relegated them to separate buildings. Catherine became more and more popular while Amanda turned in on herself, no longer under the protection of a cool older sister. Her peers became aware of it and the bullying resumed. Amanda grew quiet and studious, and eventually found Liz Green, another quirky kid with a big imagination.

When Catherine was a senior in high school, Amanda was a freshman. It was the first time they had been in the same school in six years, and it would also be the last.

Too much time had passed.

Catherine was the queen bee of the school, was dating the most handsome guy, was the envy of everyone. Amanda was a shy book nerd who walked the hallways with slumped shoulders and downcast eyes. Catherine would see her sister and wrestle with whether she should say hi or not. Despite the years that they had been close, deep inside of her was the complicated love-hate she still felt. For the girl who had stolen her parents from her; for the girl who knew her better than anyone else in the world.

Everything changed one Saturday night.

THEIR PARENTS were out of town for the weekend, at a teachers' conference in another state. Catherine took the opportunity to throw the party of a lifetime. Dozens were invited; hundreds showed up. Amanda tried to stay out of it, retreating to her room and losing herself in the fantasy book series she was reading.

The noise of the party was deafening. Things were breaking. Amanda wondered how Catherine would explain this to their parents. She loved her sister so much, looked up to her. She didn't want Catherine to get in trouble. But what could she do?

As the night progressed, Amanda realized she couldn't hide forever. She had to go to the bathroom and had no idea how much time would pass before all these strangers would vacate their home. So she slowly unlocked and opened her door, and braved the hallway. The bathroom was only a few dozen feet away.

Then *he* appeared. Scott. Catherine's boyfriend.

As she reached for the handle, he opened the bathroom door from within, stepped out, and smiled at her. Not a kind smile. He was drunk. Swaying.

"Hi," she said quietly. He'd been over before, for dinner, and had always been extremely polite, answering her dad's probing questions with tact and humor. He was on the football team and was a scholar.

"Hi," he responded, and then quickly reached out and grabbed her hand. She'd resisted but he was huge, had pulled her easily into the bathroom, and shut the door behind them. His lips were on her neck before she knew what was happening.

"Oh my god, you smell *so* good," he slurred.

"N-no," she stammered. "Stop."

Her protestations only made his kissing more feverish. He moved his lips to her face and then her mouth. He tasted like beer and cheese, and Amanda felt like she was going to throw up. She had never wanted her first kiss to be like this.

She pushed against him but he was too strong. He wrapped his arms around her and shoved her up against the bathroom cabinet, a cabinet that housed her toothbrush and dental floss and cold medicine. She tried to scream but couldn't seem to catch her breath. He was thrusting his hips against hers.

And then, suddenly, he stopped.

Amanda blinked, confused, relieved, and noticed that he was staring at the door. Which was open again. In it stood Catherine, a look of shock and anger on her face.

"What. The. *Hell*," she said in a clipped, controlled tone that was more frightening than if she had been screaming.

"She pulled me in here, babe," Scott said, shrugging.

Catherine turned her gaze to Amanda, a look of hurt appearing in her eyes.

"What? No, I…" Amanda said but she was having trouble finding the words. She hadn't done anything wrong, so why was she feeling a crushing wave of guilt? Catherine just shook her head and walked away. Scott turned back to Amanda with a look of contempt.

"Your loss," he said, and then he walked out.

Amanda made it back to her room before bursting into tears. She fell face-first into her giant pink beanbag and heaved out deep, wet sobs, blocking out the increasingly bacchanal sounds of the party.

Hours later, when she woke up to a silent house, Amanda realized she had never used the bathroom. And wouldn't, not until the safety of daylight arrived.

CATHERINE TRIED to hide all evidence of the party, but their parents were too smart for that. A slightly askew window shade was the first clue, which led to a landslide of others, their father too much of an amateur detective to ignore the increasing trail of evidence. When Amanda was questioned, she feigned ignorance even though Catherine had been placed in another room for the interrogations.

Eventually, the facts were just too hard to ignore and Catherine confessed. Her father was furious, accused her of betraying their trust. Their mom appeared unfazed by the incident, oddly so. She seemed almost proud of her older daughter.

That didn't make sense.

Regardless, Catherine was grounded for a week, including a dance she later claimed she hadn't wanted to go to anyway. After the punishment had been doled out, she quietly made her way upstairs and shut the door silently behind her. No teen meltdown, no claims of unfairness, not even any bargaining.

To her credit, Catherine dumped Scott the next day, but nothing between the two sisters was quite the same, ever again. When Amanda explained what had happened in the bathroom between her and Scott, Catherine said she believed her, but there was still something more. Amanda assumed it was sadness at Scott's betrayal—and it was. At least some of it. But another part was the rage Catherine had felt as a child, the rage that had led to her wrapping her fingers around a helpless baby's throat.

The rest of Catherine's senior year went by without a hitch. Breaking up with the most popular boy in school only increased her social capital, and she went on to date a string of other jocks, all while maintaining straight A's. In contrast, Amanda sank farther into herself, relying on Liz to get her through the perils of pubescence.

Catherine's college years were a blur. She joined a sorority and did certain things of which she was not terribly proud, but she maintained her excellent grades and found herself on a similar track to her mother, perhaps influenced by Myrna.

But Catherine's interest in history ran even darker than her mother's. She found herself going beyond the obvious flashpoints and digging deeper, into Hitler's obsession with the occult, the writings of Algernon Blackwood, the more obscure philosophies of the Marquis de Sade. The list went on and on. She looked beyond what she felt were the caricatures of these men and into their often supernatural endeavors.

After college, Catherine took a mindless office job that paid incredibly well, assisting a man who destroyed other people's dreams for a living, and she used the money to rent an apartment that was eerily similar to that first one in which she'd grown up. The one before Amanda. She visited home now and then, had dinner with her parents and sister. Amanda was dating someone, seemed incredibly happy. Her parents, less so. Her father had lost his job at the school, possibly because of his drinking, and took on whatever work he could find—though he refused to talk about it to his daughters.

Catherine tried to engage with all of them as best she could.

Yet as each day passed, she sensed that something was missing. For her whole life, she felt as if she had an itch that she just couldn't scratch, no matter how hard she clawed at her own skin. As if something inside her was desperate to escape. And then one night, after a visit from her mother, it did.

CHAPTER THIRTEEN

CATHERINE HAD just arrived home from work, had just poured herself a generous glass of wine, when the doorbell to her apartment rang. She headed toward the front hallway, down the two steps, and opened the door.

It was her mother. Looking windswept and dazed. A suitcase wrapped in her fingers.

"Mom?" Catherine asked. "Are you okay?"

Myrna didn't answer, just made her way inside and drained the contents of Catherine's glass without asking, then poured herself another.

"I'm better than fine," she said finally.

Catherine glanced at the suitcase on the floor nearby. "Are you… are you leaving Dad?"

"I'm leaving *everything*," Myrna said quietly. "Except you."

"Me?" Catherine took her mother's hand,

confused. Even a little scared. "I don't understand. What's happening?"

When Myrna spoke, it was with words and a dark conviction that Catherine simply didn't recognize. Once the truth ushered forth, it came in waves that lasted so long that there was no telling how much time passed.

She spoke of a secret life, of a cult called Demon-Fire. About its goal to cleanse the world through pain and death and fire. How she had found them during her research, sought them out, pleaded with them to accept her, and then pledged her life to them willingly when they finally did. As the years passed, she secretly helped them however and whenever she could, but it became too much for her, living a hidden life smothered beneath a false one. She'd had enough.

This would be the day she shed her skin, and became the person who she truly was. Sister Saint. She would give herself to the cult, fully and without regret.

"But what about us?" Catherine asked in a small voice. As strange as all of it sounded, somehow it also made sense. But the little girl in her didn't want to lose her mother.

They were in the living room, sitting on an elegant sofa. The distant look on Myrna's face faded, and her eyes focused and she seemed to suddenly remember where she was. She placed her hand on her daughter's cheek, pushed an errant strand of hair behind her ear.

"Oh baby," she said, tears filling her eyes. "Your father and sister are weak. It's not their fault. I knew he was inferior when I met him, and he's only become more so over the years, but I myself wasn't strong yet, not then. Not like I am now. Thanks to Demon-Fire. And as for you…"

"Yes?" Catherine asked.

"You were *always* strong. I knew it from the moment you were born. You slipped out of me like a warrior, without a single tear, and you latched onto me immediately. You were hungry. Ravenous. For sustenance. For *life*. Not like your sister, who came mewling into this world, small and scared and needy."

Catherine felt a rush of excitement at her mother's words, and then shame. Amanda loved them both so much.

"I saw you," Myrna whispered loudly.

"What?" Catherine said. "When?" Even though—deep down—she knew exactly what her mother was talking about.

"That night. When you almost choked your sister to death. I was there. In the doorway. And I was *so* proud of you, Catherine."

"Proud? For… not doing it? Or—?" She couldn't finish the sentence. For her part, Myrna only smiled. A shiver ran up Catherine's spine.

"After you let go, I slipped away," Myrna continued, "down to the kitchen, when she started screaming."

At that moment, Catherine's phone rang and she reached for it.

"No," her mother commanded. "Not yet. After I'm gone, you will play your part until I reach out to you again."

Catherine looked at her phone, torn, knowing

how distraught her father must have been. The two of them had never been all that close. He seemed to retain most of his overt affection for Amanda, but she loved him, nonetheless.

Finally, the phone stopped ringing.

Myrna took her daughter's face in both her hands now. "You are my truest offspring, the person most like me in the entire world, and I suspect that you will have more to offer Demon-Fire than I ever will. But first... you must learn."

She pulled back, stood, and walked across the dark apartment to where she had left her suitcase. Unlatching it, she plunged a hand within. Catherine noticed dark red material among the clothes. *A dress?* she wondered. Finally, Myrna held up a large, black, leather-bound book and brought it over, placing it on the counter in front of her daughter.

"What is this?" Catherine asked.

"This is *The Lesser Key of Solomon*, my love," Myrna answered, reverence in her voice. "Also known as the *Lemegeton*. It is an ancient grimoire, passed down in the shadows and through the ages, made up of—"

"Five books," Catherine interrupted in wonder, running her fingers delicately across the cover. "It's *real?*"

"It's real," Myrna responded. "And it's yours now."

Catherine slowly opened the book to a random page in its middle, ignoring her mother's soft gasp, and cut herself on the ancient paper. She yelped and pulled her hand away. The book slammed shut as if an unseen force had reacted in anger.

Myrna looked at Catherine's bleeding finger and then grabbed it, placing it in her mouth, tasting her daughter's freshly spilled blood. A smile wrinkled her face as she removed the finger from between her teeth.

"You must read the *Lemegeton* from the very beginning to the very end," she said quietly. "There are no shortcuts."

"I… I understand," Catherine replied, her mind spinning.

Myrna walked over to her suitcase, latched it again, and lifted it from the floor.

"When you are finished reading… experiencing… I will send for you."

"But how will you know?"

Myrna's disconcerting smile faded and her eyes grew dark.

"Demon-Fire knows everything, Catherine. *Everything.*" She turned to leave, but then stopped and looked at her daughter again. "I almost forgot." Myrna set down the case, reached over, and took off her wedding ring. Held it up for her daughter to see.

"I don't understand," Catherine said. "Do you want me to give that back to Dad?"

Myrna smiled. "Oh, my sweet naïve daughter. No. This is no ordinary ring. It was transformed during a Goetian ceremony, after I became a high priestess of Demon-Fire. It contains the fragments of demonic souls, thousands of them. They… they speak to me, but they have also told me that I am not the true Chosen One. That one of my daughters is."

"Me?"

"Yes, Catherine," Myrna said, her eyes ablaze. "I believe you are the Chosen One. When the time is right, when you have proven yourself worthy, I will give this ring to you and it will grant you great power. Power to heal, and to destroy."

Tears filled Catherine's eyes, but they were tears of excitement, as Myrna put the ring back on, then turned and walked toward the door. Catherine followed despite the pull she felt toward the book that sat behind her. She was desperate to start reading it, but a part of her also wondered if her mother had gone insane. If she would never see her again.

"Mommy?" she called out gently as Myrna walked down the two steps at the end of the hallway and put her hand on the doorknob.

"Yes?" her mother replied, not turning around, her figure silhouetted in the doorframe.

"I love you."

A long moment of silence stretched out. Catherine thought she could see her mother's entire body trembling, but she couldn't be sure.

"There is no more space in your life for love, Catherine," Myrna said.

And then she was gone.

Before Catherine had time to process what had just happened, her phone rang again. She ran to get it and burst into tears when she heard her father's strained voice and what he had to say. They were genuine tears, but not for the reason James could suspect. She spoke to him for a long time, pretending she knew nothing, then talked to Amanda, continuing her feigned ignorance. She was surprised how easily lying came to her in a situation like this.

At last, they said goodbye, with promises to meet up the next day, to make plans, to find Myrna and reunite their perfect little family.

Catherine stayed up as long as she could, reading *The Lesser Key of Solomon* deep into the night, but only got through the first book, the "Ars Goetia," before passing out on top of it. When she awoke the next day, several of the arcane letters had burned into her face. It was light but it was there. She was forced to use makeup to cover it.

She called in sick to work and kept reading—did the same thing the next day. And the next. After the "Ars Goetia" there was the "Ars Theurgia-Goetia," then the "Ars Paulina."

When her boss threatened to fire her if she didn't start coming in to work, Catherine grudgingly capitulated and went back in, but her heart wasn't in it. She had found her true calling. She worked her hours and then rushed back home to continue her reading. The book seemed almost to be calling to her.

The "Ars Almadel."

The "Ars Notoria."

Her father and her sister called her constantly, giving her updates on their search for Myrna. She did her best to act like she was as worried as they were, and she soon found herself giving the performance of a lifetime. The fact that she was barely eating and barely sleeping helped. They assumed it was because of her concern for her mother. In reality, it was the all-consuming need to finish the book.

And then finally, she did.

The moment she closed it—a beatific smile on her face, excitement rushing across her body—there was a knock at the door. Catherine leapt to her feet, ran down the hallway, and hopped down the two steps, throwing the door open in a burst of mad exuberance.

"Mom!" she cried.

But it wasn't her mother. It was Justin. Amanda's boyfriend. Handsome beyond belief. A smile on his face, too, though Catherine's faded as she stood in the doorway, her happiness morphing into confusion.

"Justin? What… what are you doing here?" she asked.

"Hello, Catherine," he said in a smooth voice, like a strong current running over compliant rocks. "Your mother sent me."

The smile reasserted itself. It was beginning.

She stepped aside and Justin entered. Peering past him, she looked around outside, expecting everyone in the world to know how much she had changed, how momentous an occasion this was, but the world had no idea. It kept going as if this was just another day. For Catherine, however, it was anything but.

She closed the door and followed him inside.

SHE AND Justin spent the next several days in her bed. He whispered into her ear as they lay coiled together, telling her how Myrna had planted him in their family's life. He spoke of dark rituals and blood sacrifices and the coming of a great darkness that would save the world. She hung on every word. It wouldn't be easy. She would have to say and do things that would hurt people, and even kill them, but that was the cost of change. It always had been.

A week later, the phone rang.

It was Amanda. Sobbing. Begging her to come over.

Silently, Catherine cursed her sister. She had picked the worst possible time to reach out so desperately. Catherine was supposed to reunite with her mother, and there was so much preparation needed, but one of the lessons Justin had taught her was that the sheep—people like her father and her sister—must never suspect. That was the cult's true power. They were everywhere and nowhere. They were the parent, the child, the sibling. They were inescapable.

Catherine arrived at their parents' home and Amanda threw her arms around her.

"Thank God you're here," Amanda said. "I didn't know what else to do. I can't reach Justin."

"Shhh," Catherine said. "What's the matter? Where's Dad?"

"He's gone. He left. He went after Mom."

"*What?*" Catherine barked, panicking. Had her father found out the truth? He wasn't the brightest man in the world but he *was* a top-notch researcher. She felt sweat break out all over her body. Were all her carefully laid plans falling apart already?

"He was unraveling more and more, drinking too much, desperate to find her, to save her from that coven. He didn't even know where he was going… just said he had some clues and was going to follow them to the ends of the earth if he had to. He loves her so much, Catherine."

"And he just… left you here?"

"He apologized, said he was torn, but he told me I should move in with you, and I think he's right. I can't stay here by myself. I'm dropping out of college—just for now, just until they get back. That's okay, isn't it?"

Catherine froze. It was far from okay. How could she continue her duties for Demon-Fire with this whiny child in her way? Yet there was no way around it. Saying no would raise too many suspicions. She had no choice.

"Of course it is, Amanda," she said. "Come on, I'll help you pack. And don't worry, everything will be okay."

CHAPTER FOURTEEN

AMANDA'S REAPPEARANCE in Catherine's life was a surprise in more ways than one. Despite everything that was happening, Catherine found herself enjoying her younger sister's presence. The two fell back into familiar routines, and Catherine's life snapped into two entirely compartmentalized halves.

During the day, she would spend time with her sister or at work, at a job she had managed to keep despite the interruption when Justin had appeared. At night, she would descend into the depraved darkness of the cult, finally reconnecting with her mother, learning about Demon-Fire's means and goals, and enjoying every aspect of Justin, both physically and spiritually.

Amanda and Justin continued their relationship as well, and when they would go on their "dates," Catherine was surprised to find that she wasn't jealous. Not like she'd been with Scott. Then again, she'd been a child then. Her eyes hadn't yet been opened.

She didn't love Justin, she knew. He was just part of her immersion into Demon-Fire.

On the other hand, the first human sacrifice she witnessed was difficult. Justin held her and whispered words from the *Lemegeton*, which soothed her and eventually led her to a deeper appreciation of what she was witnessing. The young woman's death was necessary and, if looked at through the right lens, even beautiful.

Each sacrifice after that had gotten easier. Catherine eventually started participating, and enjoying it. The upper echelons of the cult took notice.

One day, her mother took her aside.

"I am proud of you, Catherine."

"Thank you, Mother. I live only to serve Demon-Fire."

Myrna held out an object and Catherine took it gingerly.

"What is this?"

"This is a promotion. You are no longer only Catherine. You are also now Poison-Lark, a name that has been passed down through the generations. A high priestess capable of great and terrible things. This veil covers your face so that you can give yourself freely. When you wear it, your past identity fades away and you represent the full depth and scope of the cult. It is an honor, my love. A *great* honor."

"I am humbled," Catherine said, tears in her eyes.

"As you should be," her mother responded, "but with this honor comes your most difficult task yet."

"Anything, Mother. *Anything*."

Myrna's expression changed and she looked at the floor, as if struggling with her next words. When she raised her eyes again, however, the look there was determined.

"Is your sister still a virgin?"

Catherine hesitated. Amanda? What did she have to do with…?

"*Is she?*" her mother snapped.

"Ye-yes," Catherine confirmed. She knew as much from Justin, and from Amanda herself. The sad, trusting sister.

"As the virgin daughter and sister of two high priestesses, there is great power in her blood. It is time, Catherine. Deep down, you knew this day would come."

She didn't want to admit that it was true… but she felt in her heart that it was.

Catherine nodded.

"While we prepare for the arrival of Arachne, steps must be taken to make certain Amanda is ready for her encounter with the demon. Justin has his orders. You must continue to work with him and make sure that all goes smoothly. And you, as Poison-Lark, will supervise her kidnapping. Do you understand?"

"Yes, Mother."

Myrna helped her daughter affix the veil to her face. It felt so natural, so right. Her mother also began to put her hair up into a different style than she usually wore. She realized at that moment that it had been her chosen style when she was young. She had forgotten about it. It was tighter. More controlled.

"What are you doing?" Catherine asked, her voice barely above a whisper. She could feel something within herself changing. Hardening.

"No one must recognize you while you are Poison-Lark—especially your sister. You will reveal yourself to her when the time is right. When her fear is at its absolute pinnacle. It won't be easy—can we trust you to handle this responsibility?"

Catherine hesitated for only a moment.

"Yes," she said, staring her mother in the eyes.

Myrna put her hand on her daughter's veiled cheek, smiling. "I am so proud of you," she repeated, and then the smile was gone. "Now go. All must be ready for the arrival of Arachne."

THE EARLY stages of the plan went perfectly. Justin had continued to insinuate himself into Amanda's life, and she admitted to her older sister that she was falling in love. Catherine felt bad—slightly—but for her part stayed focused on the task at hand.

Finally, the night of the kidnapping arrived. She had been given a secret space beneath Ravenwood Cemetery in which she would carry out the sacrifice. Arachne had begun to awaken from its long slumber.

Catherine arrived near her apartment, dressed as Poison-Lark, accompanied by two of her new acolytes, including a hulking brute called Diabolik. His breath smelled like death itself but luckily he would be wearing a hood, and there was no question that he would be strong enough to subdue Amanda if she put up a fight.

And then, out of nowhere, *he* arrived.

Morbius.

He was a nightmare come to life. Which meant that, on some level, Catherine found him incredibly attractive. Yet he immediately ruined their carefully wrought plans, saving Amanda and sending them scrambling.

Fortunately, Morbius was as much a fool as Amanda, and the two of them returned to the apartment, where Catherine was able to take further stock of the man… or whatever he was. He was enigmatic, hard to read, but for some reason he chose to take Amanda under his wing. A stab of jealousy struck Catherine—this was a man of extreme power, that much was clear. Why would he take an interest in weak Amanda when someone like Catherine—like *Poison-Lark*—was standing there in front of him?

No matter. Amanda's arrival back at home made it much easier for Catherine to reclaim the advantage. Donning her Poison-Lark persona for the second time, she and her acolytes struck again later that night. This time they were successful in capturing Amanda, despite further attempts by Morbius to interfere.

They took her to the cemetery, where in the shadowy recesses beneath the ground, the dark ceremony began. Amanda was consumed with fear. Some part of Catherine loathed what was happening to her sister, but that voice in her head was distant, a distress signal that would never, ever be answered.

She shut the door on it, with extreme prejudice.

Amanda's terror reminded Catherine of something their mother had said. "You will reveal yourself to her when the time is right." With her eyes locked on her sister's, Poison-Lark removed her veil.

"Now, Amanda… now it begins!" she said to her sister, holding an ancient dagger above her head.

Amanda stared, her eyebrows beetling in confusion. Then she looked at the other cult members who stood around, their faces flush with lust and hatred and excitement.

"What did you do to my sister?" Amanda screamed at them.

The fool, Catherine thought. Amanda assumed she had been brainwashed, that she hadn't made her own conscious choice. She laughed at her sister's naiveté.

"Catherine is now but a memory," she said slowly, decisively. "There is only Poison-Lark." Realization swept across Amanda's face, then resignation. That surprised Poison-Lark, who had assumed her sister would beg pitifully until the end. Nevertheless, she continued.

"Now, as I stand protected within the Double Seal of Solomon," Catherine recited. Her acolytes murmured with excitement as the ceremony began to unfold. "Now, as the mystic black candles of Hellebore emit their intoxicating scent. Now, we offer the purity of your blood to the demon summoned from the arcane text of *Lemegeton*."

It was cruel, she realized, but necessary. For Arachne to consume its necessary sustenance, the virginal victim needed to be in a state of utter hopelessness, overwhelmed with terror. The sheer emotional energy would build to a crescendo.

And the torture was far from over.

At that moment, Morbius attacked. Again. On some level, Catherine continued to be impressed, but the plan had to move forward. As the living vampire fought, outnumbered by his acolyte opponents, Catherine used that moment to unveil yet another betrayal.

"There's one last revelation, Amanda," she said, looking down at her sister, the blade still gripped in her fingers. An acolyte stepped forward and slowly removed his hood. "Look, in your last moments, on the face of 'sweet, silly Justin'." Throwing her younger sister's naïve words back in her face—and it worked. Amanda's face froze in an expression of pure disbelief as she stared up into her true love's face.

"I'm sorry I'm so late," he said with a malicious smile. Amanda might have protested, but the time had come. Arachne's foul-smelling web pulled her up to the ceiling. Soon it would feed. Catherine's plan—*her mother's plan*—was working.

The living vampire, however, had other ideas.

Enraged, he cut a swath through the cultists who surrounded him and leapt into the air, confronting the massive demon. He put himself in harm's way, took the attack that was intended for Amanda. Catherine could only watch from the ground, watch as her future was destroyed in front of her. Watch as Arachne died from its ingestion of Morbius' foully tainted blood.

In its death throes, the demonic arachnid thrashed wildly, bringing the ceiling down on everyone. Catherine witnessed the death of her acolytes, violently crushed beneath falling rocks and pillars, watched as Justin fled.

She ran, too, made her way to a secret passage about which only a select few knew. Ascended to the surface, where she watched from a distance as Amanda and Morbius made their way up out of the catacombs. In that moment she vowed vengeance.

CATHERINE MADE her way back to the coven and told her mother what had happened. Myrna was enraged, had every right to be, but her anger was directed at Morbius. She told Catherine that she would take care of the living vampire. They would follow him. She would do whatever was necessary to kill him and sacrifice her youngest daughter for the good of Demon-Fire.

Justin was killed shortly after the disastrous ceremony. True, Morbius may not have ended him, but he was still responsible. If the living vampire hadn't interfered, he would still be alive. So much would have been different.

Her mother would still be alive, too.

Catherine almost hadn't attended Justin's funeral, but decided at the last minute to go. She wouldn't know anyone there, but it seemed like the right thing to do. She had never loved him, but they had spent many nights together, had been intimate in ways others could never imagine, and he had taught her a lot. It was the least she could do.

One of the best decisions she ever made.

After the ceremony, a man approached her. Tall. Bald. Sporting a thick beard. Incredibly handsome. He looked like an older version of Justin but more distinguished. More powerful.

"Hi," he'd said. "I'm Justin's dad. Thaddeus. I wanted to introduce myself, and thank you for coming. How did you know him?"

She'd lied at first, but he said things during that short conversation in the graveyard that made it clear he was part of Demon-Fire as well. They made plans to meet again. Which they did. Again and *again*. She told him about what had happened. With Amanda. With Morbius. She saw the rage grow in his eyes every time she mentioned the living vampire.

She told him also about *The Lesser Key of Solomon*. Even let him read it. Then she told him about a plan she was formulating, much more ambitious than the rise of Arachne, a plan that would involve her own body, and her soul. He supported her. Encouraged her. Told her she was the true leader of Demon-Fire.

All the other high priests and priestesses were weak, he claimed. Catherine had a hard time believing that. Even if she wanted to. But everything changed when her mother died.

It was Morbius. Again.

Myrna had followed him and Amanda to Maine, had disguised herself, attempted to kill her younger daughter and the vampire, but had failed. Sister Saint lost her own life as a result. The moment Catherine heard the news, that her mother's head had been split open with an ax, she decided to take Thaddeus' advice. She would implement her audacious plan. She would use the *Lemegeton*, transform herself. Invoke the power provided by the Thirteen.

Become the rightful leader of Demon-Fire.

And kill Michael Morbius.

CHAPTER FIFTEEN

"ARE YOU okay, Michael?"

The voice had a strange, distant sound, as if it were traveling through miles and miles of tunnels to reach him. He recognized it, but he wasn't sure where from. Emil? Wait, no… Emil was dead. It couldn't be him. Emil would never talk to anyone ever again.

Fresh tears streamed down Morbius' face and he blinked, the room slowly coming into focus. He was lying on his back, staring at a stone ceiling. The cell. He was a prisoner. Still. And he had just fed. On a helpless, unconscious woman. The memory reemerged like a horrible dream. Some part of him was deeply grateful that she had never woken up.

He still felt like crap.

Rolling over onto his side, Morbius prepared himself to see the woman's corpse, but it was gone. Only a large red stain remained on the ground next to him. They must have come in to retrieve the husk while he was lost in his stupor.

"I'm… fine," Morbius finally choked out, sitting up. Despite the disgust he felt at what he'd done, his wounds had almost completely healed. There was no question that he felt stronger now. A strength that came at a devastating cost.

He made his way over to the slab and sat down, staring at his palms. Would he be forced to live like this for weeks? Years?

"What is this place?" he said quietly, to no one in particular.

"That's a fair question," Jake replied, "and it took me a while to figure it out myself."

"The people in the arena," Morbius said, "the ones who were watching and screaming—who are they?"

"From what I've been able to figure out," Jake said, sitting by the hole in the wall so the two could talk quietly, "this place is run by some organization called the Demon-Fire cult, though I got the feeling from your conversation with Brother Thaddeus that you already knew that part.

"Apparently, they have chapters all over the world," he continued, "and a bunch in New York City. Including this lovely example. I've been listening in as much as I can for as long as I've been here. This facility was originally built by the city as part of an additional subway line, back in the day, but it was abandoned when the money ran out. Cult members within the government made sure that any records were conveniently destroyed, and since it was originally dug out decades ago, no one knows it exists anymore.

"Demon-Fire took it over and built the arena so they could have their games and sacrifices, all at the same time. You know, real family-friendly entertainment. It went on like this for a while, but like any organization, they needed one thing that's sometimes hard to come by."

"What's that?" Morbius asked after a few seconds.

"Sorry. I like to add drama to my stories by inserting random silences. My wife hates that about me. Anyway, they needed money. Operating capital. The New York branch was running out of cash. Hey, the city is expensive for everyone—including cultists, apparently. And then someone had a bright idea. You have this arena. You have all kinds of corrupt scientists working for you. Why not put those two things together, like evil peanut butter and satanic chocolate."

Jake let out a long sigh, then continued.

"They have this one guy working for them, I think his name is Franklin something. Anyway, he's this short round little fellow. Big glasses, wispy hair. He's some kind of genius, and he figured out a way to mutate the blood in normal humans. To turn them into something else, and then voila, instant monsters. Like yours truly."

Morbius thought back to the blood he'd been given by Liz… the blood she got from Fabian. It was all starting to make sense.

"After that, they started having monster fights, and who among us doesn't love to see a good fight, especially when one of the two fighters is guaranteed to die? Well, the one-percenters up in the real world got wind of this pretty quickly, and they wanted *in*. From what I've heard, it started small and then got big, fast. Those rich bastards bet millions on each fight. Pocket change to them, maybe, but they take it real seriously.

"Apparently I was their first guinea pig. Lucky me. So, I've been in a lot of fights in that arena, and it just gets louder and louder. Maybe because I keep winning, or maybe because there's just more and more of them every time. I don't know.

"I just wish I could go home."

"You said you have a wife," Morbius said gently.

Jake laughed, then sighed.

"Yeah, or I did. I've been down here so long, I wonder if she's just moved on at this point. Written me off as dead, or maybe she thinks I ran off on her. That part hurts the most, I think. The idea that she might assume I got sick of her or whatever.

"We talked about having kids. It's something we both wanted, but money was tight, you know? I'm a—I was a teacher. Best job in the world. My wife is a librarian. We're both book nerds, I guess. We had just bought a house before I was, y'know, before I was taken. We had an extra room we were going to make into the nursery. I guess that room is probably still sitting there, empty."

A long moment of silence played out. Somewhere, in the shadowy distance of the stone catacombs, water dripped slowly, rhythmically.

"How about you, Michael?"

"Hmm…?" Morbius responded, pulling himself out of the maze of his own thoughts.

"You got a wife up there?"

A vision of Martine flashed in his mind. He missed her so much.

"No, not a wife… but there is someone. Someone very special to me. Martine. We were in love. It was the greatest time of my life. Everything finally made sense, after a lifetime of nothing making sense, but it was fleeting. I risked everything to hold onto something that wasn't meant to be mine. Risked everything… and lost everything. When she finally saw what I had become, she was sickened—and who can blame her? I'm a monster."

There was another moment of silence, and then Jake chuckled. Morbius felt white-hot rage building in his stomach.

"You laugh?"

"Oh shoot, sorry, Michael. I'm not laughing at you. I promise. It's just, you and I are so alike in some ways. I-I've always felt like a bit of a monster myself. I've always had anger issues, you know? Ever since I was a little kid. I wouldn't get my way and I would just lose it. My parents didn't know what to do with me. They had me talk to shrinks and guidance counselors, and that helped, but that rage was still there. Deep."

Morbius thought back to his childhood, to the bullies, and he understood.

"So when these Demon-Fire guys kidnapped me and handed me over to that Franklin guy," Jake continued, "on some level I think I felt like I deserved it. And when he injected me, told me he was unleashing something that already existed in my DNA, I kind of knew exactly what he was talking about. He may have turned me into a monster, technically speaking, but the monster was already there."

"I'm sorry, Jake."

"Yeah, me too. For both of us. What's that saying? We're cursed to live in interesting times."

"Cursed," Morbius echoed. "That's how they got me."

"What do you mean?" Jake asked.

"The mutated blood. That the scientist you mention created. It gave me incredible strength, but it's also instantly addictive. They used it as bait. Lured me into a trap. I was so stupid."

Another long moment of silence stretched out. Finally, Jake broke it.

"So... where is Martine these days? I can't help but wonder if she might be more forgiving than you think. Love can forgive a whole hell of a lot."

"She's been taken... by someone named Daemond. A powerful, evil man. I'm helping a friend search for her parents, and she's helping me search for Martine."

Amanda. In the insanity of his time in this miserable cell, he had momentarily forgotten about her. He wondered again if Demon-Fire had kidnapped her, too. Again.

"Helping a friend? That doesn't sound like something a monster does, Michael."

"You are very kind, Jake, but I have done things since my transformation that haunt my nightmares. Hurt people. Battled good men and women. Taken the lives of the innocent. On second thought, perhaps it's for the best if I just rot away down here in the darkness, like the vermin I really am."

"Did you ever have any teachers you really liked, Michael?" Jake asked. "When you were a kid?"

The question surprised Morbius. He had been thinking about his favorite teacher just the other night. His mind returned to the time when he was eight. It had been a hard year for many reasons, but his teacher had made all the difference.

Mrs. Morgenthaler.

She had recognized something special in young Michael, had encouraged his love of math and science, had told him that the bullies would be weak when they were old, and that age would give Michael strength. Unfortunately, their special friendship had died the day Michael accidentally coughed blood all over her.

Still, she had been right about the bullies, though perhaps not in the way she had thought.

"Yes," Morbius murmured, thinking of his teacher's kind face. Of her cold hands. "Cold hands, warm heart," she had said. Her mantra.

"Well, I teach fourth graders, Michael. After a few years of doing that, you start to have a sense right away about which kids are inherently good and which have a bit too much darkness in their souls. I'm not saying any child is beyond being helped, but there are certain aspects of everyone's personality that I think are fundamental to who they are. I'm pretty damn good at reading people. Not sure if it's a gift or something I've developed from years of teaching, or both.

"And let me tell you something, Michael…"

Another moment of silence stretched out. Michael's curiosity was piqued, though he never would have admitted it. He sat still, waiting. Then, finally, Jake finished his thought.

"You may have done some horrible things, and I question how much of those things are truly your fault, but I can tell you one thing. Based on what I've seen of you and what you told me, you are not a monster."

Morbius smiled, his lips curling past his sharp fangs. Even though he didn't genuinely believe his new friend, he appreciated the words.

"Thank you, Jake."

There was a soft noise coming from the cell next door, and Morbius listened carefully. At first, he couldn't make out what the sound was. And then, slowly, it came to him.

Jake was crying.

Morbius' smile faded. He imagined Jake's wife, up on the surface, crying as well. Missing her husband, living in an empty house with an empty extra room that was supposed to become a nursery.

"And neither am I," Jake whispered.

CHAPTER SIXTEEN

M

AMANDA AWOKE screaming.

She sat up and looked around, blinking her eyes furiously. She was in a small room with concrete walls and a single door, and nothing else. She was lying on a metal table, similar to the ones used in morgues. The door had a window but it was frosted, though dull light pushed against the glass.

There wasn't a single sound to be heard.

Amanda sat up, and her brain swam. She closed her eyes and placed her face in her palms, the darkness soothing but discomfiting at the same time. She tried to work her way through where she was, how she had gotten here. The memories came rushing back.

The bookstore.

The apartment. Liz.

Catherine.

Amanda pulled her face out of her hands and

looked around the room again, her breath coming in fast, uneven gasps. Her sister was alive, and she had kidnapped Amanda. Again.

This time, Morbius was nowhere to be found, but Amanda was no longer the person she had been the last time Catherine and her goons had taken her. Amanda was stronger. More determined.

Pulling herself to her feet, she was shaky at first, but got her bearings and scanned the room. She needed to get a sense of her surroundings and then figure out how to escape.

She was surrounded by concrete, and there appeared to be no way out, no secrets to be found in the walls or the floor, other than the single door. She put her ear to it and still heard nothing. Slowly, nervously, she placed her hand on the doorknob and turned, expecting it to be locked.

It turned.

Clicked, and the door moved at the slightest pull.

Amanda only opened it a crack and peered out with a single eye. She was met with a long hallway that stretched out and into shadows. She couldn't see any other doorways, just a hanging light fixture outside of her cell, shadowy walls, and a low ceiling. There were more bulbs farther down the hall but they threw off very little light.

Amanda looked back into the room, and then at the hallway again. Neither option was particularly appealing. She could wait here until someone showed up and then try to fight her way out, or she could strike out into the hallway and hope for the best.

Old Amanda would have stayed put.

Stepping into the hallway, she shut the door quietly behind her.

Her shoes made no sound on the hard floor as she walked. The hallway stretched on and on, naked bulbs hanging from the ceiling every few yards or so, creating small pools of light. After walking for a number of minutes, Amanda looked back. She could no longer see the room from which she had emerged. It was as if it had been swallowed by the darkness.

Her steps and the minutes dragged on. She lost all sense of time and fought back tears of frustration and exhaustion. Finally, just as she was about to give up and turn back, she saw something in the distance.

A door.

Amanda bit back her fear. It looked like the door through which she had just walked. *Exactly* like it. Amanda peered around. She hadn't seen or heard anything, or anyone. Perhaps she had imagined the entire incident at Liz's apartment? Maybe it had just been a bad dream.

Maybe *this* was just a bad dream.

She reached the door and entered.

The room looked exactly like the one she had just left. Nothing within except a metal table. Amanda was confused. Had she somehow gone in a circle, returned to the place where she had awoken? No, that was impossible. She had walked in a straight line. She was certain of it. How could a straight hallway turn her in the opposite direction?

As she reentered the hallway, thinking it would make sense to go back the other way—perhaps she had missed an exit or a staircase—the lightbulb over her head began to flicker. Then it blinked out entirely. Amanda was consumed by blackness.

The darkness was so complete that she even lost her sense of up and down, and had to reach out to the wall to keep her balance. Fighting back the terror that was rising in her throat, she decided her best course of action was to go back into the new room—or the old room, or whatever it was—until the lights came back on. *If* the lights came back on.

Yet after taking a few steps in what she thought was the right direction, she realized that she may have been turned around, and took a few more steps in the opposite direction, keeping her hand on the wall. Despite walking multiple steps in both directions, she couldn't seem to find the room again.

She stopped moving.

There had been a sound.

Whispering.

Or was it? She wondered if it was just her imagination as the whispering suddenly stopped.

She could feel something on the back of her neck. Breathing. Someone was standing right behind her. She turned around slowly, terrified, ready to fight. Just as she clenched her fist to throw a punch, she felt something on the back of her neck again, a similar sensation. Warm breaths. Someone was standing in front of her, and someone was behind her, too.

A light abruptly clicked on somewhere in the hallway and Amanda screamed. She was surrounded by people in red robes. They encircled her, smiling, staring at her as if they had been able to see her through the darkness this entire time.

Amanda's scream turned from one of fear to anger, and she pushed against them, but there were too many. They began to laugh as they pushed her back and forth between them, their mirth louder and louder as she was battered about. It bounced against the low ceiling and grew in volume. Still she fought, but there were too many opponents in an extremely cramped space. Their shoving grew more violent as the sounds increased.

Then the lights flickered on and off, a strobe effect that turned their shadowy faces into demonic snapshots as the pushing became blows to her head. Finally, the lights went out altogether, or perhaps Amanda was slowly slipping into unconsciousness.

She wasn't sure which.

As her face hit the floor, painfully, her only thought was how cool the concrete was against her cheek.

It's so refreshing, she thought, and she actually laughed. Her laughter mingled with the laughter of her tormentors, and then there was nothing except silence and darkness.

"AMANDA? AMANDA, honey, wake up."

It was her sister's voice. For a moment, she

imagined she was back in their childhood home, and that Catherine was waking her gently to get ready for school. Amanda always had such trouble in the morning, while her older sister had jumped out of bed every day with an envious determination. While Amanda struggled to get dressed and force some cereal down her throat, Catherine would already be decked out for the day, sipping at a coffee and helping her younger sister gather her books and untangle her hair.

The moment passed quickly. That beautiful, painful memory was decades old.

Amanda's eyes fluttered open again. She surfaced fully from the nightmare of the people in the hallway, and then came to realize that it was no nightmare at all. She could feel the bruises purpling on her face.

Sitting up again, she half expected to be back on the metal table, but she was on a couch now in a small room full of religious symbols and paintings on its walls. Catherine sat on a chair nearby, smiling at her sister.

"Welcome back," she said. "I'm sorry about earlier. I was told that you would be unconscious for much longer. I would never have left you down there in our tunnels beneath the church, if I thought you would wake up so soon.

"My acolytes got word that someone was moving around down there," she continued, "and decided to pay you a visit. They're not used to seeing outsiders, and got a little overzealous. I apologize for their dramatics. They have been properly chastised.

"However, the next time you wake up in a strange room, I recommend staying put until someone in authority comes to get you. Then again, you were never the best at following directions, were you?"

Catherine stood and walked across the room, stopping in front of a painting that depicted dozens of small human figures falling into a fiery cavern. The painting was done in shades of red, orange, and yellow, and was highly disconcerting. Amanda found herself unable to pull her eyes away from it.

"Where's Liz?" she said finally.

"Your best friend betrays you, and your first words are about her? Your loyalty is impressive."

Amanda pulled her eyes away from the painting and stared. That damn smile. Amanda wanted to lunge and smack it off, but after everything that had happened, she decided discretion would be the better part of valor. Something her father always said.

Her time would come.

"What happened to you, Catherine?" she said. "How could you?"

The smile faltered, then reasserted itself. Catherine walked back across the room and sat beside her on the couch, as if they were two normal sisters who were catching up after some unexpected time away from each other.

"I know it's confusing, Amanda," she said. "I remember how difficult it was to comprehend when Mom first approached me about Demon-Fire."

Amanda's mouth went dry.

"M-Mom? Is she here?"

"Are you hungry?" Catherine asked, ignoring the question. "You must be hungry."

Amanda was about to respond "No" when she quickly took stock of herself. She was hungry. Starving, actually.

"A little," she admitted, hating herself for doing so.

"Of course," Catherine said simply. She stood up, walked to the door, opened it, and muttered a few words to someone who was standing on the other side. After a moment's hesitation, Catherine closed the door again and turned.

Silence filled the room for a few long moments. She seemed to be in no rush.

"I thought you were dead," Amanda said finally.

A darkness fluttered across Catherine's face, and then vanished. She smiled, but there was menace there. Not the smile from a few seconds earlier, the smile of a loving sister. This was a predator's grin.

"I almost was," she said coldly. "No thanks to your friend, Mr. Morbius."

Amanda felt goosebumps run up and down her arms at the mention of Michael's name.

Where is he?

"When he interrupted the ritual, when he murdered Arachne—"

"He didn't murder that disgusting spider, Catherine!" Amanda shouted, the blood rising to her face. "Michael saved me, and Arachne killed itself by attempting to feed on him."

"Perhaps," Catherine said coolly. "Regardless, in its death throes Arachne brought the temple down upon us, and many of my acolytes were crushed beneath the falling rock. But somehow I was spared, and ever since I clawed my way out of that unintentional grave—ironic, considering we were beneath a graveyard—I've slowly become grateful."

"Grateful?" Amanda echoed.

"Yes," Catherine confirmed, walking back over to the couch and sitting down again. "While I believed wholeheartedly at the time that shedding your virginal blood would serve our mission to Satan, I've realized in the time that has passed since that I may have… *underestimated* you.

"Seeing you now," she continued, "that realization is confirmed. You are stronger, Amanda. I can feel it. Your death would have brought about great things for Demon-Fire, but I think your life can accomplish even more."

"My life?" Confusion swept over her. "What are you talking about?"

At that moment, the door opened and a man in a red robe entered, carrying a tray full of food—cheese, bread, and fruit. He placed it on the desk and then exited without saying a word. Catherine stood and plucked an apple from the tray, then returned again to the couch.

She held out the piece of fruit. It was bright red, gleaming in the light that cascaded down from the ceiling. There were no filthy bulbs here.

"I want you to join me, Amanda," she said. "Your rightful place is by my side. Together, we can *rule* Demon-Fire. Everything you've ever desired can be yours."

Amanda took the apple. Considered Catherine's words. She had always looked up to her sister, had always wanted to be more like her.

"Where's Mom?"

Catherine looked down for a long moment, and then back up. Her eyes were filled with tears. The sight caught Amanda off guard, yet how could she possibly feel sympathy for someone who had tried to murder her? But still… she felt it.

"She's dead," Catherine whispered.

"*What?*"

"Murdered. Violently. Horrifically. An ax to the head."

Tears sprang to Amanda's eyes as well. She hadn't witnessed the act, but the image was easy to conjure, and seared into her mind. Her mother's surprised face as a blade entered her skull. The blood arcing out into the air. Her small body collapsing to the ground.

"By… whom?" she asked, gripping the apple even more tightly. On some level, she already knew the answer.

"Morbius," Catherine hissed.

Amanda stared deep into her sister's eyes. She had always thought she could tell when her sister was telling the truth, but given the events of the previous weeks— Justin and Poison-Lark and the Demon-Fire cult—she didn't know *what* to believe.

"You're lying," she whispered.

Catherine didn't blink.

"I know I have lied to you about many things," she said, "and for that, and so much else, I apologize. I was wrong about you, Amanda. You are my sister, and you are a Saint, and you are strong. Like I am. Like Mother was, and I am not lying to you. Morbius killed her. I assumed he had told you, and I'm sorry he didn't. That you had to find out this way. I wish it wasn't true."

Despite herself, a part of Amanda believed her. Morbius was, after all, a killer by nature. Could she have been wrong about him all this time? She knew there was some goodness within him, but was that enough?

Why hadn't he told me?

A single tear ran down her face, but she wiped it away. She was sick of crying. She was done with it.

Amanda Saint bit into the apple.

It was delicious.

CHAPTER SEVENTEEN

"DID YOU ever fight Spider-Man?"

Morbius blinked and refocused. He had been lost in a daydream about Martine. Or was it a memory? He wasn't sure, but it had been beautiful. He wished he could live within that fantasy forever, but his mind returned to the cold, dank cell. He was getting hungry again, yet feared that another feeding might be imminent.

"What's that…?" he asked.

"I know, I know… it's a weird question, but I feel like I read in the *Daily Bugle* one time about the web-slinger fighting a vampire. Was that you?"

Morbius thought back to his many battles. He regretted some, if not all.

"Yes," he said finally.

"Wow," said Jake. "What was… what was that like?"

"I don't like to talk about it," Morbius responded, "but I will tell you that he is annoyingly fast. And those jokes? The worst."

He smiled then. Despite his protestations, it felt good to talk about this. He had never opened up quite this way to someone—not since the experiment. Since his life had been destroyed. By his own hand.

"Really?" Jake said. "I saw him once on the Upper East Side, after he'd beaten up Doc Ock and a bunch of his goons. His jokes were actually pretty funny."

"Well, some of them are humorous, I suppose," Morbius admitted. "The man is still annoying, though."

Jake laughed. It was a good sound. Michael had always been able to make Emil laugh, too. He missed him a lot. Was haunted by what he had done. Murdered his best friend in the world.

At that moment, there was a noise at the door to his cell. He looked up and his face filled with rage. It was Thaddeus. A smile on his face. The jagged claw marks on his cheek had healed somewhat but were still red, a painful reminder of the hatred they shared.

"Good evening, Michael," he said, disdain dripping from each word.

"Is it evening?" Morbius replied, not looking away. A primal part of him was excited; was it really feeding time again? Yet he had no desire to murder anyone else for his own survival. The human part of him wished he could just kill himself and save everyone the agony of his existence. He shook these thoughts away. This was no time for pity or weakness.

"It is indeed," Thaddeus replied, "and today is your day."

"I have no interest in feeding again," Morbius growled. "So you can get your sick pleasure elsewhere."

"I plan on getting immeasurable pleasure today, Michael," the cultist replied. "It's your turn again. In the arena. You've caused quite a stir among our customers."

Michael looked down. Somehow, he hadn't considered that another battle might be imminent. Perhaps because he had no interest in fighting another tragic prisoner for the enjoyment of hundreds of unseen humans—if they could be called that. Still, on some level he was excited. He was sick of sitting around, rotting away in this cell.

When he looked back up, Thaddeus was flanked by half a dozen cult members, their faces hidden within the shadows of their hoods. Each held one of the electrical prods.

"I won't do it," Morbius said. Boredom was better than senseless battle. Nothing could make him *want* to kill.

Thaddeus' eyes widened, yet there was excitement there, as if he'd been hoping for such a response. He withdrew a small device from his robes and pushed a button. The metal collar around Michael's neck clicked again, and electricity shot through his entire body. He screamed and fell off the stone slab, writhing on the floor for several minutes as Thaddeus kept his finger pressed against the switch. Finally, he relented.

"That was the lowest setting," the cultist said. "Do you feel like trying the next one?"

Morbius caught his breath and rose slowly to his feet. Thaddeus watched him, silent. Waiting. The vampire stared into his tormentor's eyes. He had no choice. It was fight or be killed, and while there was breath in his body, there was a chance he could escape. Exact his revenge.

Find Amanda.

He approached the cell door. Despite the living vampire's proximity, Thaddeus held his ground. Morbius wanted desperately to give the man a matching set of claw marks on his other cheek.

"Get on it with it," he growled.

"Michael…" A voice came from behind him.

It was Jake. Morbius could tell that his friend was sitting near the hole that connected their two cells. Could feel the man's eyes on his back.

"Good luck," Jake continued. "I'll see you back here after you win. We can swap more Spidey stories."

"How sweet," Thaddeus said, staring daggers. "Now let's go, Michael. It's time for you to dance like the puppet you are."

THE HOLDING area was freezing.

Morbius didn't experience cold the way he used to, before the experiment. Something about his mutated blood made almost any temperature bearable, but he shivered, nonetheless. He had been in any number of battles since becoming a living vampire, had seen creatures and worlds he'd never imagined possible, but something felt off about this impending combat.

Perhaps it was the silence. Where was the roar of the crowd? Had he been moved into a different facility? He had been blindfolded as soon as he stepped out of his cell, and they had walked for a long time.

Morbius didn't want to fight.

But he would, and he would win, no matter what it took. There was simply too much at stake. He would do whatever was necessary to find Amanda, and then Martine.

Finally, the door opened, bright light streaming in. He couldn't see past the glare, so he took a deep breath and entered into its brilliance.

Into the arena.

After the stone floor of his cell and the long hallway, the sand felt soft beneath his feet. He walked to the center, reaching it and turning in a circle. There it was... the murmur of the crowd. He was shocked that so many people had been able to stay so quiet.

"I'm going to kill every single one of you!" he bellowed.

The murmurs grew silent, and then laughter burst forth, loud and raucous. Morbius ground his back teeth together. He had never wanted to inflict violence as badly as he did right now. He was about to shout at the faceless masses again—pointlessly, he realized—when the large door at the other end of the arena began to open.

Morbius took a couple of steps back. Took a deep breath. He was ready for this. More than ready, even if he had no wish to hurt an innocent creature for the pleasure of the wealthy bastards who sat in the shadows, wagering on the outcome.

An immense creature came bursting out, at least fifteen feet tall, covered in long, thick fur, sprinting forward on two muscular hind legs, large claws glinting in the light, fangs bared beneath a long snout. Morbius inadvertently took in a breath. This was one of the most savage-looking beasts he had ever seen.

He braced himself. The crowd screamed in anticipation.

The monster crashed into Morbius with the impact of a freight train. He felt the breath rush from his lungs as he fell backward, attempting to free himself from the creature's sinewy arms. Its teeth snapped at his face, but he managed to push the large hairy body off him and roll away.

The two monsters regained their feet and circled each other, breathing heavily.

Morbius leapt into the air, hoping to surprise his adversary, but the creature was incredibly fast, grabbing him by the ankle and slamming him down onto the ground. Pain filling every inch of his body, Morbius summoned enough energy to kick the creature in the face with his free foot. The impact snapped the creature's head back, blood shooting from its nostrils. Morbius jumped to his feet and grabbed the creature's head, deciding that a broken neck would end this fight quickly.

The creature's black eyes stared, and it seemed to hesitate for a moment. Michael attempted to break the creature's neck but it was too strong. In response, it plunged its claws into Morbius' stomach. Then it withdrew its hand and stabbed him again in the exact same spot.

Morbius screamed. The crowd roared.

He was losing a lot of blood. Fast.

Bringing both his hands back, palms open, he slammed them into the creature's ears. The most vulnerable spot Morbius could see. The creature reacted accordingly, rearing back and holding its head, bellowing in apparent agony.

Pressing his advantage, Morbius landed a series of devastating punches to the creature's gut. When it doubled over, he aimed for its face. Faced with such an unrelenting assault, the monster collapsed to the ground, a huge cloud of dust billowing up.

Morbius fell upon his opponent, hammering its face with more blows. The roar of the crowd grew to a frantic pitch. They were getting the kind of show they clearly desired. But Morbius could barely hear them.

He was lost in a blood frenzy.

"Mi-Michael…"

Morbius stopped punching. Where had that voice come from? Had he imagined it? Then he realized. It was the monster beneath him. Or what had been the monster.

The creature was bleeding profusely from its nose and mouth and ears. Dying, and in the process it was transforming. Back into its original human form.

It was Jake.

"*No*," Morbius said, his eyes widening.

"It's okay," Jake rasped. "It's okay…"

The crowd's screams grew more feverish. A chant began, quiet at first and then louder and louder.

"Finish him!"

"Finish him!"

"Finish him!"

Morbius could see cult members emerging from the two doors, electrical prods in hand. There wasn't much time.

"Michael… what you told me… the blood that they used as bait… to get you here. It's in me, too."

"What…?"

"Drink, Michael. *Feed*."

Morbius looked at Jake's neck. The vein there pulsed, beckoning to him, but he couldn't. He couldn't kill a friend… not again. Not like Emil.

"*Do it!*" Jake yelled.

Morbius bit into his friend's neck, the sweet salty blood bursting into his mouth. It wasn't exactly like the blood Fabian had procured, but everyone's blood was slightly different. It was similar enough, though. As the first gulp entered his system, he felt his mind expand, felt his muscles loosen, and then tighten. All sound fell away.

The collar around his neck suddenly buzzed and electricity coursed through his body, but it was distant, like a bee sting rather than the excruciating experience it had been before.

Morbius continued to drink.

The blood tasted incredible, filling his mouth and his stomach and his entire existence. He could feel the sand against his knee, and then it was inside his knee and his leg, crawling up along the inside of his skin. Soon Morbius was composed entirely of sand... blood-soaked sand... his body expanding with its rough moistness, and he nearly laughed. Nearly choked on the blood that rushed down his throat.

The insect on his neck kept buzzing, kept stinging him, so he reached up and wrapped his hand around it. It was bigger than he expected, thick and metallic, but Morbius didn't care. He pulled with all his strength, and the pulling hurt, but he didn't care about that either. Finally, the thing snapped and he was free of it.

Dropping it onto the ground, he sat up, his mind clearing slightly as he did so. He blinked and stared down at a dying man. No, not just a man.

His friend.

"Jake!"

"Welcome back, Michael," Jake replied softly, a smile adorning his pale face. Morbius could hear the cult members approaching but he ignored them, let the strange blood course through his system as he listened. His friend was just about to slip away forever.

"Can you... can you do me a favor?" Jake said.

"Anything," Morbius replied, his mind swimming.

"Find my wife. Jenny Radford on... Edgar Street... Tell her what happened to me. Tell her that I love her so much..."

"Of course," Morbius said, taking Jake's hand in his own.

"And remember..." Jake wheezed through his final breaths.

"What, Jake?" Morbius asked quietly. The sound of the arena was growing again, the angry crowd calling for the death of both monsters now, the cult members only feet away.

"You are... *not* a monster."

Jake went still. Morbius let go of his friend's hand. And then the cult members were upon him.

There were a lot of them and they screamed profanities into Morbius' face as they stuck him with their electrical prods and kicked him and punched him. He took it for a few moments, without moving, staring into Jake's dead eyes.

"Goodbye, my friend," he said, and then he rose.

The first cult member died instantaneously when Michael's fangs ripped the man's throat clear from his neck. Blood burst across the living vampire's face, creating a vivid, haunting tableau against the pale skin beneath, the dark and violent eyes peering out, seeking his next victim.

The cult members saw this and hesitated.

But it was already far too late for them.

Morbius picked up another man and slammed him down over a knee, snapping his spine, then threw the broken, dying cultist into another with such force that bones broke in both of them, sending them collapsing in a heap of flesh and twisted limbs.

Jake's mutated blood continued to pulse through Morbius' body, energizing every part of him. It was far more effective than the blood he'd been given by Liz what seemed like years earlier. Perhaps because it had come directly from the source. Perhaps because Jake's blood was fresh and pure.

As he sank his claws into the face of another cult member, he noticed that many more red-robed men and women were pouring in through both doors of the arena. In his current state, he felt like he could probably take on them all, but then he remembered the real reason he was fighting.

Amanda.

He needed to escape.

As the cult members converged on his location, Morbius leapt high into the air and cried out in euphoria. He had never felt this powerful. His mind was a whirl, but he retained far more control than on the night he'd first consumed the mutated blood. There were no more hallucinations as the raw power coursed through his body.

He cleared the razor wire and landed in the audience section of the arena. Though he was still bleeding from the wounds in his stomach, they were healing quickly. Peering this way and that, he found men and women in expensive suits and dresses who were scrambling to get up from their seats and out the arena. Glasses of wine and plates of food scattered across the floor.

Michael's bloody smile widened. He moved purposefully forward, slashing and biting them as he went. The screams of the rich caressed him as he strode up the stone stairs, their bodies falling to the ground as he passed. He had warned them, had told them exactly what he was going to do.

"I'm going to kill every single one of you."

He licked the gore off his fingers as he reached the top of the stairs. It tasted like bloat and excess, at first a pleasant taste, but there was rot beneath the initial sweetness, and Morbius spat onto the floor. All the money in the world wasn't going to save them from the vengeful wrath of the creature on whom they had been betting only moments earlier.

Finally, he walked out of the arena and into the shadows of the labyrinthine underground catacombs, taking to the darkness as if he was born to it.

CHAPTER EIGHTEEN

"WHERE *IS* Morbius?" Amanda asked, almost finished with the food on the plate.

She and Catherine had barely spoken while she ate. It tasted so good, and she felt guilty for having enjoyed it so much. It had been prepared by murderers, people who had tried to feed her to a demon. She couldn't afford to let herself get too comfortable here. Still, she was torn.

Morbius had killed her mother. Allegedly.

"He fled the city," Catherine answered. "According to eyewitnesses, he went into a rage and murdered a civilian. The police arrived and chased him, but he flew off into the night. My people tried to follow him but he's… gone."

Amanda stared at her sister as she spoke. She lied with such ease, Amanda didn't know what to believe. But Morbius *was* fickle… the way he spoke to her at times. And really, how well did she know him?

She let out a long sigh.

"What about Liz?"

"She's safe and sound." Catherine smiled. "We're taking care of her father as well. He'll get the care he needs."

Amanda grunted. More mixed feelings. Liz had betrayed her, but what choice had they given her? The look of fear on her face told the story. Demon-Fire had threatened her father. Wouldn't Amanda react the same way, in her place?

When this ended—if it ever ended—she and Liz would have a long talk. With luck, their friendship wasn't permanently fractured.

"So... what's next?" she asked, curious to hear the answer. Terrified, too. "You going to feed me to a giant cricket?"

Catherine laughed. Amanda didn't.

"Of course not," Catherine said, standing and moving toward the door. "You always had such a good sense of humor. I don't think I told you that often enough."

"Thanks," Amanda said flatly.

"You stay put for a little while," Catherine said over her shoulder. "I need to talk to a few people, see how preparations are coming along. Then I'd like to make you a formal proposition. It will be up to you whether or not you'd like to accept what I have to offer. And I promise you, if you come around, I'll never hurt you again. Like I said, I made a mistake, and I'm sorry." She stopped and turned. "We're family, and with Mom gone, that's more important than ever."

"Speaking of which," Amanda said, "where... where's Dad?"

Catherine raised an eyebrow.

"Honestly? I don't know. My acolytes have spotted him from time to time, but he's remarkably good at hiding from us. He's been on our trail for quite some time. I actually hope he finds us now… perhaps we can have a family reunion, and I can convince both of you to join me. I mean it when I say that I'm trying to save the world."

"Mm-hm," Amanda intoned, locking eyes with her sister. She really believed what she was saying.

Catherine smiled and turned around to leave. "You'll see."

"Wait," Amanda said. "What did you mean when you said, 'preparations are coming along'?"

Catherine placed her hand on the doorknob. She stood completely still for a long moment, and then turned again. Her face was dark, her eyes half-open with a demented kind of clarity.

Aha, Amanda thought, *so* there's *Poison-Lark*. Goosebumps of fear ran up and down her spine.

"Tonight is the night that has long been prophesied," Catherine replied. "The moment everything changes. Like I said, I was wrong about trying to sacrifice you to Arachne. I had been thinking much, much too small. I won't make that mistake again." With that, she turned and left the room, closing the door behind her.

Amanda heard a lock being turned.

She was trapped. Again.

MORBIUS CREPT through a darkened hallway, his senses expanding and retracting with every breath he took.

He hadn't encountered anyone for a couple of minutes, but distant screams of pain and fear echoed all around him. He had made his way through a crowd of wealthy spectators who were bottled up at an exit. Some begged for their lives, while others seemed resigned to their fates, as if they knew they deserved it.

Either way, Morbius showed no pity.

These were people who preyed on society, who watched as innocents turned into monsters against their will battled each other to the death. People who laughed and cheered, ate and drank while it occurred. Enabled the violence through their enthusiasm and their patronage. Usually Morbius took no pleasure in the taking of lives, actively hated himself for it most of the time.

Today, not so much.

He reached a part of the hallway that branched out in two different directions. He looked down both branches, opened his senses to the sounds and smells coming from each, but he couldn't tell which was more likely to lead to an exit.

He cursed. He needed to escape this prison… this coffin.

From the offshoot to his right, he heard the sound of angry voices. Cultists. A *lot* of them, coming closer by the minute. His fingers tightened into fists, then he released them.

No. With the strength he'd gained from Jake's blood, he felt as if he could overcome any opponents, but he had to stay focused. Morbius turned left and flowed deeper into the shadows.

This hallway went on for a long time. The pain-filled screams and the sounds of his enraged pursuers grew fainter. He thought for a moment that he could hear the distant rumble of a subway train, but he couldn't be sure. He thirsted for the night sky. Felt as if he could barely breathe down here anymore.

Approaching the end of the hallway, he saw a large metal door. Stopping, he cautiously placed his hand on it, but felt nothing other than its cold surface. Part of his mind told him that this could be a trap, but there was no way Demon-Fire knew exactly where he was. Morbius hesitated for another moment until he heard the shouts of the cultists, far behind him.

He had a simple choice.

Enter this door and face whatever lay behind it, or turn around and battle an unknown number of foes, not knowing what kinds of weapons they had. He realized then that the effect of Jake's blood was wearing off, just slightly. He had no idea if he would return to his normal strength once it was gone, or if his wounds would manifest again, leaving him vulnerable. Although it was healing, his stomach was still bleeding.

The sounds of the shouting increased.

Morbius made his decision.

The door was locked, so he threw his shoulder against it with all his strength. The lock shattered, and heavy door swung slowly open. His eyes widened when he saw where he was.

"Interesting…"

CHAPTER NINETEEN

M

FRANKLIN LATTIMER had been born several months too early.

As a result, he grew into a tiny boy with a disproportionately large head, and suffered constant ignominy as a result. Badly bullied as a child, he retreated into his studies, bolstered when his rich parents sent him away to the best private schools. He realized at some point that they may have just been trying to get rid of him, that they probably didn't like looking at him either, but by that point he didn't care.

He took great solace in being by himself. Threw himself into his studies, in particular biochemistry, where he excelled.

After college, where he graduated at the top of his class, he found it difficult to find a job. He shouldn't have needed one. His parents had *so* much money, but they wanted him to be independent, to make his own way. He told them he understood their reasoning, but secretly he cursed them. Easy for them to say, with their normal-sized bodies and heads.

Their privilege rankled him.

His résumé earned him many interviews with major laboratories, but once he arrived, his potential employers would stare at his misshapen body and verbally stumble through their rote questions. Franklin would answer them thoroughly, showcasing his brilliance and humor, but it didn't matter. The meetings would always end quickly, with the interviewer awkwardly mumbling that they would be in touch soon.

They were never in touch at all. None of them.

Franklin fell into poverty. He begged his parents for help, and they would give him meager handouts, telling him to keep trying, that he needed to be his own man. Like his father had. Eventually, Franklin said things in anger. Bad things. Nasty things.

They stopped returning his calls.

The checks stopped arriving.

Franklin lost his apartment. Began living on the street. Ate out of dumpsters—at least the ones into which he could clamber. He thought about killing himself. Was ready to try, and then he heard about a church that was looking for members. He had always shunned religion, thought it was ridiculous, but this one sounded different. Its name alone intrigued him.

Demon-Fire.

He felt like a monster, so that name felt right. His kind of place.

The first meeting he attended was in an abandoned church in the South Bronx, which also felt right. He sat in the moldy pew with a scattering of other people, water dripping down onto him from the broken roof.

A woman with a veil over the bottom half of her face stood in front of them and spoke quietly. She told them about the inequities of the world, about how the rich and the corrupt had perverted all of society, and how Demon-Fire had a plan to fix it. To fix everything.

This was like no church he had ever encountered. Franklin felt as if he was the only person in the church, like she was talking directly to him. He saw more love and caring in her eyes than he ever had from his parents. As the woman continued to speak, he had to hold back tears.

He was home.

For the few who decided they wanted to hear more, the woman in the veil led them to a shuttle that was idling outside. As Franklin took a step up into the vehicle, he chanced a glance behind. He feared he would never see her again.

She was standing there, close to him, and stared directly into his eyes.

"I suspect that you are bound for great things, Mr. Lattimer," she whispered. "Franklin." She remembered his name, even though they had spoken for maybe thirty seconds within the church. Franklin was more confident than ever that he was making the right choice.

He smiled at her, wishing he knew her name, wishing he knew what to say. But he'd always struggled for the right words, and instead he just nodded, then turned around and climbed with some difficulty into the shuttle, quickly finding a window seat. When he looked back out to the sidewalk, she was gone.

FRANKLIN PLUNGED headfirst into the world of Demon-Fire. He attended classes where they read ancient texts and discussed the failings of the modern world. They fasted. Then they ate huge meals that were nothing if not gluttonous. He made friends and realized that every single one of the trainees nursed deep emotional wounds.

However, he was the only one with such obvious physical limitations. When their training began to encompass feats of dexterity and strength, he simply couldn't keep up. Whenever he found himself alone, he would rage at his inability to compete with the other acolytes. He wanted them to like him so badly, but he could see the pity in their eyes as they advanced, as one by one they were given red robes of their own.

Each of his friends graduated, and were sent off across the country to different sects. Then a new group of trainees would be brought in, and Franklin was still there. He became something like a pet to them, and he had to fight against the hatred that started to fester.

Eventually, Franklin reached the point where he thought foraging on the streets of New York City would be better than being a joke within the cult. He was living in a small room at one of the cult's New York headquarters, with only a bed and a sink. He shared a communal bathroom with the trainees, but had been given his own room after it was clear that bullying wasn't always relegated to a person's childhood years.

Then, one day, there was a knock at his door.

"Come in," he said softly, standing up and adjusting his glasses, straightening his wispy hair. He'd never had a visitor before.

A senior cult member entered, a bald man with a thick beard. Franklin recognized him. He was new, had recently joined the sect, and walked with an air of supreme confidence. Franklin looked down at the floor and mumbled, "Good evening, Brother."

"Good evening, Franklin," the man replied, his voice deep and thick.

A moment of silence ensued and Franklin finally looked up, finding the man's dark eyes locked on him. Franklin forced a smile. He knew what was coming. Luckily, he didn't have much to pack... didn't have anything, really.

"I've heard a lot about you," the man said, and Franklin nearly jumped out of his skin. What did *that* mean? He hadn't done anything which would have generated any kind of talk. Franklin spent most of his days in the cult's mostly unused laboratory, attempting to create potions based on old occult texts, and analyzing strange fluids that were labeled "demon's blood." He'd always assumed that was a euphemism, but the deeper his research took him, the more he wondered.

"Whatever I've done…" Franklin said, his voice strained, "I'm sorry."

The man laughed. In the small room, the sound seemed deafening, and Franklin fought an urge to cover his ears.

"You have no reason to apologize," the man continued. "My name is Thaddeus. I've been keeping track of your work… quietly… and I'm impressed. I've been brought to this sect from San Francisco to help exploit the incredible resources that can only be found in this city. The amount of supernatural activity here is unprecedented, and I want your help, Franklin. So does High Priestess Lark."

The man extended his hand, a cruel yet inviting smile slipping onto his face.

"Will you help us? Will you help us save the world?"

It was the moment Franklin had been waiting for his entire life. When someone powerful sought him out, wanted what he had to offer the world. He felt as if he might cry, but marshaled himself and remained composed. This was no time to show weakness.

Franklin reached out and slipped his malformed hand into the cultist's.

"I would love to," he said as boldly as he could.

"Excellent," Thaddeus responded, squeezing hard enough that pain shot up Franklin's arm. "Come then. There's no time to waste."

THE DAYS blurred.

Under Thaddeus' watchful gaze, Franklin was given sole control of the laboratory. Anything he wanted, Thaddeus made sure he had it. He was given bizarre fluids that had highly unusual properties. When he asked too many questions about the source of such arcane materials, Thaddeus would simply shake his head and his dark eyes would say, *Just do your job.*

Indeed, Franklin knew enough to do his work, and to create formulas based on what the cult told him they desired. At first, he tested them on rats, helpless creatures whose eyes bulged when he stuck them with needles and plunged the strange-colored liquids into their writhing bodies.

Many died.

Dozens, probably hundreds.

But Franklin didn't give up. More and more strange liquids were brought to him, every color of the rainbow and more. He knew now to never ask questions regarding their origins. And then, one night, at God knew what hour, he was successful.

He injected his latest formula into what must have been his tenth rat of the day and then put it back into its cage. Sitting back, he waited for the small animal to die a violent death, like all the vermin before it.

But it didn't die.

Instead, it began breathing heavily, screeching, and ran around in circles within the small cage. Franklin sat forward, his eyes widening. Before his eyes, the rat's back suddenly split open, dark red blood spurting out, but the creature stopped screaming. Instead it bared its teeth, a low growl coming from the back of its throat.

Four boney appendages burst forth out of the jagged hole in its back, then bent and curled down to the floor of the cage. The rat raised itself up on the new limbs, shaky at first, but then seemed to find its balance. Its head turned and it saw Franklin, drool falling from its mouth. The rat leapt at him, causing him to fall out of his chair in terror, but the creature just slammed violently against the metal. Throwing itself against it again and again, a high-pitched shriek accompanying each thrust.

Franklin picked himself up off the floor and stared at the thing that used to be a rat. Its fur was falling off and its skin was blackening. It stared at its captor with absolute hatred in its eyes. Franklin smiled, and laughed.

Then he ran to tell Thaddeus.

Word of Franklin's success spread like wildfire through the cult. They had been attempting this kind of arcane breakthrough for years. He was quickly moved out of his small room and into a luxury penthouse in Katz Tower, given new clothes that perfectly fit his small body, and was assigned as many assistants as he needed.

The laboratory, which had been a run-down, dreary affair, was outfitted with all the best equipment, including refrigerators in which Franklin could store his successful formulas, alongside blood from the hybrid creatures he was creating. High-level cult members would often visit to pay their respects and watch him work.

Once, Thaddeus asked him if there was anyone in the world upon whom which he wished to visit justice, and he handed over his parents' address. From that day forth he never asked any questions about what had followed. He hated them, but he didn't want to know any details.

Then came his first human subject.

They brought him to the underground facility. Franklin didn't know where the cult got him, was reluctant to ask, but the man clearly hadn't volunteered. Several cult members dragged his unconscious form into the lab and placed him on an operating table, securing him there with thick leather straps. They nodded at Franklin and left the room. A moment later, Thaddeus entered.

"It is time," he said.

The cult's illicit scientist had known this day was coming, but still he felt ill-prepared. The experiments on the rats had become almost commonplace, and on occasion he'd graduated to larger creatures. There'd been rumors that they wanted Franklin to try with humans, but he had convinced himself that such talk was just theoretical. Now, however, that theory was lying on a table in front of him, slowly waking up.

Thaddeus said nothing more, just stepped back and waited.

The subject's eyes blinked open, focused, and then landed on Franklin.

"Please… help me," the man choked out through chapped lips. A black eye was forming on his face and

Franklin noticed multiple welts and bruises across his body. He had definitely not come peacefully. As quickly as it arrived, Franklin forced this realization out of his mind.

This was the next logical step. Unlocking the potential of the human body, and perhaps eventually the human mind. Thaddeus had told him over and over again that they were going to rescue humanity from its own excess, and that sacrifices would always be necessary for progress to occur.

"Everything's going to be fine," Franklin said to the man, walking over to him. He placed his hand on the subject's shoulder in an effort to calm him, but the man's entire body jumped at the contact.

"My… my wife, she doesn't know where I am. Can you—?"

"I said everything is going to be fine!" Franklin suddenly shouted, interrupting his patient. He had never yelled like that before, not in his entire life, not even when his parents had belittled him. God knows he wanted to.

Then he heard a chuckle behind him. Thaddeus. The sound should have angered him, but it didn't. It only made him feel more powerful. Franklin pulled away from the subject and walked over to his table of instruments. His hands were shaking as he picked up the syringe. At first, he thought it was nerves. And then he realized it was excitement.

He turned back around and approached his patient. The man's eyes bulged when he saw what Franklin was holding.

"Wait… please," the man begged.

"Shhhhh…" Franklin responded, smiling, and it was a genuine smile. Franklin was, on many levels, envious. He had offered to test the formula on himself, having no affection for his current form, but Thaddeus had categorically refused the request, saying that Franklin was too important. That made him feel powerful, too.

"This will barely hurt at all," he said, trying to sound reassuring. "And then, I think, you will thank me. For unlocking what has always been inside you."

The man thrashed against his restraints but they were pulled tight against his body. Franklin very carefully pressed the syringe to the man's vein and then plunged the needle in. The man screamed, more from fear than pain, Franklin knew. This part wasn't painful. Not yet.

"Franklin…" Thaddeus said, cautioning him with a single word.

"I know, I know," Franklin responded. He had explained this part to Thaddeus and his superiors on more than one occasion. "I'm only giving him enough to jumpstart the process, not fully engage it. This will be enough to see if the formula works, but it won't allow the change to engage in its entirety."

"Might that small amount possibly kill him?"

"Well, of course," Franklin scoffed.

"Wh-what?" the man on the table said, breathing heavily. He seemed about to ask more questions when an unearthly sound erupted from his lungs. Franklin took a step backward, grinning nervously.

Here we go.

The man continued to fight against his restraints, his screams hitting a crescendo and then fading away. Just when it seemed as if he was done, they started up again. Franklin could hear Thaddeus behind him, breathing heavily. It all came down to this. If it failed, Demon-Fire would throw Franklin out. Of that he was certain.

Peering at the subject, he swallowed nervously. The man on the table didn't look so good. Sweat had broken out all over his body, and his skin had turned a dark shade of pink.

"Franklin…" Thaddeus intoned again.

"Give it time!" Franklin barked, a bit more belligerently than he intended. He almost apologized, and then thought better of it. The experiment was either going to work, or it wasn't. They'd gone past the point of apologies.

Suddenly all was silent, and the man's head flopped to the side, eyes closing. His body went entirely still.

"God damn it," Franklin whispered. Behind him, Thaddeus sighed.

With a jerk, the subject suddenly screamed, as fur began to push through reddening skin. Short claws stabbed out through the tips of each of his fingers, causing existing fingernails to crack and be pushed away. Multiple wounds opened up, and odd-colored blood poured to the floor. It came from his mouth, as well, where several of his teeth had elongated and sharpened to points. His screams continued, but they were garbled.

Then the transformation slowed down. The man— or whatever he was now—stopped screaming and thrashing against the restraints. Slowly, he turned his head and locked eyes with Franklin. The half-human, half-creature stared with a startling mix of confusion and rage, an evolutionary halfway point between man and beast living in a single body.

"How much…?" Thaddeus asked, appearing next to Franklin but staring at the thing on the table. Franklin didn't answer. He couldn't seem to look away from the creature's eyes. A large tear rolled down its face and was absorbed by the thick fur that had just recently appeared there.

"How much?!" Thaddeus bellowed.

"Only… a quarter of a dose."

Silence filled the cavernous laboratory for a long moment, then it was finally broken by something Franklin had only heard once before. Thaddeus' laughter, still deep and booming. He placed his hands on Franklin's shoulders and smiled. Franklin wasn't sure if Thaddeus had ever touched him before. It was the kind of gesture he would have loved to have received from his father, but never had.

Franklin reveled in the moment, despite the fact that it was being witnessed by some kind of monster.

"You did it, Franklin. You *did* it. High Priestess Lark is going to be so happy. Do you know what we can *do* with this? The applications? The *financial gain*? This is a game changer, my friend. Yes, she is going to be very, very happy with you."

Franklin's chin trembled slightly and he willed himself not to shed any tears. This was the greatest day of his life, but he had to remain professional. This was the only job he'd ever had, and even though he often questioned himself, sometimes wondered if he was doing the right thing, ultimately he believed what Thaddeus told him. They were going to make the world a better place.

"Thank you," Franklin whispered.

"Prepare a full dose." Thaddeus clapped him painfully on the shoulder and then walked toward the exit. "I'll send some men down to transport him to the arena. Once he's there, you'll give him the rest, and we'll see what that ugly bastard is capable of."

Franklin nodded, even though Thaddeus was already out the door and down the hallway. He could feel the creature's eyes on his back, but didn't have the heart to turn around. A low rumble came from the monster's mouth, but at first he couldn't make it out. The subject seemed to be attempting to say something—which was incredible, considering what it had just experienced.

"What's that?" Franklin said. He was distracted, though, still staring after Thaddeus, reveling in the moment.

"My name… is Jake…" the thing on the table finally uttered, and then it went silent. Unconscious, most likely.

The words punched a hole in Franklin's gut, however, and finally the tears fell. There was a still a man inside that mutated lump of fur. Someone who had a wife, who had clearly been kidnapped and dragged to his fate beneath the earth. Franklin looked down at the floor and watched as a couple of his tears plummeted to the tiles.

He clenched his teeth and reminded himself of the importance of their mission. Thaddeus was counting on him. *Demon-Fire* was counting on him—as was High Priestess Poison-Lark. Their methods might be extreme, but they were trying to save a planet that was spiraling toward destruction. How many innocent people died in Noah's flood? It took moral courage to do the necessary things in order to bring about change. That's what he had been told, and that's what he believed. *Had* to believe.

He placed his shoe on top of the tears and rubbed at them until they disappeared. Then he looked up and wiped his sleeve across his face, drying the wetness there, too. Franklin cleared his throat, walked over to his workstation without glancing at the creature on the operating table, and got to work.

THE WEEKS after that went by more rapidly than he could keep track of. He was given even more resources, and brought more humans to work on. Each subject reacted differently to the formula; each mutation was entirely different. Franklin was fascinated, carefully charting information about each subject pre-test and then post-test, seeing if there was a correlation between what they were like as humans and then as monsters.

So far, it seemed random, but Franklin was having the time of his life trying to figure out any connection. With each subject he distanced himself more from any personal reaction. This was science, pure and simple. He had to remain aloof.

One night, as Franklin sat at his desk, working on a new variation of his latest formula, he heard screams from the arena far above. He cocked his head to the side. The yelling sounded slightly different from the usual, but perhaps it was a particularly good match tonight. Those rich people certainly enjoyed their fights, and a new creature had been added to the mix. The vampire, lured into captivity by the promise of a serum that would sate his endless hunger.

Franklin had helped them "acquire" him, and had been rewarded with samples of his unique blood. While he was curious to see what effects his formula would have on the thing's metabolism, he had no desire to witness the distasteful—and frankly alarming— carnage. He would be given a full report, as well as the vampire's corpse when it was dispatched by one of his genetically superior children.

So he got back to work. He didn't need to be there, could have stayed home in his fancy apartment and watched bad TV or made a phone call and done naughty things. These days, however, he enjoyed his work more than anything else. Besides, he was close to perfecting a new formula, something that would create an all-new strain of behemoths. Larger and more deadly than ever.

So focused was he on the work, he didn't notice the silence that had replaced the sounds of the match. He jumped, however, when there was a loud noise at the door to the laboratory. The locked door.

Someone was trying to enter but they weren't using a key.

CHAPTER TWENTY

MORBIUS FOUND himself staring into a pristine laboratory, everything white and silver. State-of-the-art equipment populated the counters and cabinets, while computer terminals sat on several workstations. Under different circumstances, he might have described it as beautiful.

Stepping inside, he closed the door behind him as best he could. The door would probably never close correctly again, but it would look normal enough not to attract attention. But the cultists would figure it out soon enough. He didn't have a lot of time.

Stepping cautiously, he moved farther into the room, a trail of blood marking his path on the floor behind him, almost artistic against the bright tiles. He scanned for a door, a vent, anything that might offer a way out of this tomb. Then he noticed a small man with wispy hair and glasses, hiding behind a stool.

Morbius bared his fangs, more than ready to feed again if necessary, and walked toward the man. Grabbing him by his throat, he lifted the man off the ground. Michael's claws dug into the flesh of his neck, drawing thin rivulets of blood.

"Wait," the man cried, holding up his hands in supplication, tears filling his eyes. "Don't kill me, I'm not your enemy!"

"Who are you?" Morbius demanded.

"My name is Franklin Lattimer." The man's gaze flicked from side to side, avoiding direct eye contact. "I'm… I don't belong here. I live in Katz Tower. I'm being held here against my will, forced to create monsters for some kind of cult. They kidnapped me and told me they would kill me if I didn't do what they said."

Morbius felt his rage subside slightly. The man was small, weak, and malformed, not the usual member of Demon-Fire. His words had the ring of truth, so the vampire let go. The man fell to his knees, grasping at the bloody cuts on his neck and struggling to catch his breath.

"What is this place?"

"It's… it's my laboratory. *Their* laboratory. I'm a scientist, so they give me the tools needed to create the monsters for their fights. I don't want to do it. Y-you have to believe me. I—"

"How long have you been down here?" Morbius barked, walking around the lab.

"I don't know… years?"

Morbius stopped in front of a glass case, his eyes widening.

"I'm a scientist, as well," he murmured. "Or I was. My name is Michael Morbius."

"Oh, yeah?" Franklin said, walking slowly toward the broken metal door. Morbius glanced over and the man stopped moving.

"Come here."

Franklin swallowed nervously and then approached. Morbius pointed at the glass case.

"What is this?"

The man peered into the case. It was full of clear, soft plastic pouches, each one containing a different-colored liquid.

"Those are blood samples," Franklin said, "from some of my more, ah, extreme experiments. My captors' experiments, I should say."

Morbius opened the case and grasped one of the pouches. It was cool to the touch. Inviting. He looked the man in his eyes. Franklin blinked rapidly, looking away. He was lying. He wasn't here against his will. There was a hint of pride in the man's voice when he discussed his work.

With his free hand, Morbius grabbed Franklin's shirt and pulled the man closer, baring his teeth.

"No… please," Franklin whimpered. At the same time, a commotion sounded outside in the tunnel.

Just as Morbius' teeth touched the man's neck, the metal door burst open and a crowd of cult members came running in. In his surprise, Morbius let go of Franklin and the small man skittered off, disappearing into the growing mass of newcomers.

Thaddeus stepped to the front of the undulating crowd, men and women alike. All of them carried weapons at the ready, and many wore cruel grins.

"End of the line, Michael," Thaddeus growled. "You've done irreparable harm to what I've built here, and now you are going to pay for it with your life. But don't worry, we'll take our time with you. No one is in a hurry, and there is no other way out… except through us."

Morbius couldn't see past the red-robed cult members. He had never faced off against this many people, especially in so confined a space. And he was weakening—the effects from Jake's blood were starting to wear off. If only…

He looked down. He was still holding the vial of strange-looking fluid, and there were several more in the case. He smiled, then looked up and into Thaddeus' eyes.

"It sounds like fun," Morbius replied.

With lightning-like speed, he grabbed a handful of pouches from the case and held them above his head. As if on cue, the cultists bore down upon him. Using his claws, Morbius ripped open the packets of mutated blood and opened his mouth wide. He was tackled from every direction, blades entering multiple points of his body, but the various packets of blood burst open and the liquids cascaded down, drenching him in a crimson shower. Copious amounts fell into his mouth, mixing together into a gory cocktail.

Pounded to the ground, Morbius swallowed. Blood erupted from cuts all over his body while an entirely different mixture slipped down his throat. He closed his eyes. The pain from the assault grew almost unbearable… and then it vanished entirely. His mind tunneled into a single pinprick of light. He heard Martine's voice whispering to him, then Amanda's, then Jake's.

Morbius… they said in unison. *Rise.*

The living vampire burst out of the sea of red-clad cult members, slicing open opponents as he did so. The white room ran red with a veritable river of blood and shredded cloth. Leaping high, he landed on the ground at the far end of lab, placing his back against the wall. As the enraged contingent of cultists surged, Morbius pointed a gore-soaked finger at Thaddeus.

"I'm going to kill you last," he hissed. "So you and Justin can be together in Hell."

Thaddeus bellowed, a sound of absolute rage, and sprinted forward. Morbius moved, too, and backhanded the man, sending him pinwheeling into a group of assailants. They all stumbled backward and one of their arms must have hit a light switch because the room was suddenly plunged into gloom, lit only by the random computer screens scattered throughout the laboratory.

As the blood raced through Morbius' system, the room was imbued with a surreal quality, the encroaching silhouettes taking on the aspects of an old black-and-white movie, tinted by intermittent splashes of red as the living vampire continued to wade through them. It became difficult to tell reality from hallucination.

They slashed at him with knives and shocked him with electrical prods, but he barely felt it, distant nuisances as he responded to their violence with ten times the ferocity. Morbius sank his claws and teeth into tender flesh, and caught glimpses of their eyes. The pure hatred they showed was staggering—these men and women were willing to die for a cause he could hardly comprehend. Did they really think Demon-Fire had their best interests at heart?

Their blind fanaticism sickened him.

Yet he wasn't going to allow these cattle to keep him from Amanda, from Martine. He would raze the entire cult if necessary, crisscross the country wreaking bloody vengeance if they touched a single hair on Amanda's head.

The thought of his friend, of what he had said to her the last time they saw each other, drove him farther into a rage, part of it self-directed, and he lashed out even more passionately, the mutated blood seeming to explode through every inch of his body. The lights began to strobe above him as he used anything he could grasp as a weapon to incapacitate his attackers, hurling equipment and opponents as if they were weightless.

A twisted ballet of chaos and gore.

Finally, the crowd began to thin, leaving the bodies of victims piled on the floor. As he slaughtered the last of the cult members who were still standing, he realized that the lights weren't strobing at all. It was in his mind, the light show corresponding to the rapid-fire beat of his heart.

The last man fell.

Morbius stood still.

He loomed above a bloody tableau of unmoving

bodies. Inhaled a deep breath and held it for a second. The room was entirely silent, a stark contrast to just a second earlier. The silence was like a beast, tensed, waiting. He could feel its hot breath on the back of his neck.

"*You're not quite done*," it whispered.

A quiet scuffling sound reached Morbius' ears. It was near the metal door, growing fainter by the second. Morbius made his way through the piles of bodies and finally reached the source.

Thaddeus.

Barely alive. Crawling toward the exit. Morbius reached out and turned him over. Thaddeus looked up at his enemy, blinked, and then spat in the living vampire's face.

Morbius wiped it away with the back of his hand, smearing even more blood across his cheek. The strobing fell away and his senses focused in on Thaddeus's face, dimly visible in the gloom.

"You've already lost," the man gasped, blood leaking from his mouth.

Morbius looked around the room, and then back at his prey.

"Really?"

"We have Amanda. She's one of us now. Even if you manage to get out of here, you're too late. You're nothing. Alone. *Pointless.*"

Thaddeus' words pierced him more than the blades of the acolytes, because on some level, Morbius suspected that the man was telling the truth. He screamed in rage and sank his fangs into Thaddeus' neck.

CHAPTER TWENTY-ONE

M

AMANDA WAS wracked with guilt.

After her sister left the room, she finished every morsel of food that was left. She had wondered if perhaps the food was poisoned, but was ravenous, and quickly reasoned that they could have killed her at any time. No, Catherine seemed to be earnest when she said she wanted Amanda to be part of…

What?

The family business?

The very concept made her shudder. She thought of her father. Was he even alive? Catherine seemed to think so, but Amanda didn't know what to believe anymore. As she sat back on the couch, she also thought about what Catherine had said about Morbius.

She didn't want to believe it, but Morbius was largely an enigma to her, in spite of the time they'd spent together. His huge mood swings were nearly impossible to navigate, and the way he sometimes spoke to her was inexcusable. Yet she sensed goodness in him, beneath the pale skin and jagged teeth and sometimes vicious sneer. She genuinely believed that he wanted to do the right thing. His curse was real, and at this point, Amanda felt like she knew a thing or two about living a cursed life.

As she gulped a glass of water, she stood up and paced the room, putting the empty glass on the small desk. There didn't seem to be any other way out, but she wasn't about to sit around and *hope* her sister was sincere. Wouldn't try to turn her into a blood sacrifice again.

Taking a deep breath, she stepped over to the door and knocked loudly.

Silence.

She knocked again. "Hello?"

A muffled voice responded.

"Yeah?"

"Hi. I need to use the bathroom. Like, ASAP." It was the truth, but she was met with another moment of silence, so she slammed her fist against the door and shouted, "It's about to get messy in here! You think Poison-Lark is going to be happy about that?"

Nothing.

Swearing under her breath, she turned to head back to the couch when she heard the lock click. Her heart raced, but she forced her breathing to remain calm. She was only going to get one chance at this.

The door swung open and she was faced with a very young-looking cult member, the red robe looking slightly too big for his skinny frame. He held a long-bladed knife in his hand, which she regarded dispassionately.

"They don't trust you with a gun?"

"Demon-Fire doesn't believe in guns," he said, sounding vaguely unsure of himself. "We're… better than that."

"Oh really? One of your buddies had a gun the *first* time your little cult kidnapped me."

"I heard about that. He was… *dealt* with rather harshly as a result. Now come on. To your left. I'll be right behind you. I've been ordered to keep you under control, whatever it takes."

Amanda nodded, doing her best to look cowed. She headed down the hallway and could hear him following directly behind her. He was breathing heavily. Nervous.

Good.

They were in a decrepit-looking hallway with small, ancient-looking chandeliers appearing above them every dozen or so feet. More religious paintings adorned the walls, many of them slightly askew. The carpet was old and stained. Wherever they were, it smelled like mildew and neglect.

"Nice place," she muttered.

"Quiet!" the kid commanded. "Up there, that last door on the right."

Amanda's heart began to race again. The time was almost here. It was now or never.

"You coming in with me?" she said as they reached the door.

"Of course not," he scoffed, "but there are no

windows in there, so don't get any ideas. If you're not out in a couple of minutes, I'll come after you, and it won't be pretty."

"Okay," she replied. "I'll be quick."

She took hold of the doorknob and rattled it.

"It's locked," she said, pretending to sound frustrated.

"What? That doesn't make—"

Without looking, Amanda lashed out with her foot, connecting with the kid's midsection. The breath exploded out of his mouth. He doubled over and fell back, but held onto the knife. She continued her motion, turning the rest of the way around, and lunged toward him, raising her knee as she moved and slamming it into his cheek. He flew back, blood shooting out of an instant cut on his face and spraying the wall. It was similar to the move she'd used on the subway... the one that Morbius had made her practice over and over again.

Why mess with something that worked?

Pressing the attack, she threw a punch toward his face but he dodged it and slashed at her, catching her just below her shoulder, slicing into her upper arm. A shock of pain ran through her.

"I'll kill you!" he screamed, stabbing at her again.

She screamed, too, right into his face, and blocked his attack with her injured limb, their forearms smashing painfully against each other. She used her momentum and head-butted his nose, breaking it instantly. The young cult member made a small, surprised sound and then collapsed in an unconscious heap.

Amanda fell back a couple of steps, breathing heavily, and then pressed her hand against the wound. The cut wasn't too deep, thankfully, but it burned like hell.

With her good hand, she grabbed the knife out of the kid's grasp, made her way back in the direction they'd come, and turned down a shadowy hallway, gritting her teeth against the throbbing pain.

If she was going to die in this place—wherever she was—she wasn't going to go quietly.

MORBIUS RAN quietly through the catacombs beneath New York City.

He heard distant screams, full of pain and anger, but he avoided the cult members as best he could. He had no wish to engage in further physical violence. During the battle in the laboratory, the monster blood had worked its way quickly through his system. He still felt its residual power, but it was fading. Perhaps his body was adapting to it, so the effects were less... dramatic. Even so, his addiction to it seemed to be increasing.

He wanted nothing more than to escape this tomb and find Amanda. Reaching yet another door, he pushed through, tensing himself for opposition, but found himself in a stone tunnel. Up ahead in the distance he could see a metal staircase. The one he'd fallen past what seemed like centuries earlier. This was it.

Escape.

He sprinted forward as a hidden door along the hallway burst open, sending multiple red-robed forms spilling out. They saw him and screamed. Morbius ran toward them, then leaped into the air, sailing over the acolytes as they clawed the air, attempting to grab, electrocute, or stab him.

When they failed, they turned to follow him, but it was too late. Morbius was already climbing the exterior of the metal staircase at incredible speed, ascending out of what felt like Hell itself. A grim smile spread across his face as the first hint of vaguely fresh air reached him. He could hear the far-off rumble of a subway train and he thought it was the sweetest sound he'd ever heard. The beautiful normalcy of it was almost overwhelming.

Moments later, he reached the top of the metal stairs and touched down. Ahead lay the door that led to escape. Behind and below there were incoherent shouts and the sound of multiple people stomping up.

Let them come.

He would be a bloody memory by the time they reached the top.

He kicked out and sent the door flying off its hinges. It smashed into a pylon across the tracks and lay crumpled on the ground, like a distorted metal corpse. A bizarre echo of everything he'd just experienced.

A train was approaching to his left. The rush of air whipped his long black hair and he raised his nose, reveling in the scent. Despite the undercurrent of urine, garbage, and decay, it was a beautiful smell, heightened no doubt by the remnants of the monster blood still coursing through his system.

He opened his eyes as the train bore down on his position. He could hear the cult members behind him. They were getting close to the top. He was vaguely impressed by their speed, but their laboring was for nothing.

Morbius had a train to catch.

As the subway blasted past him, he jumped. Dug his claws into the metal and felt himself jerked violently forward, the sudden change in speed nearly pulling his arms out of their sockets. Still he held on, allowing the train to speed him away from this horrendous hole in the ground. As the train shot through the darkness, Morbius closed his eyes.

He had escaped.

But the night was far from over.

CHAPTER TWENTY-TWO

THE APARTMENT was as dark and silent as a sepulcher.

Morbius crawled in through the still-broken window, not expecting Amanda to be there but still hopeful, nonetheless. He knew he didn't have much time. The cult would know where he went, but he had rocked them back on their heels. Still, he had to be quick.

As his feet touched the floor, a scent instantly hit his nostrils. One he knew all too well.

Blood. A lot of it.

He crouched down and scanned the stark shadows of the room. He had been attacked too many times in recent days, taken by surprise far too often, to assume that there was no threat here.

His senses were starting to normalize as the effects of the monster blood cocktail waned. Rather than reasserting themselves, most of his wounds had healed. He looked around the dark space, his eyes adjusting to their usual preternatural state.

Something had gone horribly wrong here. Furniture was overturned. The front door was slightly ajar, and dark liquid had gathered on the floor nearby, sending up a heady aroma. A pool that was very large. From it, a red trail streaked off into Liz's bedroom. Quietly, cautiously, Morbius stood and walked toward the doorway.

Liz was face down on the floor, one arm stretched up onto her bed, as if she had been attempting to get up there but failed. The trail of blood led directly to her body.

Morbius walked over to her and kneeled down, cautiously placing two fingers against her neck. He felt the slightest pulse there. Somehow, despite all the blood on the floor of the apartment, she was still alive.

Gently he lifted her and placed her, face-up, on the bed. The jagged holes in her stomach continued to leak blood, so Morbius took one of the multiple pillows strewn across the bed and placed it against the wounds as softly but firmly as he could. He had seen many knife wounds in his life, and these didn't look good.

"Liz," he said quietly. Then, louder, "*Liz.*"

The woman's eyes fluttered open and she attempted to focus. Finally, after flicking about the room, they found Morbius. Tears began to fall down her face.

"I'm sorry," she said, choking back sobs.

"It's okay," he said, unsure why she was apologizing. "What happened? Where's Amanda?"

"I thought… Catherine… was going to kill my dad. I had to…" she gasped.

Catherine. The name startled him. She could only mean Catherine Saint, Amanda's sister. *Poison-Lark.*

But she was dead. Crushed to death in the catacombs beneath Ravenwood Cemetery—or so they had assumed. If Poison-Lark had survived, she must have been the architect behind everything that had transpired over the past few days. Who knew how long she had been tracking them… hunting them.

Morbius peered over his shoulder, back at the bedroom doorway, painfully aware of how unsafe this was. Then he turned back to Liz.

"Where is Amanda?"

"They took her," she said, still crying. "I don't know where. I'm sorry, I'm sorry. Please, please make sure they don't… hurt my father."

Demon-Fire had threatened Liz's father. Liz had betrayed Amanda, and now the cult had her. Again. After Morbius had abandoned her. Liz wasn't to blame.

He was.

"I'll do what I can," Morbius said, but the light was leaving Liz's eyes. The world was collapsing around her—and yet, his curse remained. He had killed innocents before, and in this moment he thought about draining her blood. But she had housed him, had been kind to him. His heart was full of pity for her, despite the betrayal.

"Thank you, Michael… thank you." It was the only time she had ever called him by his first name. "And please," she continued, lifting her head slightly, struggling to get the words out, "tell her… that I'm sorry."

Liz's head dropped back and her body slowly went slack. Her eyes were still open, but she was gone. Morbius stared at her for a moment, silently cursing Demon-Fire for the swath of destruction they continued to cut, then gently reached down to shut Liz's eyes with his bloodstained fingers. It was the least he could do.

An instant later, he was gone.

CATHERINE SAINT took a long sip of red wine, a slight smile crossing her face.

Everything was going according to plan. Morbius was trapped below ground in Demon-Fire's arena and would spend the rest of his short, brutish life battling other sub-human creatures. Amanda was starting to crack—she could tell. The bloodsucker's part in their mother's death was enough to drive a wedge between her and her bizarre protector. And Catherine's grand plan, thanks to the genius of Franklin Lattimer, was about to come to fruition. It all hinged on the sacrifice of the Thirteen.

She had approached it from the wrong direction the last time, with Arachne. Catherine had put all her hope in a spider demon, trusted her mother's word, when she should have taken matters into her own hands. She loved Myrna with all her heart, but the elder Saint had been wrong.

Another read of The Lesser Key of Solomon had opened Catherine's eyes to what was truly possible. She would correct the mistakes of her own recent past. Her mother would have been so proud—if Morbius hadn't killed her.

Her smile faded as she thought about the living vampire. No one really knew what had occurred, but Morbius was the last person to see Catherine's mother alive. When they found her, she had a hatchet imbedded in her head. It wasn't difficult to figure out what had transpired. Morbius had destroyed everything—again—and now, finally, he was paying.

The vengeance was bittersweet but she would take it.

As she finished her glass of wine, a soft knock came from the door of her office.

"Come in," she called out, placing the glass down. She tried to keep the annoyance out of her expression. Apparently she couldn't even have five minutes to herself, to contemplate her next steps. The process would be very precise, and required finesse.

She tried not to be distracted by the fact that her sister was close by. Catherine prayed to all the darkest powers that Amanda would choose to join her—that she wouldn't do anything stupid. They could continue the work started by their mother, build upon it, exceed her wildest expectations. Perhaps even rule the cult together. The thought was invigorating.

The acolyte who entered the room had a worried look on his face, forehead wrinkled and eyes wide. This was not good.

"What?" Catherine demanded, standing up, wondering if she should have chugged the whole bottle.

"There's been… an incident. At the arena."

"Morbius," Catherine whispered.

The man nodded. He looked terrified. Of what had happened in the arena or of Catherine, she wasn't sure. Perhaps both.

"Apparently he, he broke out of the pit and… killed a number of the guests. As well as many of our brothers and sisters."

"Thaddeus?" Catherine asked quickly, the wine turning to acid in her stomach. She knew the answer even as she said his name. The man swallowed nervously.

"Slaughtered."

Without even thinking about it, Catherine snatched the glass off the desk and threw it across the room. It connected with the cult member's face, shattering, blood instantly appearing in multiple cuts. To his credit, the man yelped but didn't move, didn't even wipe away the blood, just stood there, waiting for her next instruction.

"Where is the vampire?" Catherine asked through clenched teeth.

"Just… gone," he responded, wincing, waiting for the next punishment.

"Find him!" she screamed, slamming her open palm onto the desk. The man nodded and escaped from the room, pulling the door closed behind him. Catherine collapsed back into her chair and took a long pull from the bottle of wine, her nose going tingly, tears filling her eyes.

Thaddeus had been her lover. They hadn't told anyone. Under different circumstances, she might have even called what they had love. Despite what her mother had told her about that emotion and its place within the cult. Yes, she had met him through his son, poor stupid Justin, but he was only a boy, while Thaddeus was a man.

They had spent many nights in her bed, whispering about the world to come, how darkness would reign and they would be rewarded for their work, for their sacrifices—both figurative and literal. He had lost a son, she had lost a mother. They bonded in their pain, and it didn't hurt that they connected on a physical level, too.

Thaddeus understood her on a level that no one else ever had. And they both hated Michael Morbius with a passion that transcended words. They had looked forward to watching the vampire fight for his pathetic life until, little by little, he was reduced to a fraction of his former self, until he was begging for death.

Slaughtered, the acolyte had said. Horrible images filled Catherine's mind. Of Morbius feeding on the love of her life. She would get her revenge on that disgusting pale-faced monster, even if it took an eternity. As she took another long swig of wine directly from the bottle, there was a second knock at the door.

"Damn it, *what?*"

Another cult member entered, a woman this time, looking similarly terrified.

"*What?*" Catherine repeated.

"Your sister, sh-she, she…" the woman stuttered.

"Spit it out, you moron!"

"She's escaped."

Catherine was tempted to throw the bottle this time, but reined in her anger. After a moment of silence, she actually felt an incredibly calm feeling overtake her. This could be played to her advantage, she realized.

She had made mistakes—falling in love with Thaddeus, believing her sister could change. And now her mother was gone. Her lover was dead, her sister a fool. Catherine was alone. Perhaps as she was fated to be. So much easier to be alone when confronted with this kind of crucible. Yes, this was better.

Catherine sat down and smiled at the woman.

"Assemble a team," she said. "Go get her. She's somewhere inside this building—has to be. There's no way out. And if you don't bring her to me in the next thirty minutes, I will personally cut the heart from your body. Do you understand me?"

Pale before, the woman's face went white.

"Yes, Poison-Lark," she said with a slight bow. "She will be found. Immediately." The woman left in a hurry. Catherine closed her eyes for a long moment and then opened them again, her mind clear. Everything was so much simpler now.

She opened the drawer and pulled out two items, placing them on the desk. Slowly, methodically, she pulled her hair up and back, into Poison-Lark's telltale style. Then she carefully clipped the veil to her face, obscuring most of her features.

Catherine was gone. Perhaps forever. Poison-Lark sat in her place. What little love had remained in her heart was gone. She would burn the world down if necessary, sacrifice her own life if it came down to it.

But not before she personally watched Morbius draw his final breath.

CHAPTER TWENTY-THREE

M

AFTER A time, Amanda heard the voices of cult members coming closer, and she slipped into yet another room with old and dusty religious trappings. This place was a maze, but at least she had figured out what it was.

A church.

Or a former church. It was in such rough shape that it was obvious no one had worked here in a long time. There was a fine layer of dust over everything. Why would Demon-Fire be here? They had the resources to acquire a much better, much nicer facility. Then again, she had given up trying to understand the motives of this bloodthirsty cult. They had, after all, tried to use her as a sacrificial virgin.

As the voices came closer to her hiding spot, Amanda moved as far back into the room as possible, and found a vent. She pried it open, and was just small enough to shimmy inside. As she pulled her feet in after her, the cult members entered the room. She stayed still, crammed in, and held her breath.

After a few minutes of angry arguing, the cultists left. Amanda exhaled, and then decided to see where the cramped metal shaft would take her. Her mind raced. Was she even in New York City anymore? What would she do if she managed to get out of this building? She didn't have any friends, still didn't know where her father was.

Where Morbius was.

Did she even want to find him?

Gritting her teeth, she pulled herself forward through the narrow crawlspace, leaving the knife behind. She couldn't crawl while holding it. She hoped she wouldn't regret the decision.

The farther she got from the room, the darker it became, until she was in complete darkness. The duct felt slimy, and on more than one occasion her hand slipped out from under her. She couldn't let that stop her, though, had to focus on one thing at a time. Get through this shaft and then find a way out of this hellhole. Go to the police, and then resume her search for her dad.

He was all she had left.

If he was even alive.

No. She couldn't let herself think like that. There was too much at stake.

Amanda kept moving. She had never been a fan of enclosed spaces, and worked hard now to keep her breathing even. Having a panic attack wasn't her best option in the world.

After a few minutes of shimmying forward, she saw light up ahead and let out a breath of relief. For all she knew, it was going to lead her back into the belly of the beast, but she couldn't take much more of the metal walls that were pushing against her.

Finally reaching the source of the light, she looked down through a grating to see a large, shadowy room. The grate was held in place by screws but she was able to work them loose, slowly, one by one.

She grabbed for the grate but it fell too quickly, clattering loudly on the carpeted surface far below. Amanda grimaced and froze, waited for yells or footsteps, but none came. Still she waited. Part of her just wanted to stay there forever, hidden, relatively safe, but she knew that was ridiculous. She had to keep moving. Her father had always told her that a rolling stone gathered no moss, another quote that always made her roll her eyes. But she would give anything to hear him say it now.

Crawling just past the hole in the shaft, she dropped her legs down, then her waist, her stomach, until finally she grasped the metal at the edge of where the grate had just been. Taking a deep breath, Amanda dropped and surprised herself when she was able to hold on, hanging about twenty feet above the ground. She was fairly athletic but this drop was going to hurt, there was no doubt in her mind. People always talked about "rolling with the impact," but that just seemed like an easy way to bust your head open.

"You got this, Saint," she whispered to herself, and then she let go.

Her feet touched the ground before she even fully realized she was falling, and she surprised herself again when she rolled instinctively. It wasn't pretty, though. The roll was off-center and she landed on her uninjured arm, hard, the impact sending a shock of pain across her body. For a moment, she saw stars.

She lay on the ground, catching her breath, doing a mental inventory. Nothing was broken. At least it didn't feel like it.

Get up, Amanda, her mind commanded, and she did.

Climbing to her feet, she looked up and around, turning in a circle. The room was even bigger than she had thought. This was the nave of the church. Ancient-looking pews stretched back into the darkness. She had just missed smashing her head into one of them by only a few inches. She thought about saying a little prayer of thanks but then noticed that an eerie light was coming from behind her, from the sanctuary. And a sound like liquid going down a drain.

Slowly, she turned.

The pulpit had been transformed into a nightmarish scene. Demon-Fire had erected thirteen large crosses, and strapped to each one was a woman, unconscious or maybe dead, tubes leading out of their arms, blood running through the tubes and into a large glass box in front of the altar. The blood bubbled in the container.

Nausea rose up from her stomach, but Amanda managed to swallow it down. She walked down the aisle and then up the several steps that led to the altar, and placed her hand gently on the nearest woman's arm. Warm. A slight pulse beneath her fingers. These women were alive. Being bled out for… something. Something awful.

She looked at the tube that came out of the woman's arm. She had spent enough time at St. Gabriel's to at least know how to remove it without killing the woman, or causing unnecessary damage. Which is what she did.

Once the tube and stent were out, Amanda held her hand over the hole in her arm, hoping to stop the bleeding. As she stood there, hand pressed against the puncture, Amanda looked around. She didn't hear anything, but she quietly berated herself.

What was she doing? She should be focused on escaping, not helping these women. But she couldn't. Couldn't just leave them here to die. Even if she saved just one, even if she herself had to die to save even one of these women, it would be worth it. It was the least she could do. It was what Morbius would have done for her. What he *had* done.

Morbius.

As her mind cycled through Catherine's words, she didn't know what to believe. Had he really killed her mother? Had he really left town, abandoned her? Or was he wondering what had happened to her, regardless of where he was?

"Whuhh…?"

The woman on the cross began to stir, and Amanda

pushed these thoughts out of her mind.

"What…?" the woman asked as if she was talking through a mouth full of cotton. She opened her eyes, then blinked rapidly, her head swiveling, trying to make sense of where she was.

"It's okay," Amanda said. "You—"

Suddenly the woman inhaled with a gasp, her eyes going wide as she seemed to realize where she was and the fact that she was tied up, that a strange woman was holding a hand against a bloody wound in her arm.

She's gonna scream, Amanda's brain informed her.

She reached up as far as she could and clamped her free hand over the woman's mouth. This would be quite a tableau if anyone entered the room. Her arms outstretched, covering a mouth and a hole in an arm, standing by the altar of an abandoned church. Like some kind of bizarre painting that had been lost to time.

"*Hlpff…*"

"Don't. Scream," Amanda said, quietly but firmly, attempting to make eye contact. The woman's breathing increased, but then slowed down as she looked into Amanda's eyes.

"I'm here to help you," Amanda said, forcing a grim closed-mouth smile for a moment. "You've been kidnapped, and so have I, but I'm in the middle of escaping. I need your help untying the rest of these women. Will you help me?" The woman blinked several times, rapidly, and then nodded. "And will you stay quiet?" Amanda asked. The woman nodded again, more forcefully.

Amanda slowly removed her hand from the woman's mouth, waiting for the scream, but it didn't come. The woman just nodded again, and then the two of them worked together to free her from the cross.

As the woman put her feet on the ground—with Amanda's help—she looked up at the other twelve women who were still strapped to crosses, the red tubes stretching out from them like nightmarish umbilical cords.

"What *is* this?" the woman whispered.

"It's…" Amanda started, trying to figure out how to explain everything she'd gone through during the last several weeks in as few words as possible. "It's complicated, and I promise I'll explain everything to you, once we get out of here and get you… get *all* of you to a hospital." She paused and added, "What's your name?"

"Brianna," the woman said, "but everyone just calls me Brie." She was staring at the partly filled vat of blood now and her face had gone pale. Or paler than it already had been. She looked as if she was going to be sick.

"Nice to meet you, Brie," Amanda said quickly. "Now, look at me, okay?"

Brie looked over, her eyes filling with tears. "I was walking home from a date with my boyfriend. I don't even remember them… taking me. Oh my god, we need to get out of here."

"I know, I know we do, and we will, but we need to help these other women first. We can't just leave them here."

Brie nodded again, a huge tear rolling down her cheek.

"Okay," Amanda continued, stepping toward the next cross, "I think we can—"

A noise from the vestibule stopped her. She looked up, as did Brie. The front door had opened and a dozen or so cult members entered, wearing their red robes with the hoods pulled up. In the darkness of the church, it was impossible to see their faces, other than the occasional flash from their hate-filled eyes. Amanda could hear Brie starting to hyperventilate.

"It's okay, we're not—"

Brie screamed and ran past Amanda, down the few steps of the altar, and toward the closest door.

"Wait!" Amanda yelled after her, but the terrified woman didn't hear her or simply didn't care. For a moment, Amanda wondered if Brie had made the right decision. Maybe she would find a way out through the back and make her way to safety. Maybe they both should have escaped while they had the chance—but no, Amanda couldn't leave these other women here to die. No matter what ultimately happened, she just couldn't do it.

Brie sprinted toward a door that led to the back of the church and promptly ran into the blade of a particularly sharp knife. A surprised look crossed the young woman's face and she found herself staring into the eyes of a woman whose face was mostly covered by a veil. Terrifying eyes.

Brie glanced down at her stomach, where the blade had entered her body, and touched it, looking surprised. Then she looked back up and touched her attacker's forehead, gently, as if in some kind of deranged benediction.

Catherine shoved the knife in deeper and Brie gasped, then collapsed to the floor, blood gushing out of her stomach and pooling beneath her. Amanda's sister wiped the knife on her sleeve and stepped over the dying woman on the floor.

Amanda hadn't seen her sister wearing the veil since their encounter in the catacombs beneath Ravenwood Cemetery. With the blood streaked across her forehead, Catherine looked more terrifying than ever. Amanda didn't recognize her sister at all.

The cult members moved closer, and Amanda looked around. With the crosses behind her, she was completely boxed in. There was no way she could fight this many people, and she was exhausted.

That's it, she told herself. I've lost.

"Don't beat yourself up," Catherine said as if reading her sister's thoughts, stepping up to her, flanked by her acolytes. "I'm actually impressed that you got this far. You are so strong now, Amanda. Which is why I had genuinely hoped that you would join me. We could have done so much together.

"But I see now that I was being foolish. You've been infected by Morbius' perverted sense of right and wrong. Such a shame, but since you cost me my thirteenth victim… I guess your newfound strength will do some good after all."

She nodded at the closest cult member, a huge man whose face Amanda could barely see in the shadows of the pulpit. He and the others closed in on her. She promised herself she wouldn't scream.

As the hands grabbed at her, as they roughly tied her up on the cross and shoved a needle into her arm and attached a tube to it, and began draining the life from her, it was a promise she was unable to keep.

CHAPTER TWENTY-FOUR

FRANKLIN LATTIMER sipped at his green tea as Mozart played quietly in the background.

It had been a hell of a day. He had barely escaped the underground facility where he worked most days, while Michael Morbius, the "living vampire," had wreaked absolute havoc.

Franklin worked with blood every day, had never had an issue with it, but he had never seen so much freshly spilled gore in his entire life. The sheer volume of blood, ruptured flesh, pierced necks, and spilled intestines had caused him to vomit multiple times during his ascent from his place of employment.

It was highly undignified for an intellectual such as himself. Then again, he had chosen, after all, to work for a cult. He had never fully bought into their ethos, of course. At least, that's what he told himself now. Though the world was full of supernatural creatures and men who claimed to be gods, it still seemed far-fetched, the idea that Demon-Fire was literally serving the Devil. Nevertheless, they had paid well and provided him with all the supplies he requested, no matter how ethically questionable.

Franklin took another sip of tea. This was the sort of life he deserved. He had taken a hot bath as soon as he reached home, what with the blood and who knew what else splattered across his clothing and skin. No telling what horrible diseases it carried. The cab driver had at least been courteous enough not to mention anything about the state of Franklin's wardrobe.

He's probably seen worse.

Now, as he sat in his living room, staring out at the New York City skyline, he wondered what life had in store for him next. He suspected that this particular coven of Demon-Fire had probably reached its violent conclusion thanks to Morbius. There had been talk during his months working down there that other factions of the cult operated within the city, but they all operated independently of one another, in order to keep each chapter intact should one fall.

Still, Franklin couldn't help but contemplate the idea of finding another Demon-Fire headquarters to approach them, explain who he was, what he had been doing for Thaddeus and Poison-Lark.

Ah, Poison-Lark. He had only seen her real face once, glimpsed when he was summoned to her quarters to discuss her master plan. And what a face it was! He'd been imagining what she might look like since the day she had recruited him in that old, abandoned church. She was beautiful... stunning, really. He fell even deeper in love with her in that instant—at least, that's the way it felt.

And the more time he spent in her service, the more Franklin convinced himself that she could love him, too. She respected his intelligence, valued it even, and pushed him to work harder, to perfect his formula in time for the "Sacrifice of the Thirteen," as she called it.

That hadn't been a simple task—not like the monsters. The photocopies she brought him, taken from some antique writings, were almost impossible to decipher. Or they would have been, for anyone of a lesser intellect. Franklin had broken the code, though, and recreated the formula she desired. After that, he was given even greater resources, and left to his own devices.

The day he realized the truth about her and Thaddeus, his heart had been broken. He had even considered quitting. How could a woman like that be romantically involved with such a brute? Yes, he was handsome and tall, but he was so old, and nowhere near as intelligent as Franklin.

As soon as he started to piece together that they were a secret couple, Franklin made every effort to find proof. Some may have called it stalking, but Franklin considered it smart business sense. Insurance, even. If his two employers were having some kind of affair, it was important that he know about it. It was possible their relationship was affecting their decisions, and Franklin could adjust as needed.

Still, he pined for her. Fantasized about a day when she would realize just how useless Thaddeus was, and how much Franklin could offer her. As he sat in his penthouse apartment contemplating a future with Poison-Lark that was never going to happen, Franklin suddenly heard a noise from across the room.

"Who's there?" he shouted, sitting up, spilling the tea across his patent leather couch. As he stared into the looming darkness of his own apartment, he slowly came to realize that a pair of bloodshot eyes was staring back at him. He scrambled to his feet as best he could.

"Don't come any closer! I have a gun over here!"

"We both know you're lying," a voice rumbled from the darkness, sounding as if it had just clawed its way out of the grave. Which Franklin supposed it had, in a manner of speaking. He recognized that voice.

"Morbius," he hissed.

"You got out." The eyes narrowed. "I'm impressed."

"No thanks to you. How many did you kill?"

"Not enough."

"I'm not one of them," Franklin said, his voice pitched too high. He looked around, trying to remain as casual as possible, calculating how quickly he could make it to the front door, the bedroom, or even the balcony. But he had seen Morbius in action. His speed was superhuman. There was no way he could outrun the vampire. Why had he mentioned where he lived when first confronted by Morbius?

Because you were desperate, his mind told him.

"I'm not part of that cult," he protested. "I just used them, to further my research. I was going to use my findings to help the world. I was planning on quitting soon, I swear."

Then he remembered. "And I have more of that blood. The blood that gives you that... that high. You like it, don't you? I have some here in the apartment. Locked away. I can... I can give it to you. We can make a deal."

Morbius' eyes narrowed.

"I'm a scientist, too," the voice said in a tone that was surprising. Earnest. Maybe even... proud?

"You *are*?" Franklin responded. He had not expected the monster to say that.

"Before I became... this, I received a Nobel Prize. Studied blood, as have you. You and I are not so different. Let me guess, you had a... difficult childhood."

Franklin's eyes went wide and he sat back down on the couch. His mind raced. How did the vampire know that? Franklin had been careful to keep the public's knowledge about him to an absolute minimum. It was too dangerous otherwise. Perhaps his time working for the cult had made him paranoid, though he would call it cautious.

Morbius stepped forward, his face appearing in a crisscross of light and shadow. It was like every nightmare Franklin had ever experienced, coming to life in his own apartment. He swallowed nervously.

"I did," he answered, deciding it was best to cooperate. Perhaps it was still possible that he could talk his way out of this. "I'm not exactly a perfect physical specimen."

"Nor was I," Morbius replied. "And I suffered for it. Greatly."

Franklin nodded and even smiled slightly. "So, we're *not* so different... you and I."

"Perhaps not. You've done evil things. Things for which you deserve to die."

A long silence passed. Franklin's mouth had gone completely dry. He couldn't swallow, let alone speak.

"Then again," Morbius continued, "so have I."

The creature stepped farther into the light, and Franklin got a good look at him. He was covered almost entirely in dried blood. The calm expression on his pale, deformed face was more terrifying than if he'd been enraged. Franklin was shocked to see what looked like kindness in the monster's eyes. Yes, he realized, there really was still some hope.

"Tell me more," Franklin said, forcing his smile to grow. He knew it probably looked unnatural, fake, but he had to take that chance. "About your work. Scientist to scientist. I've been surrounded by simple-minded fools for as long as I can remember. For my entire life, I suppose you could say."

"I haven't always been like this," Morbius answered, taking another step forward. He glanced around the apartment as if looking for something.

The blood, Franklin realized. *He's trying to figure out where the blood is.*

"No?" Franklin said. *Got to keep him talking.*

"I was sick… working on a cure. Trying to save a life that I wasn't meant to have, and I paid for it. As have so many others."

He took another step forward, and Franklin realized the vampire was shivering. *Withdrawal symptoms*, Franklin noted. *It has to be.* Morbius was vulnerable. Franklin looked around and noticed the heavy, metal candleholder on the table next to him. He placed his hand on the armrest as casually as possible.

Keep him talking.

"I understand, Michael," he said. "I've hurt so many people, and I regret it. I have nightmares... the most horrible nightmares. Do you?"

The vampire's eyebrows arched, and a deep sorrow came over his face. It was almost heartbreaking. Almost.

"Yes," he answered, the word barely audible. His face looked almost green and his blood-caked hands were trembling.

"I honestly thought I was helping people," Franklin continued. "I still feel that way. My work... *our* work can still benefit humanity. The people we've hurt, the ones we've killed, who were they really? *Nobodies.* Nothing they did or could ever do would help the world, not without us." Franklin sat forward slightly, really selling his proposal, and moved his hand even closer to the candle. "I remember the first man I experimented on. At first I felt guilty, but then I realized that my work was more important than his life. How many people would benefit from his sacrifice? He and his wife should have thanked me..."

"His... wife?" Morbius said.

"Yes," Franklin scoffed, confused but determined to continue. "He kept babbling on and on about his wife, how she would worry about him, how she would—"

Morbius lunged forward, catching Franklin off guard, but the smaller man managed to grab the candleholder and swing it in a fluid motion, probably the fastest he had ever moved in his entire life. As Morbius' hand reached his neck, Franklin brought the thick metal object against the side of his attacker's head. It snapped back, and a deep gash appeared. Dark blood oozed out and the vampire collapsed at his feet.

Stumbling past Morbius, Franklin ran for the front door. His entire future flashed before his eyes. He would get through this door, then make it to the elevator. Leave the building and get into a cab, check into the worst motel he could find in New York City. He'd pay for it with the wad of cash he had in his pocket. The cult always paid him in cash.

He thanked God for that fact.

Franklin would lay low in the motel. Have food delivered. Wait for weeks if necessary, until the money began to run out. Then he would take the rest of the cash, just enough, to get a bus that would take him across the country. But he wouldn't go all the way. He would get off in some random city… or even better, some small town. Get a job where he didn't need to give his real name.

He'd be poor again—at least for a while—but eventually, he'd work his way back up. And he would return to his experiments. Somehow. He would never have to see Michael Morbius or the Demon-Fire cult, ever again.

As his hand touched the doorknob, he was tackled from behind. His face crashed painfully against the wood, smashing his nose, blood bursting out and causing him to cough uncontrollably. Stars exploded behind his eyes.

Franklin gasped for breath as he was flipped over, the back of his head smacking painfully against the floor. He saw stars again and slipped into unconsciousness for a moment, beginning to slump downward, but then came roaring back to lucidity as Morbius' face filled his vision. The vampire's fangs glistened in what remained of the candlelight, saliva dripping down onto Franklin's chest.

"Puh-please, d-d-don't…" he stuttered, tears rolling down the side of his face.

"Where is the blood?" Morbius demanded, his eyes hidden in deep shadows, black buttons in the darkness.

"O-over there," Franklin responded, lifting a shaking finger and pointing to the kitchen.

Morbius lifted the shaking man with a single hand. Franklin struggled to find his balance as he was placed on his feet; his head was swimming from the blows he'd just received, front and back.

"Show me."

CHAPTER TWENTY-FIVE

CATHERINE SAINT poured herself another glass of wine, filling it nearly to the top.

She had been drinking a lot lately, perhaps too much, but these were trying times, and she had lost so much. Her mother. Her lover. And now her sister. She had wanted so badly for Amanda to join her, to become a true Demon-Fire disciple. The things they could have done together!

Catherine was alone now. Just like she always had been, she supposed. At least, ever since her sister was born. Those first early years with just her and her parents… in many ways, that was the only time Catherine felt like she belonged to something. She missed those days so much that it literally made her ache.

She pushed away the memories, drained most of her glass, then refilled it.

No. Nostalgia was dangerous. It had no place in

Poison-Lark's life. She was powerful now. Strong. And she was going to change the world.

Catherine stood up and took a deep breath. Despite the setbacks, everything was back on track. Midnight was fast approaching. The day the *Lemegeton* had prophesized. The Sacrifice of the Thirteen, performed on November 18th, and during a blood moon.

She downed the wine and placed the glass back on her desk. She felt the effects of the alcohol, but it didn't matter. Her father had struggled with addiction to alcohol. He was weak. Always had been. But she was in charge now. She was Poison-Lark, and she was so much bigger than the shadow he had cast over her life.

Once again, she affixed the veil to her face and tied her hair up, transforming with these simple gestures into a creature of power. Where Catherine Saint was burdened with the trappings and failings of humanity, Poison-Lark was a symbol of everything Demon-Fire could accomplish. Tonight, she would bring about the terrestrial victory of Satan, and she would do it using her own body—as well as the blood of her sister. She had been a fool to try to do it any other way. She laughed at her previous naiveté, and that of her mother.

Arachne was nothing compared to what Catherine would become.

Grasping the *Lemegeton*, she stalked across the room and threw open the door. The cult member on guard straightened to attention, gripping the blade in his hand more tightly. She didn't even look at him, just kept moving forward, heading toward the center of the church.

Along the way, she passed several more guards, all of whom tensed as she approached. Their fear, their reverence was as intoxicating as the wine. She was addicted to that. The terror she inspired. It filled her with a euphoria that she could never truly explain, not even to Thaddeus. When he was alive.

The thought of him shifted her emotions to rage.

Morbius.

She had never hated anyone as much as she hated the living vampire. He had ruined her plans, murdered her loved ones. Again and again, and there was no doubt in her mind that he would be coming to save Amanda. Inevitably. Stupidly. She didn't know how he would manage it, since she had kept secret the details of the ceremony, but Morbius had proved to be an inexplicably smart and dangerous opponent. She almost admired him.

Almost.

But time was running short. If he did arrive, he had no idea what was in store for him. He would wish he had just stayed in the arena, fighting other monsters and being fed innocent victims as a reward. He should have *thanked* her!

Catherine cleared her mind as she entered the vestibule. Thinking about Morbius wasn't good for her. She could feel her heart racing, and she needed to be calm for the ceremony. Everything needed to proceed precisely as planned, or all her careful preparations would be for naught.

Those preparations stretched back years, back to when her mother had appeared in her apartment that night, handing her the *Lemegeton* and changing her world in an instant. That night felt like a thousand years ago. In many ways, it was a different life altogether. It was the night that a version of Catherine had died, and that Poison-Lark had been conceived.

Her acolytes had followed her instructions, lighting the entire nave and pulpit with candles. Moonlight streamed in through the windows. It was a cloudless night and the full moon hung in the middle of the clear sky, just as the book had predicted. The Earth's shadow had already begun to cut into it, and within an hour or so the eclipse would be complete. The disc would turn red—a blood moon.

Everything was perfect.

Beneath her veil, Catherine smiled.

She strode up the center aisle and toward the altar, holding the ancient book in the crook of her arm. It was the first time she'd carried it in a long time. It felt so good in her grip. So natural.

The thirteen crosses still stood, throwing huge shadows across the floor and the first several rows of pews. The sight sent shivers of pleasure up her spine. Tubes snaked out, tendril-like, from each sacrifice, blood slowly pumping from them and into the tank in the center of the pulpit. At the end of the row of victims, Amanda was lashed to one of the constructs, her eyes closed, unconscious.

She looked so young up there, like the little girl Catherine remembered from when they were growing up. Even though they hadn't always gotten along, they'd had some good memories. Interspersed throughout the fights, there had been moments of tenderness, of raucous laughter, of teaming up against their parents during arguments that seemed absurd now. There were even several years when they had become all but inseparable.

Regret crowded in around her heart, but she hardened herself again. This was her sister, yes, but Amanda had made her choice. It was her own fault. Her own responsibility.

Demon-Fire acolytes milled about the church, preparing the space and the equipment for what was to come. Only an hour or so away from the ceremony, their timing had to be precise. Catherine had butterflies in her stomach, felt like a child again, in many ways. As if she was going to her first dance or a job interview.

This particular life event was going to involve a lot more blood.

Catherine stepped up to the pulpit and got the attention of a cultist who was checking on one of the unconscious victims tied to a cross.

"Yes, Poison-Lark, how may I serve?" he said, carefully avoiding eye contact.

"Wake her," Catherine responded, nodding toward her sister.

"At once," he responded, and he stepped over to Amanda. Withdrawing a syringe from within his red robe he plunged it quickly, efficiently, into her arm. The task completed, the instrument disappeared back into his robe and he turned away as Amanda's eyes began to flutter open.

"Wake up," Catherine said in a tone she might have used decades earlier, on a school day. *The bus is almost here, Amanda*, her memory whispered. *Tie your shoes, get your backpack.*

No, it was a lifetime ago.

That girl didn't exist anymore.

"Ca-Catherine…?" Amanda said groggily, trying to focus her eyes.

"I'm here," Poison-Lark replied, stepping closer.

"You… you don't have to do this," her sister said, her voice sharpening much more quickly than Catherine expected. Once again, she was impressed. Amanda was made of sterner stuff than she'd anticipated.

"You're right," Catherine said, reaching up and brushing her sister's hair out of her eyes, "I don't have to do anything I don't want—but I want to do this. So very badly."

Amanda's eyes flitted to the glass case. The blood within continued to churn and bubble.

"What… is that?"

"It's beautiful, isn't it?" Catherine answered, following her sister's gaze. It had taken her a long time to decipher the *Lemegeton*, to understand what she must do, and finding Franklin Lattimer had been key to the completion of her plan. His formula was essential, was so much more than just a device to create monsters for the amusement of the rich. Yes, that was an advantageous benefit, there was no denying that. The money that had poured in as a result of the fights in the arena had made possible their preparations.

the way as Carnage's razor-sharp tendrils snaked out, tearing out huge gouges of the massive tree to which the web-slinger had just been clinging.

"Stand still, bug!" the symbiote and his host screamed, pulsing with hatred.

It was two o'clock in the morning in the middle of Central Park. No one was around to witness their savage battle. Spider-Man had tracked Carnage to this otherwise-peaceful part of the city and had hoped a surprise attack would result in a quick victory.

So much for that.

"You know, I used to get in trouble in third grade for never sitting still," the web-slinger quipped. "If only Mrs. Willicker could see me n—*argh!*"

In the undulating shadows, he had failed to notice two of Carnage's tendrils, which snaked around his chest, squeezing tightly and almost snapping several of the wall-crawler's ribs. In a desperate attempt to regain his breath, he flexed, but Carnage was incredibly strong—even these small, slithering parts of him.

"If you… wanted a hug…" Spider-Man gasped, "you should have just… said so!" Carnage stalked closer, his fingers transforming into deadly claws.

"You won't be joking once I disembowel you."

"Heh… you… you said 'bowel'."

As Carnage slashed toward Spider-Man's face, the web-slinger tensed his powerful legs and leapt over his opponent's head, twisting as he did so, causing the tendrils to wrap around Carnage's neck. Carnage tried to apply further pressure, but only succeeded in choking himself. Reluctantly, Carnage released his grip, and the two tendrils coiled back up into his black-and-red body.

He leveled a sharp finger at his enemy.

"I look forward to ripping you apart piece by piece, tearing you to shreds with my teeth."

"Just make sure you floss when you're done, Carnie!"

Carnage screamed in rage and lunged with inhuman speed, barreling into Spider-Man too fast for the wall-crawler's spider-sense to warn him and knocking the breath of the already-winded super hero. Carnage battered him with blow after blow until he stopped moving.

Spider-Man was barely breathing.

Central Park was still and silent.

"FINALLY!" CARNAGE screamed to the heavens. He had dreamed of this day. The infuriating wall-crawler, unconscious at his feet. One focused blow would obliterate the spider from existence. He thought about removing the hero's mask, discovering who it was beneath the thin layer of fabric, but decided against it.

What did it matter? He was about to die, regardless.

"Goodbye, bug." Carnage's tendrils formed into a battering ram of deadly spikes, and he held it in front of Spider-Man for the briefest of moments. "I wish I could say it's been a pleasure."

He drew back to land the killing blow, then hesitated as he heard a strange *whoosh*. There was a sudden stinging pain in his chest. He looked down and saw a small dart sticking out.

"What the h—?"

A group of seven figures burst from the shadows. His head was spinning, and they tackled him before he could react, grabbing his arms and legs, two of them immobilizing the spiked limb.

What was in that dart?!

Carnage lashed out at his attackers, but they were incredibly fast. Their movements seemed coordinated with a military level of efficiency, though none of them appeared to be carrying weapons of any sort.

He'd been an idiot... letting his moment of triumph over Spider-Man distract him. That would never happen again. He would take care of these new assailants, and then there would be a reckoning. Their deaths would be quick, but painful.

Seeking to focus, Carnage tried to get his body and the symbiote to respond to his mental commands. He managed to lash out with a tendril, which caught one of the men in the shoulder, splitting it open in a bloody burst. The man fell to the ground, biting down on a scream, and Carnage chuckled inwardly.

"I'm going to enjoy feasting on your innards!" he yelled, gaining a grip on another of his attackers and throwing her across the clearing. Two down, five to go, but more and more he was struggling to concentrate. He screamed with frustration as he picked up two of his attackers and smashed them together. They fell together at his feet.

Three left.

He whirled to face them but was shocked to discover himself staring instead at a small man with glasses and a quixotic smile on his face. For a moment, Carnage thought he was seeing things.

"Who… who are you su… supposed to be?" he slurred, blinking several times, trying to keep his balance. He'd been so close to killing Spider-Man, and now he was face to face with the least imposing adversary he could have imagined.

"Hello," the little man said. "I'm Franklin Lattimer, and I'm sorry to drop in like this. It looks as if we interrupted a very big moment for you."

"Bite me," Carnage growled. "I'm going to sh-shove those glasses where the sun don't shine!" He moved forward and could literally taste the fear that radiated from the man despite his confident words. He'd probably assumed the seven thugs would do the dirty work, that he wouldn't need to show his stupid face.

Oh, how wrong the little worm was.

Still, Carnage found himself having more and more trouble concentrating. Whatever was working its way through his system, it was strong as hell. The three remaining thugs had flanked him, yet Carnage didn't take his eyes off of the man who appeared to hold their leashes. It was the smile. It was *infuriating*.

The world began to tilt, but Carnage lunged

forward, a trio of tendrils snaking out from his body and puncturing the three figures simultaneously. They collapsed with little more than a gurgling sound. But he wanted to kill this "Franklin Lattimer" with his bare hands. The little man had earned that honor for leading this little band, for interrupting Carnage's long-desired murder of Spider-Man.

To his surprise, Franklin stood his ground.

He was brave. Or stupid. Or both.

Just as Carnage's claws were poised to tear the man's head from his body, Franklin's hand appeared out of nowhere and plunged a syringe directly into Carnage's neck. Instantly, more chemicals went rushing through his system, and *again* he cursed himself for being the idiot. Franklin had *wanted* Carnage to attack, had wanted him to come in close for the kill.

It was kind of brilliant, really.

Carnage collapsed to the ground, unable to feel his arms or legs, his tendrils flowing back to his body. He tried to speak, but couldn't find his voice. The little man knelt down and gently caressed his head, as if he was a beloved pet who was being put to sleep.

"Shhh," Franklin said. "It's alright. Don't fight it."

This dude is creepy, Carnage thought. He managed to turn his head and found himself staring at the still-unconscious form of Spider-Man.

He had been so close… so close…

FRANKLIN AND Fiona stood over Carnage's unmoving body.

They had pumped him full of enough modified sedative to keep a rhinoceros unconscious and affixed an updated version of the control collar to his neck, but they were still nervous. The Extractors were lying on medical beds in other parts of the lab, recovering from their encounter with the deadly symbiote. Most of their wounds were serious, and Fiona could do little more than stop the bleeding and stitch them up. It wasn't pretty, but at least they were likely to survive.

"Even asleep he looks dangerous," Fiona said quietly, admiringly.

"I suppose," Franklin responded, a tinge of jealousy in his voice.

Fiona reached out and touched Carnage's arm. His skin, or whatever it was, reacted to the contact, oozing over her fingers. Yet she didn't jerk back.

"That is *so*… fascinating," she murmured. She withdrew her hand and placed it against Franklin's cheek. "Feel how warm."

He placed his own hand against her face and smiled. "We've got an arena to fill."

"More monsters to make," Fiona confirmed.

CARNAGE AWOKE with a start.

It took a moment for his eyes to focus; when they finally did, he was staring at a floor made up of packed dirt. Something was attached to his neck, his brain felt like it was stuffed full of cotton, and his entire body ached. Wherever he was, it smelled of mold and mustiness, as if he was underground.

With increased consciousness came an insane rage as the memories from Central Park came rushing back in. He *had* Spider-Man, was an instant from caving in his skull in a delicious explosion of gore. Then came the seven assailants, and the little man with his stupid smile and damn needle.

Someone is going to die today.

Carnage leapt to his feet and took in his surroundings. It was a huge open area, indoors, surrounded by concrete walls. Beyond them, everything fell into shadow, but there appeared to be a lot of people gathered as an audience. There was an excited murmuring that increased as soon as he was upright.

He turned in a circle, taking it all in, giggling. Were these people for real? Did they think this pathetic arena could hold him? One leap and he would have a smorgasbord of victims to kill, offering some solace for his lost web-slinger. He tensed, and just as he was about to spring, his eyes landed on the little man from Central Park.

"Franklin Lattimer!" he shouted, and a grin spread across his face, teeth growing and extending outward. "I was hoping I'd see you again!"

The little man was wearing a suit, and there was a woman sitting next to him. She grinned confidently and placed her hand on his arm. This was something

Carnage might be able to exploit. Even if Lattimer didn't fear for his own life, he might balk at seeing her entrails spread out on the ground.

"I don't know what you think is gonna happen down here," Carnage continued, "but let me tell you... you're gonna die long before I do." Tendrils began to snake out of his body, waving in the air, and his fingers transformed into razors. He was ready for some sweet, sweet vengeance.

As he watched, however, Lattimer smiled that infuriating smile and removed a small device from inside his suit jacket. He gently pressed a button.

The device around Carnage's neck buzzed, and an unbearable burst of pain radiated outward, sending him writhing back down onto the packed dirt. Simultaneously he laughed and screamed in pain. He had never felt anything quite like it.

He begrudgingly began to admire Franklin Lattimer.

The pain subsided, and Carnage lurched back to his feet. As he did, the people in the audience began *clapping*. They were applauding Franklin, he realized— this was all some sort of show, and apparently Carnage was the star.

Nope. Screw that. Not having it.

He reached up to tear the device off of his neck. At that moment, however, he heard the grinding of rusty hinges as two huge doors on either side of the arena began to lumber open. The crowd above Carnage roared.

A half-dozen creatures emerged, three from each side, a motley crew of fangs and talons and grotesque muscles. Each wore a similar collar, and a couple of them began attacking each other. Then they screeched and began to claw at the devices, one of them falling to its knees. When they stopped squirming, they focused their attention on the figure at the center of it all.

Carnage.

"Heh—"

Then the creatures were upon him. Within an instant, he was being bitten and clawed from all sides, yet through it all he could hear the roar of the crowd. Once again, he silently saluted his captor. This had to be one hell of a show for those in the bleachers.

Forming his right arm into a scythe, he lashed out, catching one of the creatures—a huge hairy mass with a pair of bloodshot eyes—right in the stomach. The creature fell back, blood shooting like a geyser from the wound, then rolled up into a bleeding ball and stopped moving.

Multiple tendrils shot out of Carnage's sides and wrapped around two of his other attackers, lifting them up and throwing them to opposite sides of the arena. They struck the wall with bone-jarring impacts, but quickly recovered. It didn't matter—he just needed a minute to clear his head and catch his breath.

These odds weren't great, but he'd faced worse.

A tall, sinewy monster with an elongated head and six eyes bit down on one of the tentacles and ground its oversized teeth, tearing the tendril in half. Pain radiated up Carnage's arm; in response, he lashed out at the tall creature with his scythe and nearly took the monster's head off. It fell in a heap next to its shorter, hairier brethren, blood shooting out of its cleaved neck.

Two creatures on either side of him backed off in unison, perhaps realizing this wouldn't be as easy as they expected. A moment later they both howled and clawed at their necks, and Carnage surmised that Franklin was leaning on that little button of his. He chuckled, but it was short-lived as the two monsters leapt at him faster than he thought possible.

One was covered in oozing flesh; its fatty skin engulfed Carnage's lower half, tripping him up, while the other monster—its skin crystalline and reflective— wrapped long fingers around Carnage's throat and began to squeeze.

Both creatures pressed their attack. He fell to the ground and glimpsed the other two monsters running back from where he had thrown them. As black spots danced in front of his eyes, Carnage wondered whether he was fated to die on this dirt ground.

No.

Cackling, he focused on one of the creatures that was barreling toward him. Its cracked skin was rock-like and looked incredibly hard, as if it was made entirely of concrete. A smile slithered onto Carnage's face.

"You know what they say about glass houses!"

As the pressure on his neck increased and the blob creature continued to engulf him, he sent out as many tendrils as possible. They wrapped around the concrete monster and lifted it off of its feet, plate-like eyes widening in surprise. Carnage used all his strength to pull it through the air until it smashed into the crystalline creature, shattering it into a thousand pieces and sending what must have been diamond-hard shards into the concrete monster. It fell writhing to the ground. All around it the shards vibrated.

Two more down.

The blob had risen past Carnage's waist now and was squeezing his ribs, making it hard for him to breathe. The crowd's bellowing grew louder and louder. Carnage made eye contact with Franklin, who nodded approvingly. Sucking in as much oxygen as he could, Carnage laughed and shoved his hands into the blob as it covered Carnage's chest, approaching his face, then engulfing him completely.

All was blackness and silence.

Then Carnage slashed out with two scythes and a dozen sharpened tendrils, all at once. The blob exploded outward. Fatty goo splattered a section of the audience, sending them fleeing, while the rest laughed and cheered at the sight.

And they say I'm *a monster…*

Carnage stood and faced off with his final opponent, chuckling as he did so. Despite everything, he was having the time of his life. The creature in front of him was huge, with dark-green scales on its upper half and arms that ended in deadly looking claws. Its bottom half showcased muscular, hair-covered legs with massive hooves that dug into the dirt as it sprinted toward its opponent.

"You seem nice," Carnage said, then the thing reached him, slicing him across the chest. The crowd cheered its approval. The beast was unreasonably fast and sliced Carnage three more times before he could even register what was happening.

Not sure how much more damage he could take, Carnage quickly reached out, even though it gave the creature even more of an opportunity to slash at him with its deadly claws. He grabbed one of its arms and used all of his waning strength to hurl it into the air, then leapt up after it.

Once again, both hands became scythes.

As the creature fell back down toward him, its limbs pinwheeling, Carnage screamed and lashed out, slicing the monster into three separate pieces, raining blood and gore and body parts all over the arena.

The audience went silent as Carnage landed in a crouch. He slowly stood to his full height and locked eyes with Franklin as the crowd erupted, its applause louder than ever. Grinning wildly, he began to walk slowly, inexorably across the arena toward where Franklin was sitting with his lady friend. Franklin raised the device and shook his head. "*Don't do it*," the little man's eyes said.

All around, the audience tensed, poised to head toward the shadowy exits.

"Not gonna happen, Frankie-boy!" Carnage shouted. Still silent, the audience looked to the master of ceremonies, pleading with their eyes for him to hit the button. Which he did. Pain lanced out, but

Carnage ignored it, leaping up and climbing the tall wall. He reached the top in seconds and hopped over the barbed wire, landing right in front of Franklin—who was pressing the button as hard as he could.

"You're going to break that if you're not careful." Carnage did his best to pretend the pain wasn't bothering him even though it was. A lot.

The audience scattered.

Carnage reached out and delicately plucked the device out of Franklin's hand, silently thankful when the pain abruptly stopped. Then he popped it in his mouth and ate it, chewing slowly while staring at Lattimer.

"Aren't you going to introduce me to your girlfriend?" he said, using a sharpened finger to pick pieces of plastic and metal out of his teeth. To his surprise, the woman stood and showed no fear.

Damn...

"I have a name. And it's *Fiona*," she replied.

"Ooooh, I like you," Carnage replied.

Then Lattimer spoke up, his voice nowhere near as steady.

"You can kill me," he said, standing up and looking Carnage in the eyes. "But let her go. Please..." The little man was shaking. Carnage laughed and pushed him back down into his seat.

"Kill you?" he said. "Are you kidding me? I loved every minute of that. Whatever your gig is here, I wanna invest, Frankie-boy! I mean, come on! A monster fight club? This could be my home away from home. You bring me more playmates to kill, and I'll make you very, very rich."

Carnage held out his hand, the huge toothy smile widening across his inhuman face.

"Deal?"

Franklin looked over at Fiona, and the two locked eyes for a moment. Around them, those audience members who remained had stopped fleeing and were watching the encounter with rapt interest. A cunning smile appeared on Fiona's face, and she nodded. Franklin's eyes widened, and then he nodded, too, and mouthed the words "*I love you.*"

Carnage almost killed him right then and there.

No, he was in too good a mood to ruin the moment.

Franklin took hold of the much-larger hand.

"Deal."

A BRIEF HISTORY OF *BLOOD TIES*

WHEN I got hired to write a Morbius novel, I was incredibly excited, to say the least. I've been reading Marvel comic books since… well, since I could read. My oldest brother had been a pretty avid collector in his early teens, in the late '70s, which would have made me around six or seven when I started reading his digest-sized Spider-Man reprints (the ones by Stan Lee and Steve Ditko), plus whatever comics he had picked up at our local Dairy Mart. And let me tell you, I was hooked.

My brother eventually outgrew comic books, but I never did. He bequeathed (or I stole, depending on who you ask) his collection of 200 comics and that collection eventually ballooned to 15,000 issues by the time I went to college and gave up the medium for about seven years.

Thinking back to the years where I bought and organized comics like my life depended on it, I realize that I was always drawn to dark stories, especially ones that featured the more obscure characters. I was particularly fascinated with those heroes and villains who could easily wear either label... like the blind vigilante The Shroud who first appeared in, of all places, *Super-Villain Team-Up*; or DC's incredibly bizarre team book, *The Night Force*. (I bought the first issue of this series, which featured an orgy and a demon sacrifice, at the self-same Dairy Mart, which was a family establishment, by the way.)

And then there was Morbius. I was too young to have read his first appearance in Amazing Spider-Man #101—in fact, it was published six months before I was born—but I became aware of the character very quickly as soon as I immersed myself in the ever-expanding world of Marvel. There was just something very cool about him... something undeniably tragic and cool... a living vampire. I followed the character over the years, intrigued by him, but never imagined that I would someday write a novel starring him.

I've made a bit of a writing and editing career on rebooting characters and finding "side" stories to explore. I wrote a *Flash Gordon* comic book reboot after reading literally every single Alex Raymond comic strip; told an *Island of Misfit Toys* side story that slots perfectly into the original *Rudolph the Red Nose Reindeer* stop-animation Christmas movie (which I watched every year growing up); co-plotted and co-published the Atlas Comics reboot (from a company created by the founder of Marvel, Martin Goodman), and even co-wrote one of the titles, *Phoenix*, with Jim Krueger. I conceived of and edited a *Psycho* side story book that takes place in the *middle* of the *Psycho II* novel; and I edited eight *Walking Dead* novels/side-stories, as well.

In other words, I'm a big fan of playing in other people's sandboxes, and of doing the necessary research.

Blood Ties was no different. After landing this gig, I took it upon myself (with Titan and Marvel's generous help) to read every single Morbius story from 1971 to the present, many of which I had never encountered before. It was a rare treat to see this character in action over his formative years, and that's exactly where inspiration struck.

After appearing in Spider-Man comics and spending some time in *Adventure into Fear*, Morbius then appeared in a black-and-white magazine called *Vampire Tales*. It was an edgier Marvel title, featuring a number of horror characters, and Morbius really took flight in those pages (pun only slightly intended). In *Vampire Tales* #2, dated October 1973 (published when I was one and a half), Don McGregor (writer), Rich Buckler and Pablo Marcos (artists) introduced Amanda Saint, a relatively innocuous supporting character who is Morbius' intended victim on the opening page of the short story.

However, Amanda is beset upon by members of the Demon-Fire cult, and for some reason, Morbius decides that he will save her life, to become her guardian going forward.

As Amanda continued to appear in *Vampire Tales* with Morbius for the next several issues, as the living vampire helped her find her mother and then her father (spoiler alert: neither reunion ends well), I became fascinated with the dynamic between the two of them. Amanda started out as a potential meal, but then became the closest thing he had to a friend in any of those early issues that I read.

Thus, the idea of *Blood Ties* was born. A Morbius "side story" about the complicated friendship between a vampire and his once-intended victim. And also a story about Amanda: a woman who had been betrayed by almost everyone in her life, and the unlikely companionship she finds in someone who might choose to murder (and eat) her at any time.

Who says relationships aren't complicated?

ACKNOWLEDGEMENTS

I'D LIKE to first and foremost thank Steve Saffel at Titan, who read my previous horror novel, *The Chrysalis*, and saw something in those pages that said, "This guy deserves a shot at Morbius." This was a dream gig and I had a blast writing it. Thanks again, Steve.

Thank you to Jeff Youngquist at Marvel for his additional notes and edits, and to Joanna Harwood at Titan for helping shepherd the book along.

Thanks to Mark Manne for originally coming up with the idea of Morbius drinking "enhanced" blood—that kernel was the thing that really got this plot going in my head, and I appreciate it.

My deep appreciation and admiration go to composer Hans Zimmer, even though he has no idea who I am. I listened to the *Blade Runner 2049* soundtrack while writing this book; it is phenomenal mood music when writing both horror and deep emotion. And speaking of that movie, I didn't even realize when I picked that album to write to (unless it was subconscious?) that Jared Leto is in both *Blade Runner 2049* and *Morbius*, so I guess I should thank Jared, too. He doesn't know who I am either, though.

My everlasting thanks to every teacher I had who encouraged my love of writing. It's incredible what a few positive words can do for a kid's esteem and creativity.

A big thank you, as always, to my mom and my dad for always supporting my dreams. It may seem like an obvious thing but not every parent does it, and it's been a lifelong lesson to me that I'm now passing on to my daughters.

Finally, thanks to those selfsame daughters and to my wife, Kim. They are my own personal blood ties, and they mean everything to me. To paraphrase the end of my own novel, Michael Morbius may be cursed, but I am truly blessed.

ABOUT THE AUTHOR

BRENDAN DENEEN is the author of the award-winning novel *The Ninth Circle* as well as the horror novel *The Chrysalis*. He's also the author of the *Night Night Groot* picture book series for Marvel and the *Green Arrow: Stranded* original middle grade graphic novel for DC. His graphic novel work includes multiple volumes of *Flash Gordon*, an original *Island of Misfit Toys* book, a *Casper the Friendly Ghost* reboot, *Phoenix*, *Solarman* (a reboot of a Marvel/Stan Lee series), and the original graphic novel *Scatterbrain*. His short stories and essays have been published by St. Martin's Press, Reader's Digest Books, 13Thirty Press, and Necro Publications. Brendan has also been working in the publishing industry for two decades, having worked for Scott Rudin Productions, Miramax, Dimension Films, William Morris, and Macmillan, where he was the editor of the *New York Times*-bestselling *Walking Dead* series of novels, among dozens of others.

For more fantastic fiction, author events,
exclusive excerpts, competitions, limited editions and more

VISIT OUR WEBSITE
titanbooks.com

LIKE US ON FACEBOOK
facebook.com/titanbooks

FOLLOW US ON TWITTER AND INSTAGRAM
@TitanBooks

EMAIL US
readerfeedback@titanemail.com

His formula would allow Catherine to take full control over her destiny and the future of Demon-Fire. The blood of thirteen virgins, combined during the blood moon with a very specific mixture that only she possessed, would yield her magnum opus—her greatest achievement.

She was a high priestess, but that didn't mean she told her superiors everything. Not since her mother's death. They would interfere, attempt to take control of the ceremony. Most certainly they wouldn't allow a woman to ascend to the highest level of power.

Not even Thaddeus had known the full extent of her plan. She had wanted to tell him, had almost done so more than once while they lay in each other's arms after hours of passion. But no. Through Myrna—Sister Saint—Catherine knew the cult's history of misogyny. They would try to keep her from her birthright, and that she would not allow.

The power was *hers* to possess. No man—or woman, or even her sister—would hold her back.

"That?" she replied to Amanda's query. "Let's just say I'll be taking a midnight swim." She had no interest in explaining her plan. However, she wanted her sister conscious for a reason.

"Please, Catherine, listen," Amanda began. "I—"

"Catherine is dead!" she shouted into her sister's face. Then she blinked several times and smiled beneath her veil. "I am Poison-Lark, and you won't be talking your way out of this. Tonight, you will take part in something glorious, something far more important than you realize. I woke you because I want to thank you."

"Thank me?"

"Yes. By betraying me this final time, by slapping my hand away when I offered it to you, you made me realize that I am truly alone, and how much power that solitude gives me. If you had joined me, I think it would have made me weaker." She stepped even closer and looked up into her eyes.

"As you fade into unconsciousness for the final time," Catherine murmured, "I want you to know that you helped bring about the end of all that is wrong with the world, and the beginning of all that will be right and just. I am going to burn away the weak and the corrupt, and your blood will help make that happen. In many ways, yours is the most important blood of all. So yes, Amanda, yes. *Thank you*."

Tears began to fill her sister's eyes.

"But Dad, he's out there. He's still looking for Mom—for *us*."

Poison-Lark burst forth with laughter and pulled back, shaking her head.

"Still worried about Daddy, eh, Amanda?" she said. "What a waste—so pathetic!" Her eyes blazed. "After tonight is over, he won't need to find me, because I will find him. When I do, what I do to him will be a *hell* of a lot more painful than what you have coming. And I'm going to enjoy every minute of it."

Before Amanda could protest, Poison-Lark turned

away and approached the cult member who was still busy preparing the machinery.

"Shall I put her back under?" he asked, reaching into his robe.

"No," Catherine responded. "I want her awake for this. Now get back to work. We have less than an hour until midnight."

"Yes, High Priestess," he responded.

Standing at the pulpit, Poison-Lark slowly turned in a circle, taking in the entire church, its dark beauty and promise. Beneath the veil, she smiled once again. The time was nigh.

Less than an hour before everything changed.

Forever.

CHAPTER TWENTY-SIX

M

MORBIUS WANTED the mutated blood. *Needed* it.

Each time he consumed it, each time its effects began to lapse, his craving for it was even stronger than before, more desperate. After his feeding frenzy in Franklin's underground laboratory, it took a Herculean effort just to function.

He couldn't remember ever feeling like this before. Yes, he had been a slave to his thirst since the moment he had performed that damn experiment on himself. He'd felt weak with hunger, in an animalistic way, but he had never before experienced anything like the withdrawal symptoms that were currently wracking his body.

Franklin was walking slowly toward the kitchen, swaying slightly. It was possible Morbius had hit him too hard, both times, against the door and then against the floor. He hadn't meant to, not really, but he wasn't fully in control of himself. Besides, the wretched man deserved it. Even if Franklin claimed he wasn't a cult member, he had certainly been helping Demon-Fire achieve its goals, and his own as a result. By his actions, he had killed who knows how many innocent people. Like Jake…

Yet Morbius couldn't exactly point fingers. He knew that. How many innocents had he slaughtered to slake his unquenchable thirst?

Surely this was different…

He wasn't so sure.

What if Franklin was speaking the truth? What if he genuinely believed that through his work, he was helping mankind?

Morbius shook his head as he followed. *No,* it wasn't the same. His every instinct told him so. Michael killed to survive, and sought a cure that would put an end to the cycle. The cult—and through his involvement, Franklin—selected victims and murdered them to achieve their own ends. Goals that had nothing to do with the common good.

He and Franklin were nothing alike. Morbius didn't need another blow to the head to convince him the man wasn't trustworthy.

The scientist slowed and Morbius gave him a shove, keeping the man moving. Who knew how quickly Demon-Fire would figure out where Morbius had gone. He had to locate Amanda, as well. If they had her, he had to save her. She was a strong woman, and resourceful, but she was only human. Even he would need an edge to face them.

He needed the mutated blood. His pulse was racing and he felt as if he might vomit at any moment.

Franklin led him to the industrial-sized refrigerator and opened it, withdrawing a metal box sealed with a spin dial lock. The nervous man placed the box on the kitchen counter and began applying the combination, his stubby fingers slipping on it and forcing him to start over.

"Faster," Morbius instructed with a growl.

"I'm trying!" Franklin replied, his voice high and whining as he spun the dial again. "It's dark in here, and I'm nervous, and you scrambled my brains back there. Yelling at me isn't going to make this go any faster!"

Morbius chuckled darkly. There was some fire in the little man after all. Maybe the two of them really were similar in a grotesque way. Two scientists who had lived life as misfits, and who found solace in science. In another world, they might even have been colleagues.

There was the slightest clicking sound and Franklin stopped fiddling. Slowly, he opened the box, revealing several pouches of dark red blood, sitting in a rack. Without hesitation Morbius shoved the man to the floor and grabbed one, biting into it and feeling the cold delicious liquid run down his throat, trickling out the sides of his mouth.

His body reacted immediately.

The trembling subsided, and he felt a certain amount of his strength return—but not all of it. His senses expanded, as well, but not to the degree they had previously. Something was different. Something was *wrong*. He glared at Franklin, who stared up at him from the floor, the slightest hint of a smile on his face.

"Not working quite as well, eh?"

"Why do you say that?" Morbius responded, anger building within him. He grabbed another packet and held it up, ready to drink its contents, when the other scientist's words stopped him.

"I designed the formula used to manufacture that blood, Michael. I know everything about it, and I've studied your blood, too. While you were Demon-Fire's... guest. It was my idea to bait you with it in the first place. I had suspected what it would do to you. Thaddeus was dubious—he never really believed I was any good at anything—but Poison-Lark believed me. She always believed me."

Morbius heard the lust in his voice... or maybe it was love. He almost pitied the man in that moment. But not quite.

"You're addicted, Michael, and the effects of the blood will continue to lessen... you'll need more and more of it to maintain any 'high' at all. So by all means, enjoy what's in there. After that, there's not very much left. Except for, well..." With that, Franklin seemed to lose track of what he was saying.

Morbius tried to convince himself that the man was lying, and consumed the contents of the next packet. Then the next, and then the next. Until there was no more mutated blood to drink.

He closed his eyes for the briefest moment and allowed the power to run throughout his body. True, it wasn't as potent as it had been, but he felt more like himself now. Opening his eyes, he stepped closer to the scientist, who was shakily getting to his feet. His eyes were glassy and he was having trouble focusing.

Most likely it was a concussion.

"I suppose you're going to kill me now."

"That would be a mercy," Morbius hissed, his bloody spittle hitting the man's face, causing him to wince. "Demon-Fire has Amanda Saint. You're going to take me to wherever she's being held, and *maybe* I'll let you live."

Franklin peered at the ground, and Morbius thought he was trying to decide whether or not to attempt a lie. When he looked back up, his eyes had cleared.

"They're at an abandoned church. In the South Bronx. Where they first recruited me, in fact." He paused, then added, "Tonight is the night. It's all Poison-Lark could talk to Thaddeus about when they thought they were alone—the night prophesied in some sort of spell book she's obsessed with. She called it *The Lesser Key of Solomon*, and a few other names I can't recall. It contained a formula that I deciphered for them—no one else could have done that.

"I'm not supposed to know about the book, and worked from photocopies," he continued, sounding bitter. "I'm just a lowly scientist, toiling away with their blood experiments, but I stay quiet. I listen. I stand right next to them and they don't even see me."

"What do you mean, 'this is the night'?" Morbius asked, ignoring Franklin's self-consumed train of thought.

"They called it the Sacrifice of the Thirteen. Tonight. At midnight." He looked at his watch. "In forty-five minutes. In order to bring about Satan's victory on Earth, Poison-Lark is going to drain the blood from thirteen virgins and turn herself into some kind of incredibly powerful demon—and thanks to *my* formula, the powers of darkness that she will possess will be magnified a hundredfold.

"It sounds like pure nonsense," he continued, "but my formula will do its part. Poison-Lark will be transformed—such a waste—into what remains to be seen."

Morbius clenched his jaw. Amanda would be one of the thirteen. Of that he was certain.

Forty-five minutes. He couldn't fail her.

Not again.

Grabbing Franklin by the back of his shirt, he headed toward the closest window.

"What… what are you doing?"

"It's time you and I took a little trip."

CHAPTER TWENTY-SEVEN

M

IT WAS nearly midnight.

Catherine entered through the nave, now wearing the traditional red robes of Demon-Fire. Her face was still obscured by the veil, which was good since it also hid the quickness of her breath. This was it. The moment she had anticipated for months... if not years.

The pews were filled with acolytes, those who had been carefully chosen and had come from across the country, across the world, to witness this event. Word had been spread through whispers, of a secret ceremony that had been kept hidden from the upper echelons of Demon-Fire.

Many considered their current leaders weak, unwilling to take the organization to the next level. More and more acolytes had pledged their undying loyalty to her. The pendulum was shifting in her direction. Soon, she would possess immeasurable dark and supernatural powers, derived from Satan himself, and she would take her rightful place as the leader of Demon-Fire.

If only her mother could have been there to see it.

As Catherine walked up the aisle, she banished thoughts of her family. She was no longer a daughter or a sister. She was Poison-Lark. She was the Chosen One, who would bring a thousand years of darkness to the Earth. Her name would be spoken in hushed tones, inspiring fear and reverence.

Reaching the pulpit, she walked up the several stairs to the altar. Twelve of the thirteen victims were unconscious, the blood still draining from them, ever so slowly. Barely alive, but they would survive just long enough. Give her the power of their pure blood. Silently, she thanked them for their sacrifice.

Number thirteen was awake. If looks could kill…

"Amanda," she said, "you're still with us. I'm pleased, and impressed."

"Go to Hell, Catherine," Amanda spat, her face pale, huge circles under her eyes.

Catherine bristled. None of the cult members knew her true name. But then she relaxed. What did it matter now? She would only be "Catherine" for a few moments more, and then she'd be…?

She wasn't quite sure. More than Catherine.

More than even Poison-Lark.

Something entirely new. The thought sent waves of pleasure running through her body.

"If you don't mind, I'd rather bring Hell to Earth," she replied, turning away from her sister and facing the congregation. Despite the numbers—at least a hundred of them—they were utterly silent. It was as if none among them dared to breathe.

"My acolytes…" she intoned, raising up the *Lemegeton* for them all to see. There was a euphoric murmur at the sight of it. "Thank you for your support, for believing in me when the leaders of Demon-Fire didn't. You understood my vision, helped me make it reality, and I will remember. When the new age of darkness descends upon this planet, you will be granted everything you have ever desired. I swear this upon *The Lesser Key of Solomon*."

She nodded to a nearby acolyte, who stepped over and took the book from her, a look of awe on his face as he grasped the ancient grimoire. The murmuring grew louder from the red-hooded masses in front of her. She smiled beneath her veil, and then reached up to her face.

"Before the ceremony begins, I would like to bequeath upon you one last gift before I give myself over to Satan, and all that He heralds." She unhooked the veil and removed it, revealing her face to the assembled cultists for the very first time. The murmuring grew louder.

They found the gift pleasing.

"I bare myself to you. The thirteenth sacrifice has revealed to you the name I was given by my frail human parents, and now you see the face that was given to me by a frail and flawed God." She removed the robe and stepped closer to the blood-filled tank, completely unclothed. The murmuring rose in volume, and she had to speak over it.

"I stand naked before the true and pure darkness

of this world, and the previous and the next! I am Poison-Lark, the one true leader of Demon-Fire, and I commend my body and my soul to Satan so that He may live through me on this terrestrial plane, and make His will be known!"

The crowd voiced their approval as Catherine climbed the small stepladder that would allow her to enter the tank of blood. Somewhere in the distance, a bell began to chime.

It was midnight.

"Catherine!" Amanda screamed, pressing against her bonds. "Please! *Don't!*"

She looked over at her sister and gave a small smile. *You fool*, she thought. *It's already done.*

She stepped into the warm blood, and her skin instantly began to tingle. The acolytes began the chant she had distributed among them, the words taken directly from *Lemegeton*. As she lowered herself farther and farther into the tank, slowly, reveling in the moment, she found herself in complete disbelief.

It was really happening.

Her chest sank beneath the liquid, then her neck, and finally, her head. She tried to keep her eyes open but the blood stung, so she shut them. It tried to rush up her nose, but she fought it for just a moment. She knew she had to drown in order to complete the ceremony, but every instinct in her body was trying to prevent that from occurring.

Despite her attempts at keeping her mind clear, her mind raced back to her childhood. To those years when it was just her and her mother and her father. A small part of her wished she could go back and live in that time. Before Amanda. Before the true complexities of life took hold. It had been so beautiful, so perfect.

But life was neither beautiful nor perfect. The world had been perverted beyond belief, beyond reason, by those whose greed and selfishness were all-consuming. They needed to be eradicated by any means necessary.

By fire. By blood.

By Satan. By Poison-Lark.

For the final time, she cleansed her mind of everything that tethered her to her past. At the same moment, her body demanded that she inhale, and she opened her mouth. Blood poured in, running between her teeth, up her nose, filling her stomach and her lungs. White dots filled the darkness behind closed eyelids and then her consciousness slipped away.

Her body convulsed violently, and then went completely still.

Catherine Saint was dead.

MORBIUS LANDED on the roof of the church, carrying Franklin. The huge orange moon filled the sky above them.

The vampire dropped his burden as he landed gracefully on his feet, and Franklin tumbled across the gravel-strewn surface, rolling a few feet and then stopping, a crumpled mass of arms and legs.

"Ow," he said far too loudly.

"If she's not here, your death will be a painful one," Morbius promised, ignoring the man's lamentation.

"That's what I overheard," the scientist protested. "I can't make any promises." He came shakily to his feet and put his glasses back on.

Morbius ignored him and looked around. They were in what must have been a warehouse district, on top of an abandoned church that was surrounded by gutted, burned-out buildings. Somewhere nearby, another church's bells had just finished ringing twelve times. If Franklin was correct, if he wasn't lying, the ceremony would be under way at this very moment. There was no time to lose.

The church was a huge building, probably built at least a century earlier, with multiple doorways and sections to sort through. The last time Poison-Lark and Demon-Fire had abducted Amanda, they took her underground, but based on what Franklin told him, Morbius suspected that Catherine wasn't looking to hide herself away.

No, she was going big this time, and would seek to do it in the splashiest way possible.

His eyes landed on the huge stained-glass window that had been built into the church, near the back. Yes. The pulpit. Where the most sacred part of Christian masses took place. It made perfect sense, considering Demon-Fire's inverted logic. What better place to murder thirteen innocent people?

Walking over to Franklin, Morbius grabbed him by the back of his shirt.

"Wait… what?" the smaller man protested, his eyes widening with fear. He had confessed during their initial flight that he was scared of heights, had nearly thrown up more than once. "I got you where you wanted to go!"

"Let's just say that I've grown accustomed to your presence," Morbius said and he leapt, riding the wind with stomach-dropping speed. They moved without slowing toward the largest of the stained-glass windows. Franklin closed his eyes and prepared himself for impact.

CHAPTER TWENTY-EIGHT

AMANDA FOUGHT to remain conscious.

She blinked furiously against the encroaching darkness. Her sister had submerged herself in the case of blood. For the first few moments, she could see an occasional arm or leg pressed against the glass, but then she had vanished entirely within the opaque liquid.

Too much time had gone by. No one could survive that long without oxygen. Like their mother, Catherine was dead, and no dark miracle had occurred. All the death and the pain and the loss… it had been for nothing. Despite the betrayals and lies, and the fact that she herself was dying—or perhaps *because* of it all—Amanda was overwhelmed with sadness.

She loved her sister. She wished things could have been different, that she could have gotten through to her, to her mother. But both of them had kept their hidden lives so perfectly secret. Maybe it was her fault. For being so naïve. So trusting.

No, she refused to give in to such thoughts. She would rather die with trust in her heart than hatred in her soul.

The cult members who had been sitting in the pews had risen and surged toward the pulpit. Her head spinning, Amanda laughed. Such idiots. Did they really think—

CRACK!

A fist suddenly smashed against the case—from within. The glass cracked in a spider-web pattern. Amanda's dry, cracked lips opened in surprise.

"Catherine," she said, the words barely forming.

In the next moment, a crash from above echoed throughout the cavernous chamber. Amanda and all the cult members looked up with equal surprise on their faces as Michael Morbius burst through the largest of the stained-glass windows and descended rapidly toward the pulpit, snarling savagely, his teeth bared. Multicolored glass surrounded him as he fell, catching the candlelight and sparkling.

It was almost beautiful.

Strangely, in his grasp, Michael held a terrified-looking man whose limbs were twisted and whose eyes were shut tight behind crooked glasses.

A smile crept onto Amanda's face.

"Michael…" she whispered, and then she gave in to the darkness.

MORBIUS LANDED on the floor and once again released Franklin, though more gently this time.

The little man *hadn't* been lying. They were here—at least a hundred of them. A huge glass case had been placed in the center of the pulpit, full of dark blood, and thirteen female victims were strapped to crosses. One of them was Amanda, her skin paler than his own. The sight of her like this sent him into a frenzy, rage clouding his mind and turning his vision red.

The cult members surrounded him but didn't move, momentarily shocked by his dramatic arrival. Though the multicolored glass crashed to the ground and the tank of blood continued to bubble quietly, the church was otherwise silent.

One of the cultists was braver than his comrades. With a cry he ran forward toward Morbius, his voice rising to a scream, withdrawing a long, wicked knife from within his red robes. The living vampire regarded his attacker with a moment of curiosity. He actually admired the man's courage, misplaced as it was.

Reaching out, he grabbed the man by the throat and snapped his neck. The crack sounded like a gunshot in the cavernous church. The robed figure crumpled to the ground like a pile of old rags.

Again, no one dared make a sound. Out of the corner of his eye, Morbius saw Franklin take a step behind him, perhaps thinking he could avoid the conflict that was inevitably approaching.

"Listen to me!" Morbius shouted, facing the throngs. He could already feel his enhanced strength fading. He wanted more of the blood... *needed* it. The wounds he had received in the past few days were beginning to reassert themselves. Deep down, past his rage and the chemicals running through his bloodstream, Michael Morbius was *tired*.

Yet he had work to do.

"I have killed dozens of your members today," he continued, "have bathed in the blood of your brothers and sisters! I have no interest in killing any more of you! Walk away now, and let these women live. Or stay and be slaughtered, one by one. The choice is yours."

Uncertainty rippled through the throng like a physical wave. It was several minutes past midnight. Whatever dark cataclysmic event they had thought was going to transpire had refused to manifest. They'd been duped.

Of course they had.

Morbius allowed his body to relax. Perhaps he and Amanda would get out of here without a—

CRACK.

As one, everyone in front of him shifted their gaze, peering at the blood-filled vat. The liquid inside had begun to swish about—slowly at first, but then more violently. Morbius noticed a break in the glass, and watched as a large fist pounded the same spot, the crack growing larger, drops of blood starting to spill out.

A murmur rose among the crowd, quietly at first, but increasing in volume and intensity. Morbius pivoted slightly, uncertain whether the greater threat would come from the cult members or whatever was hidden by the viscous fluid.

Could that be Catherine Saint?

His preferred course would be to untie Amanda and get her out of here, yet that would mean abandoning the other twelve women. If they still lived.

Whatever lay within the case lashed out again and the glass finally shattered, gallons of blood pouring out, covering the floor and sloshing against Morbius' feet. The smell of the blood—and Franklin's formula within it—filled his senses. He fought an urge to drop to his hands and knees and lap it up like a dog.

Something the size of a human fell out of the case. As it hit the floor, it curled into a fetal position.

The cult members reacted by screaming. Chants erupted and a cold wind filled the church, putting out many of the hundreds of candles, plunging them all into gloom. Dark clouds suddenly roiled the sky, visible through the broken window, covering the blood moon as rain began to fall, coming through the jagged hole that Morbius had just created. Lightning arced overhead, illuminating the world in a shock of white and then vanishing, only to reappear moments later.

Morbius looked to Amanda and was surprised to see Franklin approaching her. Michael prepared to leap over and rip the man's throat out with his bare hands, when nearby laughter pulled his attention away. It came from the creature that had fallen out of the glass case. Still curled up in a ball, it was growing. The sound of its skin stretching and bones creaking echoed through the large room.

The creature raised its head and stared directly into his eyes.

"Hello, Michael," it rumbled, its voice the guttural sound of a nightmare.

As it rose to its feet, the chants increased. The figure was at least ten feet tall and still growing. Its skin was no longer human flesh, but dark green and leathery, with pulsing veins and tiny black spikes appearing every couple of inches. The creature's ears were long and tall and pointed, and its face was elongated into an almost wolf-like snout, huge teeth growing out of gums, dark blood flowing freely as the few human teeth still left in there were pushed unceremoniously out and onto the wet floor.

There was a horrible ripping sound as flesh and bones made way and small wings appeared on the creature's back, close to the shoulder blades. Its legs twisted until they were arched almost like an insect's, and they ended in hairy hooves which stood firm in the pool of blood. At the ends of each arm were three-fingered hands and foot-long claws glimmering in what remained of the candlelight.

A smile broke out onto the creature's twisted face. If indeed this *had* been Poison-Lark, her features had been swept away with her humanity.

"You're too late," it said, taking a step closer to Morbius, its body continuing to expand.

"Catherine…" Morbius replied, the rain pelting him, lightning flashing in the sky again, illuminating the two monsters as they faced each other. Then he added in a sardonic tone, "What happened to your face?"

The creature bellowed in rage, echoed by its red-robed sycophants, who surged forward. Morbius ducked as the thing that used to be Catherine swiped its claws, raking him across the back. He grimaced against the pain and rolled forward through the wash of blood, but immediately found himself surrounded on all sides by cult members. He was overwhelmed. Outnumbered.

Yet if this was going to be his final night on Earth, then he was going to go down fighting.

Morbius burst up and out of the enraged cluster of cultists, slashing several of them as he did so. They screamed and fell back, blood spraying out and spattering everywhere as he leapt into the air. The wind continued to flow through the large hole in the ceiling, a product of the rising storm, and it enabled Morbius to hover above their heads. From a couple of dozen feet in the air, the odds somehow looked worse. More cultists were streaming in through multiple doors, the entire church full of angry men and women who wanted just one thing.

The death of Michael Morbius.

As he contemplated his next move, Morbius watched the creature's wings grow and spread out, and then begin to move. Flapping slowly, and then faster. Before he could react, the monster came through the air directly at him.

"Great," he muttered, seconds before the violent impact.

FRANKLIN TRIED to keep his breathing under control. It wasn't easy with a smashed-in nose.

He watched, along with hundreds of Demon-Fire members, as the living vampire known as Morbius jumped into the air above the pews, followed by the monster that apparently used to be the woman upon whom he had a major crush.

He was pretty sure he was over it now.

No one seemed to know he was even there. Which was perfectly fine with him. Cult members were still entering to his left and his right and from the nave, too. He knew that they had been actively recruiting during his time working for Poison-Lark and Thaddeus, but even he was surprised by the sheer number of them. He recognized a few faces here and there, when he could see past the hoods and shadows, but thankfully no one seemed to care that he was there to witness what might be the most important ceremony in the cult's history.

If he waited for exactly the right moment, he thought he could slip out unnoticed. Morbius had forgotten about him completely—he had other matters on his mind as he battled the winged monster up near the ceiling.

Trying to decide which door would allow for the easiest escape, his eye was caught by the thirteen crosses behind him. Against his better judgement he looked up, and was filled with remorse when he saw the women strapped to the huge beams of wood, their eyes all closed. Even in the limited light, he knew enough about physiology to realize that twelve of them were already dead, their faces pale and their chests still.

His stomach sank.

He was a hypocrite who had been responsible for his own fair share of dead innocents, but since the arrival of Michael Morbius, something had begun to awaken in him. He wasn't sure what it was, or why it was happening, but Franklin was starting to regret what he had done. All of that work, and for what…? So Poison-Lark could transform herself into a hideous monster and bring more hurt and terror into the world?

Franklin had fallen for the pitch she and Thaddeus had fed him, about a better world, but that particular world wasn't looking so very appealing.

His eyes landed on the thirteenth sacrifice, the woman who was right behind him. At first, he thought it was Poison-Lark. He looked up at the creature in the sky, and then back at the woman on the cross. No, it wasn't Lark, but it looked a lot like her.

The sister! The one Morbius had been babbling about. Even before that, Franklin had heard rumors about a sacrificial virgin who had been there when their plans were thwarted in San Francisco. He knew Demon-Fire had been hunting for her ever since.

It all made sense now.

He stepped closer to her. She was so beautiful. Like Poison-Lark, but softer somehow. Without even really thinking about it, he reached up and gently touched her hand.

Her eyes opened.

His jaw dropped.

"Help me…"

CHAPTER TWENTY-NINE

M

MORBIUS WAS outmatched. Significantly.

He couldn't believe how strong the creature was. Or the fact that it still had Catherine's eyes—and those eyes seemed to be enjoying the airborne battle, even if it was still getting used to its new wings. For the moment, Morbius' experience was keeping the battle even, but that wouldn't last long.

As he grappled with his opponent, Morbius looked down by the altar and was surprised to see Franklin talking to Amanda. What was the little man saying to her? If he even thought about hurting her…

While he was distracted, the creature took the opportunity to bite down into his shoulder and neck, ripping out a chunk of flesh and spitting it into the growing shadows of the church. Blood burst from the gaping wound and Morbius screamed in agony.

"Now I see why you like doing that," the monster

said, licking his blood off its lips. "Ahh, and you still have some of Franklin's formula rolling around inside of you. Good, isn't it?"

Morbius had already been losing strength, and this accelerated the process, so he did the only thing he could think of. Quickly—faster than the creature could expect—he wrapped his arms around its body, including the wings, and they both plummeted. As he had days earlier—he wasn't even sure how long ago it was at this point—Morbius twisted his body so the creature would take the brunt of the landing.

The impact was staggering. They crashed into the pews, killing at least two cult members, shattering them in an explosion of wooden shrapnel.

The creature was stunned, and Morbius took the opportunity to grab a piece of wood that had broken away. He shoved it into the monster's shoulder. It screamed and batted him away, sending him flying into an ancient cloth-covered piano, shattering that as well.

Cult members watched in awe, frozen in place as he climbed to his feet, teeth bared. And then they, too, attacked. Regardless, Morbius roared at their approach. He might have been weak, might have been bleeding from multiple wounds, but he wasn't about to give up the fight.

AMANDA CLAWED her way back into consciousness. She felt like she was going to throw up, and her arm hurt like hell. Glancing down, she saw that the blood was still being pulled out of her, through a tube that was pouring uselessly out onto the floor. The case had been destroyed, shattered into broken glass and twisted metal.

And there was a strange-looking man looking up at her. Misshapen, his forehead wrinkled in confusion or concern, or both.

"Help me…"

He was frozen, perhaps terrified by the battle raging around them. She slowly realized that this was the man Morbius had been holding during his dramatic entrance. But who the hell *was* he?

A loud crash distracted her. Looking over, she saw Michael lying in the ruins of a shattered piano.

Michael.

Despite everything, a smile worked its way onto Amanda's face. Catherine had lied. He *hadn't* abandoned her, had probably been trying to get back to her this entire time. Then her smile faded, and she remembered.

Had Morbius really killed her mother?

Amanda shook her head. She had to get free, struggled against the binds that held her, but they were too strong. And her head was spinning. She didn't know how much longer she could stay conscious. *Damn it.*

She looked back down at the twisted man.

"Hey!"

He blinked, and then seemed to focus on her. Opened his mouth, but didn't say anything. He glanced at a nearby doorway, the one that led to the area behind the chancel. It was empty, no more Demon-Fire members coming through.

He was weighing his options.

"You came here with Morbius, right?" she asked.

He shifted his gaze to the living vampire, who was trying to pick himself up from the rubble. As he did, he was swarmed by several of the cult members. They kicked him and stabbed at him with huge knives.

The twisted man looked back at Amanda, and nodded.

"He needs our help," she said. "Which means *I* need *your* help." She licked her dry lips with a tongue that felt like leather. "Untie me. *Please.*"

The man took a step toward the doorway, toward escape, but then stopped. It almost looked as if he was being tugged in two different directions at once, by an unseen force. Finally, he moved to the altar and lifted himself up onto it. His movements were awkward as he leaned forward, nearly falling off, but he managed to grab hold of one of the wooden beams that held Amanda. His fingers fumbled with the rope that kept her arm immobile and, after what felt like hours, managed to untie it.

Amanda pulled her arm free, gasping at the agonizing combination of pain and numbness, but she powered through it and reached up, working to free her other hand.

"My feet!" she said, and the man jumped down to untie the rope around her legs. As Amanda worked at the bindings around her other arm, she looked back to where she had last seen Michael. The creature that had once been her sister barreled toward him, while those cult members who still lived scrambled to get out of the way.

The monster—*Catherine*—slammed into him with incredible force, sending them both crashing through a pillar, bringing a huge section of the ceiling down on top of them. Torrents of rain fell through the new opening, mixing with the broken concrete, shards of glass, and pools of blood. Once again, a jagged vein of lightning burned itself across the sky and then disappeared, its visual echo remaining for a moment before that too vanished.

The peal of thunder was almost deafening.

Amanda freed her arm at almost the exact same moment that the man finished untying her legs and she fell forward, surprised and unable to move her limbs and body quickly enough to jump down. She prepared to slam face-first onto the gore-soaked floor.

But the man surprised her again by rushing to catch her, though it was more of a cushion than a catch as they both went sprawling down the altar steps. Amanda blinked and looked down into his face. He gave a small, apologetic smile.

"I'm Franklin."

"Amanda."

"I know, I—"

Abruptly, she lunged up and struck an incoming cult member with a nasty uppercut to the bottom of his chin. The man went flying back, his arms outstretched, losing his grip on the knife he'd been holding.

The exertion took its toll, however, and she fell back into Franklin's arms.

"We need to get you out of here," he said as she pulled the tube out of her arm, grimacing at the pain.

"No," she said through gritted teeth. "We have to help Morbius."

Franklin seemed to think about this for a moment, and then nodded.

"Okay," he said. "But… how?"

THE CREATURE'S strength seemed to be increasing every minute, and it was still growing.

The partial collapse of the roof had given Morbius an opportunity to think. The monster that was formerly Catherine had taken the brunt of the impact, and was still trapped under a huge section of the pillar that had smashed down on them. He made his way out of the debris and watched as Amanda punched a cult member, and then fell back into someone's arms.

Franklin.

The little man was helping her. Morbius shook his head. People continued to surprise him. Usually in bad ways, but every once in a while, the surprise was pleasant. Still, what the man had done to Jake…

Morbius' conflicted thoughts were interrupted as two cult members came charging at him, one from each side. He glanced at both, then took a half step back as they neared and grabbed both of them by the scruffs of their necks. He slammed their faces together to the sound of cracking bones and ruptured flesh. He let their corpses drop into an unmoving heap, and moved toward Amanda.

"Michael!" she shouted as she saw him approaching. "Look—"

Something grabbed him around his ankle and he went down, face-first, and clawed at the ground as he was pulled backward, leaving huge scrapes gouged into the blood-covered floor. He managed to flip himself over and saw that the creature had taken hold of him, was leaning down to take another bite out of his neck.

Pulling from every reserve of energy in his body, Morbius lunged forward, under the gaping maws of the monster, pulling his foot out of its grasp. He grabbed its neck with his forearm and flipped himself up and onto the creature's back, digging his sharp claws into its muscles to ensure his purchase there.

The monster roared in pain, then flapped its wings and took to the air again.

MANY CULT members watched the creature as it ascended with Morbius on its back, while others turned their attention to Amanda and Franklin. She bent over quickly and scooped a machete from the ground. Franklin stared at her with huge eyes.

"What are you waiting for?" she asked. "Grab a weapon."

Shocked into action by her words, Franklin obeyed and found a blood-soaked knife of his own. The two stood back-to-back as the cult members approached, laughing at the pitiable display of defiance.

FROM THE back of the creature, Morbius saw the danger Amanda faced, and bared his teeth in frustration. The tide was turning, and not in his favor.

The monster still tried to claw at him, but he was perfectly situated in the middle of its back. His fingers were still embedded in his opponent's flesh, and when he dug in, its flight pattern change slightly.

Which gave him an idea.

He pulled his claws free and grabbed onto both wings, attempting to keep them from flapping. They were incredibly strong, and Morbius fought against their movement with all his strength, causing them to stop almost entirely. Once again they plummeted, and he tried as hard as he could to force their descent toward the group of cult members who were bearing down on Amanda and Franklin.

They crashed just as another bolt of lightning lit the sky. This time, the pounding thunder was instantaneous. A half-dozen cult members were crushed beneath the weight of the creature, killed instantly. Amanda and Franklin threw themselves backward, out of the way of the impact, though more blood now ran at their feet.

Morbius was still perched atop the monster, its head twisted at an unnatural angle as it struggled to get its bearings. Several pieces of shattered pew had pierced its body. Black blood spewed forth.

Franklin stared at the scene with a strange look on his face.

"Its neck!" he cried. "Morbius! Look!"

At first he didn't understand what the man meant, but then it hit him. It was so obvious. The creature's neck was in full view, stretched taut, glinting in the light that came from the sky outside. Despite the spikes that covered the monstrous form, its veins still pulsed.

It was vulnerable.

The scientific part of Michael's brain reasserted itself. The blood in the vat had been taken from the thirteen women, to mix with an alchemical version of Franklin's formula. So the blood currently pumping through the creature's veins would be infused with incredible strength. It could change the course of the battle in an instant.

He looked to Amanda, but couldn't read her expression. Did she know what he was contemplating? She knew how addicted he had become to the mutated blood, but still...

The creature began to stir, its muscles tensing for an attack. Morbius bent over and placed his teeth against its neck. The skin was thick, almost like armor. He'd have to bite down with incredible force to get through.

The thought of drinking the monster's blood— not cold and stored in plastic, but warm and fresh within a living creature's flesh—was enough to make him almost giddy.

Morbius began to bite down.

Prepared himself for the rush.

Then he stopped.

"Do it!" Franklin screamed.

No.

Morbius' desperation, his *need*, was the thing that was making him weak. No matter how the blood made him feel, how much strength it gave him, it wouldn't last—and it was turning him into a slave. Who knew what this creature's demonic blood would do to him? How much more addicted he would become.

Was that who he was? He was cursed, yes, had been gripped by events that raced inexorably out of his control. He had killed the innocent, fought against the good, but deep down, he had never lost his humanity.

Not all of it. He clung to it fiercely.

At this moment, however, he felt it slipping away. There was only a sliver left.

Despite its initial promise as a cure, each time he'd drunk the blood mutated by Franklin's formula he'd felt less and less like himself. Less like Michael the man. Less even like Morbius the living vampire. The world might see him as a monster, but he was always a choice away from regaining his humanity. Or enough of it to keep hope alive.

Michael pulled back without penetrating the monster's neck. In response, the creature rolled to its left and Morbius jumped off, barely avoiding its flailing claws. He landed next to Amanda and Franklin and crouched, ready for the next assault.

"Hi," she said, smiling grimly.

"Hello," he responded, frowning. He might have just saved his soul, but he had also doomed all three of them. A group of cult members surrounded them and began to close in, while the creature rose up to its full height, beating its wings, and launched itself into the air.

"I'm sorry," he added.

"For not drinking my sister's probably poisonous blood?" she replied. "I forgive you." She looked around them. "If this is how I die, at least I'm doing it with my best friend."

"Ummm…" Franklin intoned, his voice rising a couple of octaves. "That's very sweet. but we have a situation here." A low rumble of laughter filled the church. It was the creature, hovering twenty feet up. Lightning appeared in the cloud-filled sky above it. The bolts were coming more frequently.

"It's *over!*" the creature bellowed as the cult members stood ready, tense with anticipation, bloodlust in their eyes. "You have managed to escape me again and again, Amanda. And Morbius, you have killed *so* many. Katabolik, Arachne, Justin, Thaddeus, countless of my acolytes… and my *mother*."

Morbius flinched.

"He *murdered* her, Amanda," the winged monster cried. "And still you stand with him? You *forgive* him?!"

"I trust Michael more than I will ever trust you, Catherine," she answered, "or *whatever* you are."

The creature let out a scream of rage and flapped its wings violently, swooping closer to the three of them on the pulpit. The cult members drew near, as well. Another bolt of lightning filled the sky.

"Very well," it said, an evil smile spreading across its face. "Then you'll die together, and I will make sure that it is a long, torturous, *enjoyable* death."

The mention of Amanda's mother jogged something in Morbius' memory. His mind flashed back to Malevolence, Maine, where the cult had again tried to kill Amanda. Sister Saint had died... violently, horribly... but not by his hand. There was one item that had confirmed to him who she was, and he had taken it off her still-warm corpse. Had kept it hidden within a small pocket inside his belt, waiting for the right moment to tell Amanda the truth of that night, and bequeath it to her.

What better time than the moment before their death?

Digging into the pocket, Morbius withdrew the item and held it out to Amanda. A small piece of jewelry. She stared at it with confusion, and then sudden recognition.

"How... where did you get that?"

"Catherine wasn't lying," he said. "I was there when your mother died—but I didn't kill her. I took this off her body and waited to give it to you."

Amanda lifted the jewelry from Morbius' palm. As if on cue, the monster and the cult members charged toward them. They were moments from pain and death, but a smile appeared on her face as her fingers closed around the ring.

"What are you doing?" Franklin asked. "Are you proposing to her? *Now?*" He gaped and brandished his knife.

"Shut up!" Morbius yelled without bothering to glance over at the small, confused man. "I'm sorry I waited so long," he said to Amanda. "And I'm sorry for the things I've said to you since we met. I don't always choose my words or actions wisely."

"Thank you, Michael," she said. "For everything." Holding the ring in one hand and the machete in the other, she closed her eyes—appearing ready for death— when her fist began to glow.

Michael stared at her hand, at the raw energy emanating from it. And then he smiled, too.

Maybe this battle wasn't over after all.

CHAPTER THIRTY

IT FELT as if her hand was on fire.

The energy raced up Amanda's arm and filled her body with a heat that was both transcendental and deeply terrifying at the same time. Guttural voices emerged in her head, speaking some kind of ancient language, and she thought she could hear her mother whispering, too.

"*Mom?*" she said. Or did she think it?

She wasn't entirely sure.

The entire church went silent and a jagged slice of lightning froze in the sky. The monster—her sister… whatever it was—was impossibly unmoving up in the air, its wings halted. Morbius was as still as a statue, staring at her, and was that a *smile* starting to appear on his face?

Shadows crept in from every corner of the chamber, covering the candles and the mostly destroyed pews and the cult members and the monster and Franklin and Morbius, until Amanda was entirely alone on a plane of utter darkness. Except for the glow that emanated from her fist.

Her next thought was that she should be afraid— should be consumed by fear at this unexpected turn of events. But she felt no fear whatsoever.

After a moment, a voice called out.

A young girl. She recognized that voice.

It was Catherine.

Her sister stepped out of nothingness and appeared before her. Nine years old. Maybe ten. Wearing her favorite dress. Her hair back in a ponytail. Amanda had forgotten that it was her preferred hairstyle back then. Shades of Poison-Lark to come.

"Catherine?" Amanda said, her voice barely above a whisper.

Young Catherine smiled and stepped closer. Something about her didn't look right, though. The whites of her eyes were more like gray, and her smile was just a little too big for her face.

"What's happening?"

"It was you all along," Young Catherine said, though now that she was closer, the voice wasn't quite right either.

"Who are you?" Amanda demanded.

"I'm exactly who you want me to be," her little older sister said. "I'm the thing that has always been inside her, and your mother, and is now inside you. I *like* it here. The other two wanted it more, but this is where I've always belonged. I bet you can feel it, too."

"I don't want this…"

"Yes. You do. And a part of you always has. That part of you that emerged on the subway with that man. All you have to do is say yes.

"Say it. *Now*."

"I… I can't," Amanda stammered.

Black blood began pouring out of Young Catherine's eyes and ears and nose and mouth, but the little girl was laughing.

"Stop it!" Amanda screamed.

"NOW!" the little girl screamed and she kept laughing, the noise echoing against the surrounding blackness.

"YES!" Amanda shouted, the word washing over her, along with a feeling of absolute power and the unmitigated wrongness of the utterance. She loved it. And she hated herself for loving it.

Amanda Saint blinked, a blink that lasted less than a second and a hundred thousand millennia, and when she opened her eyes again, she was back in the church. Time had resumed, but the creature in the air and the enraged cult members had stopped their attack. They were all staring at her outstretched hand. Her mother's ring sat in the middle of her palm, glowing brightly, casting sharp shadows across them all.

"Where did you get that?!" the monster screamed, its dark wings beating furiously, the resultant wind sending debris flying. One unlucky cult member was impaled from behind by a jagged piece of wood. "It's supposed to be *mine*!"

"Then come and get it, bitch," Amanda said with a slight grin on her face.

The monster bellowed again and dove at them as Amanda closed her fist around the ring. The cult members surged forward as well. Though he looked exhausted and was in excruciating pain, Morbius dove into them, gutting two of them before they could even register his movement.

As the creature came within striking distance, Amanda swung her fist and caught it across the face, a blow that was accentuated by a burst of light, and it went flying into a corner where it landed in a disheveled heap. Startled at what had happened, but ready to finish this once and for all, Amanda sprinted toward it.

She reached the creature and brought her glowing fist back for another blow, but the monster reacted quickly, slashing out with its claws and catching Amanda in the stomach. Three long gashes appeared there and blood poured out. Amanda stared at the holes in her body with genuine surprise, but something told her to hold her iridescent hand against the wounds, which she did for a moment. When she removed her fist, her skin was whole, as if she had never been injured in the first place.

She looked up at the monster, and smiled.

MORBIUS CONTINUED to make his way through the cult members, but quickly realized that it was hopeless.

There were just too many of them. He was subduing them at a stupefying rate, but he was also suffering cut after cut, and he was slowly bleeding out.

He wouldn't last much longer.

Glancing over, he saw Amanda battling the creature. A tableau that should not have existed. It was incredible to see her like this, though, to see her fist glowing with raw energy. Even so, the sisters were too evenly matched. They rained blows upon each other, the kind that would destroy normal humans, but nothing seemed to have sufficient effect to shift the balance.

He had to do something.

A trio of cultists jumped on top of him, landing punches and cutting into his leg, but Morbius threw them off without even bothering to see where they landed. He took a broad leap and sped toward Amanda and the monster. He knew what he had to do. He knew what it would cost. And knew that it was worth it.

He thought of Martine. If this worked, he would never see her again. The idea nearly made him stop, but she would want him to do this. She would be proud.

Morbius struck the creature at full speed, knocking it to its side. It roared and swiped at him, catching him with its claws along the side of his head, nearly taking his ear clean off. He screamed as blood burst out of him, nearly passed out but clung to consciousness as if it was all that he had left in the world. Which, he realized, it was.

Twisting wildly, he positioned himself on top of the creature, holding onto its shoulder, and glanced back quickly at Amanda. He hoped she understood.

"Michael… what are you—? No!"

Morbius bit down into the monster's neck, using all the strength he had left, and felt its blood explode into his mouth. He had expected it to be delicious, like all the other mutated blood he'd consumed since that first pouch given to him by Liz and Fabian.

He couldn't have been more wrong.

This blood was like acid. It burned his mouth and his throat and his stomach. It felt like it was eating him alive from the inside out. Yet Morbius kept on drinking.

The creature clawed at him, doing more damage, but Morbius held on. Amanda ran to his side and attacked the monster as well, battering its face with blow after blow that should have wrecked her fists. Its face split open, and after one particularly damaging blow, one of the monster's eyes burst like an overripe fruit being hit by a hammer.

It screamed in pain and rage.

Still, Morbius drank.

Until his body revolted and he fell away from his poisonous meal, collapsing onto the gore-soaked ground. Then, at last, the blackness of death consumed him.

AMANDA PULLED her hand back from the latest blow she had landed, her fist covered in blood and mucus and who knew what else. She was out of breath but it wasn't from exertion. It was from pure excitement.

The strange voices in her head told her to keep attacking but she fought them, realized they were growing stronger with every minute that passed. Even so, she refused to give in. She wasn't her sister. And she wasn't her mother.

The creature was motionless on the ground in front of her. Barely breathing, and it was shrinking, its green leathery skin turning softer and pinker. Catherine's features were starting to take shape again.

Amanda crouched and looked around. The cult members were watching her, watching the creature, confusion etched across their features. Half of them seemed ready to fight; the other half were scoping out the exits.

She stood straight and faced them. The rain fell on her and the wind whipped her hair around her face, and her fist continued to glow.

"Who's next?!" she shouted.

The cult members turned and ran. Within minutes they were gone, leaving only carnage and death in their wake.

"Typical," Amanda muttered.

She turned back around. The monster was gone as well, replaced by her sister. Naked. Small.

Dying.

Amanda kneeled next to her. She pushed the hair out of her face. For a moment, she saw the little girl that Catherine had once been, and it broke her heart. She cried. Not for the Catherine in front of her, but for the girl who once was.

"Amanda…" she said, her breath coming in labored gasps.

"I'm here, Catherine. I'm with you."

"I-I'm sorry…" her sister replied, her face wet.

Tears rolled down Amanda's face as well, but she couldn't find any other words. A moment later, her sister was gone. As her head lolled to the side, Amanda noticed two bloody holes in her neck.

"Michael!" she yelled and quickly got up.

He lay several feet away from her, sprawled out on the ground, arms thrown up over his head. Amanda reached him in seconds and shook him gently. He didn't respond. She placed her ear on his chest, but heard nothing. Moved her head to his mouth. Felt nothing. He wasn't breathing.

Morbius was dead.

"No," she said and pounded him on the chest. "No!"

Suddenly there were voices whispering in the church, and she stood up quickly and spun, ready to face this latest danger. Had a cult member been stupid enough to return?

No… there were red eyes staring at her from the shadows. Dozens of them. She couldn't see any bodies, but the glowing eyes bore into her soul. They wanted her.

And part of her wanted them, too.

Wanted everything they offered.

The whispers grew louder. All she had to do was walk toward them. Let the darkness envelop her.

It would be so easy.

She raised her fist and stared at it. It was glowing brighter, and she could feel the power filling her entire body. She liked this feeling. A *lot*. And why shouldn't she? She had been betrayed by everyone she had ever loved. She *deserved* this.

But as she looked closer, she saw dark veins spreading out from where she was holding the ring… her mother's ring. Her entire hand was slowly turning black. It almost looked as if it was… rotting.

Amanda looked over at Morbius' corpse. He had held onto this ring for her. He'd had no idea it was anything more than a keepsake, a connection to the family she'd once had. He had done it out of friendship. Despite everything, he was the best friend she had ever had.

Amanda Saint turned her back on the eyes in the darkness. The whispers grew louder, infuriated, demanding that she join them. They could give her so much. She could rule the world.

Kneeling down, she placed her fist on Morbius' chest. The light from the ring seemed to grow weaker, as if it knew what she wanted to do. She closed her eyes, concentrated, bent the energy to her will.

"Come back to me," she whispered.

The glow increased again until the entire church was filled with it. Amanda bent over farther and hugged the dead body that used to be her friend, the living vampire, Michael Morbius.

The shadows burned away, the eyes disappeared,

and then the light itself vanished in a burst. All was silent and dark except for the rain that continued to fall through the holes in the ceiling, and the half dozen candles that had survived the battle.

CHAPTER THIRTY-ONE

MORBIUS SAT up and vomited black blood across the floor.

"What the hell…?" he said, looking around. The church had been devastated during the fight, the bodies of slain cult members strewn everywhere. As well as Catherine. Returned to her human form. Dead.

Shakily, Morbius got to his feet.

Amanda stood on the pulpit. She took the last of the twelve other sacrifices down from a cross and then laid her on the ground. All twelve of the sacrifices' corpses were now on the floor, waiting to be covered.

Amanda noticed that Morbius was awake and she walked over to him, a grim look on her face. Her right hand was clenched in a blackened fist. She had a look in her eyes that he'd never seen before. It was more than sadness, more than strength.

"You're alive," she said.

"Thanks to you, I'm guessing," he responded, looking at her fist. "The ring?"

She opened her fingers and dust fell out, drifting to the floor and being absorbed by the rivulets of blood that continued to flow.

"Gone."

"I'm sorry," he said. "I know it was your mother's. It meant something to you."

Amanda laughed, but there wasn't a trace of happiness in that laugh.

"Honestly, Michael? It means more to me that you took it, that you kept it. So… thank you." They stared at each other for a long moment. In the far-off distance, they could hear sirens heading their way.

"But I have to ask," she continued. "Catherine said… she told me that you murdered our mother. I won't be mad at you, I promise, but is it true?"

"Yes," he replied. "And no. It was when we were in Malevolence. After the woman who claimed she was Mrs. Agnes attacked us that final time, you passed out."

Amanda smiled ruefully. "Yes, well, I was a very different person then. But wait, are you saying—?"

"Agnes was your mother, Amanda. In disguise. When I defended myself, she fell back and onto her own ax, splitting her head in two. She died instantly. I'm sorry."

Amanda looked down, but quickly back up. Her eyes were hard.

"No, it's okay. I wish you had told me sooner, but that's not something I need to understand—it was your call." She paused, then added, "I guess I never really knew her at all. Or Catherine. The only family I have left is my father, and I'll do everything in my power to find him."

"Of course."

"You don't have to help me any longer, Michael. You've done *more* than enough."

Morbius stepped closer to her. "You just saved my life. I won't rest until we've found your father."

"And Martine."

"And Martine," Morbius confirmed, nodding. He suddenly cocked his head and looked around. "Where's Franklin?"

Amanda turned and looked, too. "With everything that happened, I completely forgot about him. I guess—I guess he's gone."

"He was the source of so much evil," Morbius mused, walking amidst the blood and the bodies. "But maybe he earned his redemption tonight by helping us against Demon-Fire."

The sirens grew louder.

"Time to go," Amanda said.

Morbius nodded one more time, took a last look at all the death and destruction, and took hold of Amanda. Then he jumped up and through one of the holes in the roof of the church. The clouds still hovered overhead, the rain continuing to fall, but the full moon was beginning to peek through. No longer a blood moon, it was a beautiful sight.

They looked each other in the eye, and their expressions spoke volumes. The things they had been through to get to this moment. The things that they knew, on some level, would come next.

As the police cars approached the husk of a church below, Morbius twisted into the wind, riding it. Their bodies were swallowed by the darkness while the rain still fell.

EPILOGUE

MORBIUS AND Amanda sat by the window in a coffee shop, staring at the house across the street.

It was evening, the sun just beginning to set in the west, its red-tinged rays burning across the sky in a beautiful display. It had been several days since the events of the church. The news had gone haywire with the story of a horrific cult-related sacrifice. Very few of the facts were accurate, but one was incontrovertible: the families of twelve innocent local women were in mourning.

Amanda still beat herself up over that fact, even though she knew she had done the best she could.

No one had placed her or Michael at the scene of the crime. Their names were never so much as mentioned during all the news coverage, or even in the rumors that followed. Neither was Franklin's. Morbius wondered if he'd ever see the little man again. If he did, he was unsure if he'd consider him a friend or an enemy.

He decided it didn't matter right now, and refocused on the task at hand.

He was wearing a baseball cap pulled low over his face to hide his features, as well as a trench coat. The last thing they needed was for some friendly neighborhood nuisance to bother them while they completed their final mission in New York City.

"Do you think she's home?" Morbius said absentmindedly, staring out the window and clutching an untouched cup of coffee with both hands. Amanda stared at him and smiled. It wasn't often that she had seen the living vampire nervous.

"There's only one way to find out," she replied, sipping at her tea. It was hot, and the heat felt so good on her throat.

She and Morbius had spent the last several days holed up in a dingy motel in Queens, nursing their wounds and sharing each other's stories from when they'd been separated. Neither could believe what the other had gone through to finally reconnect at the abandoned church. Liz's betrayal and death, which brought Amanda to tears despite everything. The underground arena. Secrets unearthed and exposed to the light of day, and to the darkness of the night.

Sins spoken and forgiven.

If nothing else, their friendship was stronger than ever.

"So, after you work up your courage and do this, are you ready for the next step in our search?"

Morbius continued to stare out the window.

"Las Vegas?" he murmured, still stuck on the task he was about to complete. If he could summon the nerve. In many ways, he would rather take on another hundred Demon-Fire cultists than do this.

"Yep," Amanda confirmed, shaking her head. "But Demon-Fire has been badly damaged, and that's where my research says many of the surviving leaders have gathered, including those from the church. There are still plenty of local chapters, but their hierarchy has been hurt.

"Once I had that focal point for my research, plus that note that was left for us in Maine, I found evidence that my father might be there, too," she said. "This may be it, Michael. We may really track him down, once and for all. And then we can focus on finding Martine."

Morbius' attention was drawn away from the window by the mention of Martine. He closed his eyes for a moment and saw her clearly, every nuance, every detail. It was as if she were so close that he could actually touch her. Quickly, he opened his eyes and her image vanished. No. He was past losing himself in false hope, in manufactured happiness.

"Well then," he said, "Las Vegas it is. Back across the country, and who knows what kind of trouble we'll get into on the way."

Amanda shook her head. "I've had enough trouble to last a lifetime." She took a sip of her tea. "And so have you."

"Do you miss it?"

"Hmm…?" Amanda intoned, now the one staring out the window. She looked back at Michael. "Miss what?"

"The ring," he said. "The power."

She thought about it for a second, even glanced at her hand. The blackness had subsided for the most part. It would probably be gone in another day or so.

"No," she said. "Not the power, at least. I mean—don't get me wrong—it felt pretty amazing to be able to do those things. But there was a darkness beneath all of it that I… I just didn't like. I'm glad it's gone."

"Ah," was all the response Michael gave.

"But the ring itself?" she continued. "On some level, I miss that, but then again, I don't. Once upon a time, it represented the love between my parents. The 'incorruptible bond' they shared, but I guess that bond was built on a lie. Who knows if she ever really loved him? If that evil was always there. If it wasn't, if Demon-Fire corrupted her and turned her away from my dad, then I hate them more than ever.

"Anyway, to answer your question… yes. And no."

Morbius nodded. "I understand."

Amanda stared at him for a long moment. "I know what you're trying to do, Michael."

"Oh yes?" he said, aware of exactly what she was going to say. "Enlighten me."

"You're stalling. Put down that coffee you're pretending to drink and go across that street. I'm *ordering* you."

Morbius smiled and pushed the cup away. She was right and he knew it.

"Fine," he said, and he stood up. "I'm going. Wish me luck."

"Good luck, Michael," she said, but he didn't move right away. He stared at Amanda with a strange look on his face.

"What is it?" she asked.

"After…" he began, and seemed to struggle for words. She had never seen him quite like this before. So vulnerable. "After all we've been through," he continued, "I just wanted to thank you, and to apologize."

"Michael, you don't have to apolo—"

"No, I do," he interrupted. "The way I speak to you sometimes, the way I treat you. I don't mean to, but ever since the experiment that changed me into… *this*, I haven't always been able to control myself. Verbally. Physically. But no matter what I've said or done to you—in the past but also in the future—know that I care deeply about you, Amanda. You are the closest thing I've had to a friend since I cursed myself with this condition, and I deeply appreciate that friendship."

Amanda took Michael's hand in her own. "I feel the same way, Michael. Almost everyone I've ever loved has betrayed me, but not you. Not when the chips were down. You've saved me, I've saved you. In more ways than one, I think that's the truest definition of friendship. And trust me, if you lash out at me in the future, I promise to forgive you—and give it right back to you. Deal?"

Morbius smiled at his friend.

"Deal."

"Now stop stalling and cross the street!" she demanded. She turned away, indicating that she was done with this particular conversation.

Morbius turned and walked out of the coffee shop.

It was a beautiful evening, cool but not cold, with almost no breeze whatsoever. Traffic stopped at the red light, and Michael walked slowly across the street. There were dozens of people milling about on the sidewalk but he didn't see them at all. He felt entirely alone in this moment as he approached the house. He didn't want to do this—it wasn't the kind of thing he was good at, but he had to do it. He knew that.

Reaching the front door, he hesitated, his pale white finger already touching the glowing doorbell. He could feel Amanda's eyes burning a hole in his back. Morbius inhaled a deep breath and then let it out.

Do it, he told himself.

He pressed down and heard the chime ring within the house. After a moment, a voice called out.

"Coming...!"

A few seconds later, the door opened and Morbius found himself facing a woman in her thirties, hair pulled back in a messy bun, drying her hands on a dishtowel. As she took in Morbius' face, her eyes widened with the slightest suggestion of horror, but she stood her ground.

He liked her already.

"Can... can I help you?" she asked.

"Hello, Jenny," Morbius responded. "My name is Michael. I'm sorry to bother you but I... I was a friend of Jake's. I... I was with him when he..." He wasn't sure if he should say the words, but this woman had strength in her eyes, and she deserved to know the truth. "When he died." He let that sink in, then continued. "He had a message he wanted me to pass on to you. I can just tell it to you and then walk away. I know you don't know me. I know how I look. Just tell me what you want. It's just, as he was dying I gave him my word that I would find you."

The woman stared at him for a very long moment, tears filling her eyes. So long, in fact, that Morbius almost turned and walked away. The last thing he wanted was for her to call the police. He desperately wanted to get out of New York without incident.

Then, a sad smile crossed her face and she stepped back, opening the door a little wider.

"Please, come in, Michael," she said. "Any friend of Jake's is a friend of mine, and I've missed him so much. I want to hear everything."

Morbius nodded and quickly glanced back. Sure enough, Amanda was watching, a sad smile on her face, too. He gave her the slightest wave and then entered the house, removing his baseball cap as he did so.

He had always been so ashamed of his face, since the experiment, but for some reason, here, in Jake's house, that shame vanished. Jenny ushered him into her living room and the two of them sat down. After a long moment of silence, she began to ask questions. As he spoke, quietly, answering every query, he thought of the friend who had given his own life to save Morbius.

He thought of Amanda, waiting patiently for him across the street.

There was no question about it. Michael Morbius was most assuredly cursed. Yet in this moment, in the sad stillness of this home, he realized his blessings were abundant.

The story continues…

CAGED CARNAGE

M

FRANKLIN LATTIMER burst out of the church doors, his breath coming in ragged huffs.

The crashing sounds of unearthly conflict raged behind him, but he didn't look back. He never wanted to see a cult member, or a living vampire, or even stained-glass windows ever again. He'd had a lifetime of blood and sacrifice.

His short legs pumped, but it wasn't long before a nasty stitch erupted beneath his ribs and he stopped running. He leaned down, nearly falling over, and placed his palms on his knees, trying to catch his breath—a nearly impossible task. As he crouched in the middle of a South Bronx street, the blood moon's light shining down on him, he thought back to waking that morning in his penthouse apartment.

He'd been looking forward to the day. Another opportunity to run tests in his lab. To perhaps steal a conversation with Catherine Saint. To live the kind of life his parents had denied him, even though he deserved it more than them, fought for it more than they ever had. It was supposed to be a good day.

Now here he stood, in the middle of a cracked street, surrounded by burned-out warehouses and with an inhuman battle raging a few blocks behind him. A battle for which he was at least partly responsible. Franklin felt his lungs returning to their normal rhythm and slowly stood up, realizing that his hands were shaking uncontrollably. He willed them to settle, but was only partly successful.

Against his better judgement, he looked back at the church from which he had just escaped. Surreal bursts of light pushed against the windows and guttural screams came from within. He didn't know who he was rooting for at this point, and when he thought about it, he ultimately didn't care. The woman he'd known as Catherine was gone.

Perhaps this night was retribution for the things he had done while a "guest" of the Demon-Fire cult, but that was a conversation he would need to have with himself over the coming days and nights. He knew it wouldn't be an easy one.

Franklin shook his head and started moving again. He wasn't sure exactly where he was, but based on the skyline, knew he was heading south, toward Manhattan. He had enough money in his pocket to at least get out of New York. He'd worry about the rest later, once he was on a bus. He'd imagined a future somewhere in the middle of America. Perhaps he could still make it come true.

THE MIDTOWN Port Authority Bus Terminal was eerily quiet, deep shadows partially hiding people with bloodshot eyes and disturbing smiles.

Franklin held his hand beneath his nose to block some of the more pervasive smells of this place. He'd only been in this building once before, when he was a teenager, before his parents had abandoned him.

He'd been on his way to a camp in Pennsylvania. Even then, his parents seemed relieved to be rid of him for the summer. Franklin had a horrible time there—bullying of the sort he'd experienced at school was even worse in the wild expanse of a campground. The counselors didn't seem to care that the "normal" campers were ruthlessly picking on the small kid with a slight deformity.

When Franklin returned home, his parents barely asked how his summer had gone and he didn't volunteer anything. If they didn't care that he was mercilessly bullied at home, why would they care about it while he'd been away?

Franklin arrived at his gate, slightly out of breath. It felt as if he'd been running forever. He looked forward to settling down in a comfy seat on a dark bus and looking out on the city that had housed him for his entire life. He would sleep, and when he woke up he could start his new life. A life free of super heroes and the supernatural.

But as Franklin placed his foot on the first step, the reality of his situation struck home. His mind flashed forward on a more likely fate. He sat in a tiny apartment. Poor. Depressed. Alone. On some level, he knew this was the truth of what would happen if he fled.

No.

Franklin Lattimer was destined for greater things.

"Are you comin' or what?" the annoyed bus driver barked at him.

"No," Franklin replied, a smile crossing his face, "I most certainly am not."

FRANKLIN STOOD on the platform of the 2nd Avenue subway, nervously biting his bottom lip. It was late at night. He'd spent the day at his apartment scanning the news and came to the realization that there were no survivors of the massacre at the church.

He *did* see a clip of one of the crosses from the altar as men in S.H.I.E.L.D. uniforms carted it away—at least before an agent shoved his meaty palm into the camera and told the reporter to *"Get the hell out of here!"*

Demon-Fire was no more.

Franklin was safe.

After a few hours pacing his apartment, trying to figure out what to do next, Franklin's curiosity got the better of him. As night fell on Manhattan, he made his way back out into the city.

There were only a few other people on the platform, a couple businessmen and businesswomen chatting in a tight cluster, and a young man who could best be described as "goth." Franklin chuckled to himself—he wondered what this morbid kid would say if he knew the things Franklin had witnessed. He'd probably go home, wash the black gunk off of his face, and try out for the tennis team.

The train arrived. The other people boarded it, and Franklin was alone again. He took a deep breath, headed down the steps at the north end of the platform, and quickly made his way along the tunnel until he reached the door that would lead him back down into Demon-Fire's underground facility.

On some level, he knew it might be a mistake to return here—there was a chance not all of the cultists had died in the church. With both Thaddeus and Catherine dead, however, he suspected their minions would have scattered. Regardless, it was worth the risk. There was equipment and data in his underground laboratory that would be impossible to replicate.

The walk down the metal stairs took forever. His short legs were still aching from his earlier frantic flight, but he powered on. The darkness and silence of his descent almost convinced him to turn him around. Almost.

When he finally reached the bottom, Franklin stood for a moment and caught his breath. Looking around, he realized that he had never before been in this antechamber by himself. Alone, he found it absolutely terrifying. Only a few of the lights were still on, and the gloom wrapped itself around him. Clearing his throat, he moved forward, forcing himself to ignore the shadows where anything could be hiding.

Reaching the far wall, he felt along the stone, attempting to locate the secret lever that would open the door to the innermost reaches of the cult's hideout. His fingers fumbled for several minutes and he started to hyperventilate. He had never actually opened this door himself—had only seen others do it. What if he was looking in the wrong place? How long would he stand here, like an idiot, pawing at the wall?

Then he thought about clambering back up all of those stairs and emerging unsuccessful. That was not acceptable.

Franklin kept looking.

Finally, his fingers found a small hole under the slightest outcropping of the rock. After a moment wondering what might be hiding in that dark space, he slid them in. There was some give, and a faint clicking noise reached his ears. A couple of feet away, a stone doorway opened slightly, soft light emanating from within.

Franklin entered.

The hallways were empty. He saw streaks of blood here and there, but no bodies. Making his way through the tunnels, he headed to his lab. The lights had been knocked out in several places, plunging certain areas into darkness, but he could literally get there blindfolded, so he pressed on.

At last, he reached his lab. Nervous, ready to be met by the sight of dozens of dead cult members, he slowly opened the door, holding his breath.

There was blood everywhere—but still no bodies.

Franklin let out a surprised breath; when he inhaled, he nearly vomited. The smell of iron and decay was overwhelming, and he almost turned and left, but instead placed his forearm against his mouth and nose. Blinking rapidly, he walked forward, doing his best to avoid the puddles of gore. Some of his equipment had been destroyed during the battle with Morbius, but there was more than enough that could be salvaged. He wouldn't be able to take all of it, but whatever he *did* manage would ensure that he would live a very, very comfortable life.

Some of the experiments down here had been absolutely groundbreaking.

He expected the floor to be slippery, but the blood was sticky, pulling at his shoes—which he found more disturbing. Crossing the room, Franklin took a seat at his desk, placed his hands on his computer keyboard, and closed his eyes for a moment. If he breathed through his mouth, it was almost as if time had reversed, like he was still working on his experiments for Catherine. Life had been so much simpler…

"Dr. Lattimer?"

The voice shocked Franklin out of his reverie. He opened his eyes and stood quickly, his legs banging unceremoniously against the bottom of his desk.

A young woman stood in the doorway, wearing a Demon-Fire robe with the hood pulled back. She looked even more terrified than Franklin felt, which caused him to immediately relax. She looked vaguely familiar.

"Do… do I know you?" he asked, stepping around the desk, his shoes making a unsettling sucking sound on the floor. He ignored it and kept his composure, unwilling to show any weakness in front of this stranger.

"I'm sorry, I didn't mean to startle you," the woman answered, looking at the floor for a moment and then back up, locking eyes with Franklin. He noticed at that moment that she had a long scar on her face. It was faint but it was there, unmistakable. Beautiful.

"My name is Fiona," she continued, "and I joined Demon-Fire a couple months ago. I'm… I majored in biology in college—before I dropped out. I've been watching you. Wait, sorry, that sounds creepy. Admiring you. Ugh. That's worse. What I'm trying to say is—"

"Where are the bodies?"

Fiona's eyes went wide at the question, and her gaze dropped to the floor again. After a moment, she looked up. Her features were harder now, more resolute.

"We… what's left of us… dealt with them. It wasn't pretty."

Franklin nodded. There was something about this young woman that he found impressive.

"I understand," he replied, then added, "You said 'we.' How many cult members are left?" Fiona bit down on her lip for a second and her forehead scrunched up, as if she were counting.

"News from the church massacre came in pretty quickly, and a lot of people ran as soon as they heard that Poison-Lark was dead." A look of confusion crossed her face. "It was the most devout who fled. Those who stayed behind, like me, have been lost… unsure about our allegiance to the cult. I think we've had our eyes opened, but we still don't know what to do."

"Hm," Franklin responded, looking around the lab. The damage was significant but not insurmountable. There was potential here.

"Fiona, would you do me a favor?"

"Of *course*, Dr. Lattimer."

That was the second time she'd called him that. He wasn't technically a doctor, but he chose not to correct her.

"While I clean up in here and take stock of what's still operational, please gather the remaining acolytes in the arena. I'd like to speak with everyone about a way forward."

"Of course," she replied, the slightest wisp of a smile appearing on her face for a moment. "I'm on it."

Franklin smiled back, and then she turned and was gone. He let out a long breath. He didn't feel at all as confident as he had just sounded, but he was starting to.

FRANKLIN HAD never stood on the arena floor before.

It was much bigger than he'd realized from the few times he'd spent in the audience. The bright lights gleaming down were intimidating. He could still see splotches of different colored blood—and other fluids—spattered out across the packed dirt floor. He felt a pang of guilt, but pushed it away. What he planned to set in motion would more than balance the scales. At least so he hoped.

There were several dozen cult members in the audience, which surprised him, though only half of them were wearing the signature red robes. At its peak, this particular chapter boasted hundreds of members. Franklin wondered absently how many had perished at the hands of the living vampire.

While most of the remaining cultists were young, the group sitting above him in the "bleachers" had several older members and people of diverse backgrounds. Franklin smiled for a moment. If he could pull this off, he might be able to do something very important from deep within the bowels of the city. He opened his mouth, then stopped and swallowed nervously. Public speaking had never been his strong suit.

"Thank you for coming," he finally choked out.

"Louder!" someone in the shadows above yelled.

Franklin looked down at his shoes. *What am I doing?* He was no leader. He had joined a cult because he was, fundamentally, weak. Had let both Catherine and Thaddeus manipulate him to do what they wanted. Had turned off his moral compass to please them, and had blood on his hands as a result.

No, Franklin knew he should turn around and walk out of the arena. Stop pretending to be anything other than what he was. A misfit.

He looked back up, ready to apologize and shuffle out of the arena, out of the underground hideout. But he made eye contact with Fiona, who was sitting in the front row of the audience, staring down at him with huge eyes. She gave him a slight smile, bigger than the one she'd flashed in his lab, a smile that seemed to have the slightest tinge of... something. At that moment, everything changed for him. He felt a renewed strength, stood up straighter, cleared his throat, and spoke. Loudly.

"Thank you for coming!" he shouted. Several cult members sat up as his voice boomed around the cavernous arena. "My name is Franklin Lattimer. As you may know, I worked closely with Sister Catherine and Brother Thaddeus. In my heart, I believed in the core of their mission, as misguided as it was." Some of the audience murmured, but quieted when he continued. "They wished to rid the world of evil. I would like to do the same thing... but I think there is a better way to accomplish this." He paused and took a deep breath. He had everyone's attention now. He could *feel* it.

Franklin stepped closer to the group. Fiona was still smiling at him. He smiled back and even winked. He couldn't believe it. Franklin Lattimer had never *winked* at anyone in his entire life.

"I would like to lead everyone here in a new venture. It will *not* be Demon-Fire. It won't even be a cult. It will be... a collective. We will work together to better the world, doing so from the shadows. Using logic, and science, and yes—sometimes—violence. But only on those that themselves choose violence as a way of life."

He took another deep breath. This was it. The moment of truth.

"Are you with me?!" he shouted, waiting to be answered with resounding silence.

Instead, the small group yelled "Yes!", standing and clapping, led by Fiona in front. It was her turn to wink at him. He wasn't one hundred percent certain, but he was pretty sure he was blushing as the shouts and clapping grew louder and spread through the crowd.

WEEKS PASSED.

Franklin, Fiona, and their loyal crew cleaned up the entire facility, wiping away all traces of Demon-Fire. At one point, Franklin read in a news story that Morbius had been spotted in Nevada and, despite everything that happened, he silently wished the living vampire the best. There was a noble soul trapped behind that twisted visage.

Fiona helped Franklin restore the underground laboratory to its full capabilities, and he found himself astonished by the way her mind worked. She approached scientific problems from wildly different angles, and seemed to love hearing about his experiences, taking his base of knowledge and building on it.

They were quickly becoming, in his opinion, the perfect team. Working on a new transformation formula—one that wouldn't, in theory, cause as much physical torment in the test subjects. Once again they began with rats, and success came much quicker than before. Soon they completed their first successful experiment, yielding a living subject.

They also shared a gentle kiss.

It was Franklin's first ever, and it was better than he had ever imagined. The way she looked at him afterward was almost better than the kiss itself.

"What's next?" she whispered. It took him a moment to realize that she was talking about the experiments. He laughed at himself, and she laughed, too. She was still staring down into his eyes, and he fought to organize his thoughts, despite the fact that he didn't want the moment to end.

"Next…?" he replied. "I think it's time for a human subject, but we're going to do it differently this time." Franklin had come to regret his involvement in the torture of innocents. At the time, he'd believed that he was doing the right thing, that his advancements would benefit the world. But now, with the clarity of time and tragedy, he realized the price they had paid, and that there was a better way forward.

In a city of masked vigilantes, how would they be any different?

He outlined his plan, and she agreed that it was a good one.

They held interviews with each of the former cult members who were now loyal to their new leaders. Franklin and Fiona were looking for former police officers, military, security guards—anyone who had experience with physical confrontations. They put together a small squad of seven highly trained individuals, a mix of women and men, and people of varied ages and backgrounds. The interviews involved a battery of mental tests to make certain they were intellectually and emotionally equipped to handle anything they might encounter.

As they began training, the team gelled quickly. Franklin and Fiona perfected a new formula they would use to take down prey. At night, after long days of work in the lab and overseeing the training of the "Extractors," as they began to call them, they would spend exhausted downtime together, revealing to each other their pasts and their plans for the future.

A few weeks into their rigorous routine, Franklin told Fiona that he loved her.

She admitted the same.

FINALLY THE Extractors were ready. The underground facility was running like a well-oiled machine, and their followers were ready for the arena to come to life again.

All they needed were the subjects.

Whereas Franklin had come to consider the arena a barbaric place, as costs piled up he realized what a valuable resource it had been. And when he remembered the wretched human beings who had patronized it, he found himself entirely willing to separate people like that from their wealth—all in the name of science.

Despite the fear that bubbled in his stomach, Franklin insisted on leading the first aboveground mission. Fiona kissed him goodbye with a fervor that shocked him, and told him to be careful. He nodded, afraid that if he spoke he might become inappropriately emotional. Then he turned and walked toward the exit that would lead him to the surface, followed by his mercenaries, each one stone-faced and silent.

Franklin felt oddly powerful as he emerged into the shadows of nighttime Manhattan, flanked by seven highly trained Extractors. They would do anything he said, follow any command.

They made their way to Chinatown, and patrolled the streets in a planned pattern. As they did, they must have looked like a particularly strange group of tourists, a small man flanked by seven larger individuals who constantly looked to him for confirmation. They paused in Columbus Park, he nodded to them, and then they dispersed in different directions. Franklin headed down a small dark street, smiling as he found himself engulfed in the darkness of this quiet corner of the city.

His relationship with the shadows had changed.

Franklin had done his research. He knew the nooks and crannies of the city. Franklin watched as two men emerged, their cruel smiles practically glowing in the gloom. He was vaguely impressed by the nature of their arrival; they hadn't come from either end of the street—instead had appeared as if from thin air. There must have been an entrance hidden somewhere in the darkness.

They were big. Intimidating.

Clearly used to committing violence.

They were perfect.

"Can I help you?" Franklin said, a note of genuine fear injecting itself into his voice. He knew he would be okay, but these men looked fast. *Maybe this was a mistake*, a voice called out inside his mind. He clenched his jaw as the men stopped in front of him, those unnerving smiles plastered onto their faces.

"We were thinking *we* could help *you*," one of them growled. He threw a punch so hard, so fast, that Franklin didn't even see the fist approach and connect with his eye. He went down in a heap, tiny bursts of light dancing in his vision. He clung to consciousness and flipped onto his back, shuffling away from the two men, both of whom pulled out knives.

"Look at how tiny he is!" the taller one said with a strange giggle.

"Seriously," the other laughed. "Like a little kid."

"Gentlemen…" Franklin managed to say, placing his palm against his damaged eye. He could feel the skin puffing up, and he couldn't open the eyelid on that side. "You're only proving my decision to be the right one."

"What the hell are you talking about?"

"Just give us your wallet," the tall one said, "and we won't cut you up too bad."

They both stepped forward, and Franklin was certain they were going to "cut him up" whether or not he complied. As the knives came closer and closer to his face, he wondered again if he had miscalculated. Maybe his Extractors had decided to play him for the fool he really was.

He only wished he'd said more of a goodbye to Fiona.

As one of the blades slashed toward his face, Franklin closed his one good eye, but the knife never landed. Instead, there was a slamming sound, followed by a crack and a scream. Franklin opened his eye and saw that two of the Extractors had filled the space between their boss and his attackers. One of the criminals was supine at the base of the nearby wall. The other lay near Franklin's feet, whimpering quietly, his arm jutting out at a weird angle from his body.

Franklin lurched to his feet and got into the face of the Extractor who was standing over the second mugger.

"I told you quite clearly—*no* broken bones!" he growled through clenched teeth.

"I'm sorry, Mr. Lattimer," the huge man said, eyes downcast. The other five Extractors appeared from the shadows and began to bag the two criminals. Franklin sighed.

"It's fine, Lawrence," he said. "Just… don't let it happen again. It makes our work that much harder."

"Roger that, sir," Lawrence answered, then he joined his comrades to help with the exfiltration. Franklin watched his team work. Despite the throbbing pain in his eye, he smiled.

Everything was going according to plan.

FRANKLIN AND Fiona watched with silent fascination as the two men transformed.

It had been several days since the Chinatown encounter, and while still black and blue, Franklin's eye was healing nicely. Fiona told him she liked the way it looked, and he secretly liked it, too. The Extractors had tousled his hair on the way back from the mission, saying the black eye was proof that he was one of them. Though he didn't say so, he liked that praise, too.

He and Fiona had spent the interim prepping their subjects and making sure the two men could withstand the transformation. The new formula was much improved. Fiona had noticed tiny flaws in the molecular structure of the original, and they had worked together to correct them. The creatures they created would be much more powerful, and easier to control.

Fiona wrapped her fingers around Franklin's as the two criminals thrashed against their restraints. The struggles were pointless. They had invested in the best equipment money could buy—or steal from corrupt companies.

The two criminals began to transform. One's skin stretched, his limbs elongated, and tiny spikes erupted all across his flesh. All the hair fell from his body. The spikes on his knuckles grew longer than the rest, and his fingers sharpened into nasty-looking claws, while his face extended out like a melted plastic Halloween mask.

The other one, whose arm had been broken, screamed in pain as more of his bones began to crack and reform, emerging from his skin and creating what looked almost like a cage around him, with sharp edges at every single angle. Fiona inhaled a sharp, delighted breath and glanced to Franklin with a huge smile on her face, which he found to be slightly unnerving. She looked back at the men as the transformations entered their final phase.

He was shocked by her excitement. Franklin had witnessed many similar transformations, and it had taken him a long time to watch them without turning away, let alone getting excited. Still, he found her fortitude impressive. Attractive even. Fiona stood with her eyes locked on the writhing creatures, a look of absolute scientific euphoria written across her face.

As the creatures calmed down, she leaned forward and gave each an injection that would put them to sleep. Then she placed the syringe down and turned back to Franklin.

"Well… that was productive," she said, the smile lingering on her face.

"Tonight, we celebrate," Franklin responded. "Tomorrow, we arrange for the first show at our new and improved arena."

"Sounds like a plan, Mr. Lattimer."

Fiona leaned forward and they kissed, while the unconscious behemoths breathed quietly next to them.

MOST OF the seats were empty.

The fight between the two monsters had already begun, and it was quite a spectacle. The improved formula was working wonders. The creatures were incredibly fast and strong and pliant, and the battle was as impressive as any that had graced the arena during the time of Demon-Fire. In addition, the Extractors had captured several more criminals. Each creature was more impressive than the last. They had enough combatants to last for the next couple of weeks at least.

But still—most of the seats were empty.

"Why aren't they coming?" Fiona asked from the front row, where she sat next to Franklin. There was frustration in her voice.

"It's Morbius' fault," Franklin said angrily. "The last time people attended one of these battles, too many were killed. It's causing any newcomers to shy away." As the fight raged below, he sat back and wracked his brain. They needed to do more… to up the stakes.

At the climax of the battle, as the larger monster snapped a half dozen of his accomplice's external bones, an idea came to Franklin. It seemed risky as hell. Dangerous.

Perhaps even insane.

He smiled.

"YOU KNOW, you really should do something about that skin condition. Exfoliating every night might help with those blotchy red spots." Spider-Man leapt out of